SEALED WITH A LIE

Book 2 in the Moms Who Lie Psychological Thriller Series

Brett Monk, McKenna Langford

FOREWORD BY BRETT MONK

Welcome to *"Sealed With A Lie"* the second book in the *"MOMS WHO LIE"* series. McKenna and I have turned up the heat even more as Amelia, Maddy, and their kids get pulled even deeper into the web of mystery, deceit, and danger.

In addition to the five full-length novels in the series, there's also a special FREE bonus novella called "The Lying Begins" that's not available on Amazon or anywhere else other than the link below. It tells the story of just what happened twenty years ago, the night of the prom when Maddy and Amelia were in high school together. Once you're thoroughly hooked on this story, you're definitely going to want to read it, too.

https://www.brettmonk.com

When you join my reader's community, you will not only get free books and other content by me and some of my friends, but you will get the inside scoop on discounted products and upcoming releases. Plus, I share some personal thoughts and "behind the scenes" photos and notes about my life, media adventures, and favorite grilling recipes. :-)

Community members also get to vote in polls and make suggestions for upcoming books and projects. You might even want to consider being a "beta reader" or an "advance review reader", both of whom get to read the books before they're available to the public.

But for now, enjoy *"Sealed With A Lie"*.

- Brett

Contents

CHAPTER 1

WARNER

You know those websites where you can ask any question and you'll get a list of responses to it from both amateurs and experts? Well, my question is this: what should I do if I'm being blackmailed, and it turns out that the person who I originally thought was behind it has been dead this entire time, and now I have no idea who the real culprit is?

It's a bummer because I don't think my question is actually something that I can put out there on the internet. I don't think anyone would be able to help me answer it. I don't even think Lyla or Audrey—my two friends in a similar situation—could help. Up until this point, we all assumed Sydney Hutton had been the person messing around with us. We thought she somehow got a hold of all of our secrets and was threatening to release them. But just a few minutes ago, I got a notification on my phone from the Toxey news app letting me know that Sydney Hutton died the very same night she first disappeared. She drowned in Lake Oshwana during our upperclassmen camping trip. Unless ghosts are real and can somehow send texts and hack people's phones, I think I can rule out the possibility that it was her.

I'm sitting on the hood of my jeep in my "spot." It's the place I go to think. The place I go to be alone. It's an abandoned train station. Trains still go by all the time, but none of them ever stop here anymore. And the only trains that do go by are cargo ones. The train station had been an outdoor one; it's basically a brick gazebo with benches drilled into cement blocks and small rooms on either side that serve as the ticket booths. Now, everything is wildly overgrown. Weeds force their way through the cement and vines crawl up the brick. Some of the benches have been ripped out from where they had been drilled in. A couple still stand, and sometimes I lay on them and look up at the stars through the crumbling holes of the top of the structure. Right now, I'm just in the nonexistent parking lot. I can only tell it used to be the parking lot because of those cement block parking space holders that are still strategically placed throughout this grassy field. I felt too tired to make the short walk over to the gazebo when I first got here. And my eye still hurts from Jackson punching me in the face this morning. Every step I take makes my head pound in protest.

Thinking about my best friend punching me in the face makes my stomach roll. I get on my phone again, even though I desperately don't want to. It's blowing up with everybody Snapchatting and messaging me about Sydney's death. My mom has called me a million times, too. I'm not answering those because I am angry with her. She's dating a cop. An evil cop. And she let him into our home. If this had been the first time she had done something like this, I wouldn't be as upset. But we made an agreement that she would stop having guys over and stop forcing me to meet her boyfriends as long as the relationship wasn't serious. She claimed that the relationship with Detective Craig Fritz was serious, but I have since learned, given the fact that Craig is also talking to Amelia—Lyla and Audrey's mom—and he seems especially interested in figuring out what happened to Sydney, I get the feeling that it's not as serious of a relationship as she might think.

But I'm really on my phone right now because of Audrey. She texted me a few minutes ago that she had to tell me something in person and that it was an emergency. I've already replied multiple times asking her where I should go, but she hasn't replied. I'm not usually a person that calls people, except for maybe Jackson because he is my best friend—was my best friend. I don't really know where we stand now.

But I am curious about what Audrey wants to tell me, and I'm slightly worried about her, too. So, I call. It rings twice and goes to voicemail. I don't know if she declined the call or if her phone is just dead.

"Come on," I say out loud, staring at the phone screen and willing her to call me back. Every few seconds, it seems like my phone is buzzing with another message or social media notification. I groan and look up at the cloud-covered sky. As much as I want to stay out here all night, I know I shouldn't. I still have school. I still have football practice and my part-time job as an assistant soccer coach.

Even though it feels like my world has frozen, it hasn't. I just have to face it.

I hop off my car and get back in the driver's seat. As I head back home, my mind is clouded with thoughts. It's one of those situations where I find myself stopped at a red light and don't even remember how I got there in the first place. Had I missed any stop signs or run any other red lights? I don't even know.

The light turns green, and I continue on my way. The person driving behind me is obnoxiously close, their headlights blaring as they shine and reflect into my eyes from my side mirrors and my rearview mirror. It's annoying me, so I tap my brakes a little bit to hint to them that I want them to back away. Only, it doesn't work.

I look at my speedometer. I'm already going ten miles an hour over the speed limit. "What do you want for me?" I snap, knowing the person in the car can't hear me. People aren't usually in such a rush in small towns like Toxey.

I turn right, hoping that the person behind me will speed past me. To my dismay, they turn right as well.

I groan and purposely take a left at the next turn to see if they go that way, too. The turn enters a neighborhood, and the chances of this car going that way should be pretty slim.

But when I turn, so do they.

That's when the question finally forms in my head. Are they following me?

I speed up slightly, even though I'm in a residential area. They stay right on my tail. I leave the neighborhood and drive on a nearly deserted stretch of road. They're still on my tail out here. I don't know what to do. How am I supposed to get rid of them? Who is following me and why?

I decide to pull over. Maybe if they're just trying to talk to me, they'll pull up beside me and we can unroll our windows.

It doesn't happen. They stay back, still out on the road, their brights on and their engine revving.

My heart picks up speed. This could be the person that's been messing with us. The person who knows I was the last person to ever talk to Sydney. The person who sent the text message to Jackson telling him that I was in love with his girlfriend.

So, I do what I think anyone would do in this sort of situation. I put my car back in drive and take off, my foot pressing the gas pedal all the way down. It's an old jeep, and it doesn't go very fast, but hopefully it's enough. This stretch of road goes on for miles until it nears the base of a small mountain where Toxey's fancier homes sit on the cliff side, then it curves to the right and takes you to the more grungy, poor area. Where I live. On the wrong side of the tracks.

But the base of the hill is still a while away. So, I speed, hoping that a cop or anyone will notice that I'm being chased if they see me.

The car gets in the lane next to me finally, driving against the way of traffic, and I'm hoping that they are going to speed past, bored with tormenting me, then get back over in the right lane in front of me.

Instead of this, while driving almost directly beside me, they start merging into my lane. It happens quickly, and in order to avoid being hit by them, I have no choice but to swerve off the road. I'm driving so fast that I lose control when the right side of my tires hit grass, rocks, and dirt while the other side is still on the pavement. My car swerves violently and then suddenly, I am driving perpendicular to the road, away from it. I yell out in fear as I realize I am driving headfirst into a fence.

CHAPTER 2

LYLA

It's around nine p.m. on a Saturday night. I'm driving my new precious white BMW. Trinity, my best friend, is in the passenger seat beside me. We just finished seeing a horrifically awful horror movie at the theaters.

"I mean, we should have known it was going to be bad," Trinity says to me as I drive along the route to take her home. "It was only rated PG-13."

"Oh, come on, that's not true," I argue, even though the both of us are giggling. A lot. That's usually what we do every time we hang out. We giggle. "There's some good PG-13 horror movies out there."

"I bet you can't even name one."

"Well, there is..." I don't trail off because I'm trying to think of some options. I stop talking because I've just gotten a text message on my phone. Even though it's raining outside, I'm driving a car, it's dark out, and I'm responsible for driving safely with my friend in the car with me, I check the message anyway. Curiosity got the better of me. I just want to know what it says.

I read the message while driving.

It ends up being a text that I desperately want to reply to, but I won't be at Trinity's house for another ten minutes. I decide I'll just be quick about it. I've been driving for a long enough time now that I feel confident in my ability to multitask.

"Lyla, the light is red!" Trinity shouts, her voice full of alarm.

I look up from my phone just in time to see that I am speeding through a red light. I don't even make it all the way through the intersection. A car's headlights shine in through Trinity's passenger seat as it hurls towards us. Trinity screams, but it's abruptly cut off as the car plows into us and my head hits my door's window. There is a horrible crunching noise. The smell of burning rubber. A flash of Trinity's long dark-chocolate-colored hair. My BMW has completely lost control. It's spinning in circles, and I can't make sense of anything. I feel the car go over a barrier. It crashes into something and the airbags slam into my face and torso. Something impales me, and a metallic scent wafts through my nostrils. I look at Trinity beside me. She's not moving.

My eyes fall shut. I see nothing but blackness. Then I hear a voice. A girl's voice, crying to me. "Why did you let this happen to me, Lyla?" Then they're screaming and crying and repeating themselves. "Why!?" More screaming. "How could you?!" More crying.

I try to say I'm sorry. But no words come out.

My eyes snap open and I realize I am the one screaming now.

I'm back in my bedroom. Light from the rising sun is shining in through my bedroom window. I am sweating and shaking all over. I sit up and put my head in my hands and let the tears fall.

There's a soft knock on my bedroom door, but I don't say anything. Still, my aunt, Nora, cracks it open and peeks her head in. "Lyla?" Her voice is timid. "Are you okay?"

I keep my head in my hands and shake my head. She walks in all the way and comes over to my bed. She sits down at the edge of it and puts her arms around me.

I'm not entirely sure if I've ever been hugged by Aunt Nora before. She doesn't exactly come to visit very often. If ever. She showed up at our house unexpectedly a few weeks ago, and she still hasn't left. None of us know why she suddenly wants to get to know us all better, but I don't mind having her here.

"It's all my fault," I hear myself saying. Nora shushes me.

"No, it's not, no it's not," she says in a soft voice while she rocks us both back-and-forth.

But she doesn't even know what I'm talking about. She thinks I was just having a bad dream. Well, yes, it was a bad dream—but it's more than that. I had just relived the night of my accident. The night I killed Trinity.

It ended up working out in my favor that the car that hit us that night had a drunk driver inside of it. That nobody else had been around to see that I had actually been the one who ran the red light. The drunk driver died as well. I went into a coma for a few days, but I made it through. That left me being the secret keeper of the horrible thing I did. Me and only me.

Except that wasn't true. Somebody else did now. Somebody else knew that not only was I responsible for what happened to Trinity, but I was also responsible for what happened to Sydney Hutton as well. I was supposed to hang out with her the night she drowned in the lake. But by the time I finally decided to go meet her—which was way past when she asked me to—she was already gone.

"You were just having a bad dream," Aunt Nora says to me. I finally lift my head from my hands and look at her. She pouts at me and wipes away one of my tears. "It's over now."

I wished Aunt Nora was right.

But this nightmare I'm living feels like it's far from over.

CHAPTER 3

AMELIA

Mothers are supposed to be comforting and reassuring to their children. They're supposed to have all the right words. They're supposed to have the ability to make their children feel like everything is going to be okay.

For some reason, I severely lack those abilities.

The news about Sydney Hutton's death was shocking for all of us last night. I wanted to be up early enough this morning so that I could make everyone breakfast and try to be the one that helps everyone continue on with their lives. It's devastating what happened to that poor girl, but at least the mystery of her disappearance has been solved, and now Lyla and Audrey can move on.

When I get to the kitchen, Nora is already prancing about, whipping open cupboards, taking out ingredients, and looking bright-eyed and cheery.

Lyla is also already out here, and she's currently sitting at the kitchen counter. Audrey is probably still in her room getting ready, as is Joey. When I left my bedroom, Gentry was in the shower.

"How are you feeling this morning, Ly?" I ask my daughter as I walk behind her and massage her shoulders. She's wearing a hoodie and leggings, and her hair is back in a tiny ponytail because of how short her new haircut is. She has no makeup on and dark circles under her eyes.

"Miserable."

"You don't have to go to school today," I tell her. "If you need to take some time, it's understandable." I still don't know what her relationship was with Sydney. She told me they weren't friends. But I've since learned otherwise. I also don't understand why she felt the need to keep it a secret.

Lyla says nothing. I eventually give up rubbing her shoulders because she still has tons of tight knots and she's not relaxing.

I expect when Joey comes in that he will be the liveliest one out of my children. My sixth-grade foster son didn't have any relations to the Sydney girl, and therefore shouldn't be as upset about the fact that she drowned during his sister's upperclassmen camping trip.

But Joey walks right past me when he enters the kitchen and sits at the breakfast table, not even meeting my eyes.

"Good morning?" I try, standing between the table and the counter, feeling like I don't know what to do with myself.

"Morning," Joey says, taking his phone out and turning it sideways. That usually means he's about to watch YouTube.

Okay, so he's just grumpy this morning. It's fine.

I look at my sister. "Do you need any help?"

"No, I got it. I figured this morning would be a perfect time to make my roller coaster pancakes again. Everyone loved them last time."

"You mean Mom's?"

She raises an eyebrow at me to show her confusion as she stirs some batter in a bowl.

I clarify. "It's Mom's recipe. Mom's famous roller coaster pancakes."

As far as I know, Nora doesn't even have a relationship with our mother or our father. Why she would even want to make any recipes that would remind her of them is beyond me.

"Oh... whatever." Nora rolls her eyes at me and continues preparing.

By the time Audrey comes down, everyone else has already nearly finished eating. She looks as beautiful as she always does. Her makeup seems professionally applied, her hair is in loose waves cascading around her shoulders, and she's wearing a trendy outfit.

"Roller coaster pancakes?" she asks Nora. "You're the best!" She walks into the kitchen and grabs a plate of food, then she starts smothering it and butter and drenching it in syrup.

Lyla is watching her with an expression of panic. I feel slightly confused, too, by Audrey's behavior. She's acting like it's just another day. Like one of her classmates wasn't just discovered dead. I already know a little bit about how Lyla handles death and grief because of what happened to Trinity. I haven't had to see it with Audrey yet.

Audrey moves to sit at the table with her plate, but freezes in her step and stares around at all of us. "What?" she snaps.

"Nothing," Gentry says from his seat beside Joey.

"Are you doing okay today?" I ask her.

She sits down next to me and stabs at her meal with her fork. "Yeah. Fine." Then she takes a large enough bite to where I can tell she's going to be chewing it for a while. I get the feeling she did it on purpose so that I won't ask her any more questions.

Lyla stands up and carefully takes her plate over to the sink. "We should probably get going soon, Audrey," she says to her sister in a small voice.

"Like your mother said," Gentry throws in. "You really don't have to go to school today. You can take the day off. If you feel like you need it."

"It's fine," Lyla replies.

Audrey shovels three more bites in her mouth for standing back up and taking her plate over to the sink. "Thanks for breakfast!"

The two go into the mudroom, disappearing out of sight. Then the door to the garage opens and closes. The girls are gone.

Gentry stands. "I should go, too." He's dressed in business attire, ready for his workday. He gives Joey a kiss on the top of his head and grabs his plate from him, as well as mine. He puts them in the sink and gives Nora a nod. I can tell he is also trying to offer her a smile, but it comes out pinched and insincere.

"Have a good day at work," I call to my husband, who has barely even acknowledged my presence all morning.

"See you guys later," he says, looking at everyone in turn instead of acknowledging me individually. Then he is gone as well.

Joey leaves for the bus about forty minutes later, and it leaves me alone in my house with my little sister.

"So, what do you have planned for today?" I ask her as I lean against the countertop while she cleans up after herself. I'm thankful she's at least a neat freak. That she at least picks up after her messes and does it make it feel so much like I have a fourth kid. She mostly keeps to herself—watches TV on the couch or stays in her room. Sometimes she takes her faded jalopy for a drive but never tells me where. She likes to hang out with Lyla, too, when she can, but I've noticed that she doesn't seem as invested in getting to know Audrey or Joey.

"Why are you asking me?" she replies.

"I don't know," I say with a shrug. "Just curious about what you do all day long when we're all gone."

"Pretty much nothing. I've told you that before."

"Right. So then…" I want to ask her when she plans on leaving. But Nora can be pretty sensitive. Sometimes it's best to not trigger her.

"Are you trying to ask me when I plan on leaving?" she asks, a hint of venom in her voice.

Even though she's basically caught me red-handed, I try to backpedal. "No, not at all. I think it's good that you want to get to know the kids."

Ugh. If Gentry witnessed this conversation, he would be undoubtedly upset with me. He's been nagging me to get her to leave or to figure out what she wants from us for weeks now. She's my little sister. I should be comfortable with confronting her and asking simple questions. Maybe I just feel guilty. Maybe I feel like I owe it to her to let her stay here as long as she wants. Maybe our relationship has been strained for so many years that I lost the closeness I once had with her.

Not maybe. Definitely. If we were still teenagers, I would have been snappy right back with her. I would've told her to get out. I would have yelled at her for not trying to get to know her nieces and nephew earlier. We would've argued back-and-forth but eventually made up and continued on like the fight never happened at all.

Everything between us is so different now.

CHAPTER 4

AUDREY

I wonder if they are buying my act.

I am more terrified than I have ever been in my entire life. I feel awful about what happened to Sydney Hutton. I don't know who chased me through the hallways at school yesterday in that creepy mask while holding a flippin' knife like I had been transported right in the middle of a bad teen slasher movie. But when I woke up this morning, I did what I always do. I got ready for the day. I acted cheery around my sister and my family. I'm the one that puts on the brave face. I'm the one that acts like everything is fine. If Audrey Bailey can't handle or deal with something, then the entire world might as well come crumbling down around us.

"Everything is going to be okay," I say to my sister as I drive us to school after an awkward breakfast with our family. I desperately wish she would say it to me, too, but I don't expect that from her anymore. Lyla is a pessimist.

"It just doesn't make sense."

It's exactly what she told me yesterday.

"I know. But we'll figure everything out. And even if we don't, things have a way of just working themselves out eventually."

But here's the thing—or, several things, starting with: Sydney Hutton is dead. The news said last night that it was most likely an accidental drowning. But there's a chance that it wasn't.

Before this, Lyla and I had been working with Warner Carpenter to try and figure out why our mothers hated each other. Only, as of last night, Lyla and I found out that not only are our mothers actually *friends*—and for some reason, they're keeping it a secret—but also that Warner had seen Sydney the night she died. He had lied to us and told us he never talked to her. He said that she texted him and asked him to meet her, just like she texted

Lyla and just like she texted me, but Warner told us he never went. We learned the truth when an anonymous number texted Lyla a picture of Warner with her. The timestamp was on the photo and everything.

On top of that, Mr. Reeves, my high school English teacher, is Warner Carpenter's biological father, and for a while, I was the only one besides his mother, Madeline Carpenter, And Dean Reeves himself, who knew about it. Last night I decided to tell Lyla, and now the both of us have the secret. Madeline, or *Maddy*, doesn't want Warner to ever find out about his father. But I happen to know that Mr. Reeves wants the opposite.

Excuse me while I try and piece all of this together.

The person who tormented me yesterday had a figure of a man. The texts I had received from an anonymous number before my attack had told me to *confess my secret*. What if Mr. Reeves was trying to get me to tell Warner the truth about him since Maddy had told him he couldn't?

Ugh. It's all too much pressure to put on two teenage girls.

I don't know how this situation could *ever* possibly "work itself out," but I'm saying it for Lyla's sake.

Lyla scoffs at my words of wisdom. She doesn't buy it.

I take a deep breath and turn some Pop music on my Spotify through the speakers of my Mini Cooper. We drive the rest of the way to school in silence. When I pull into the parking lot and turn the car off, I unbuckle my seatbelt, but Lyla doesn't.

"We're avoiding Warner, right?" she asks me.

I nod my head.

"And we don't know for sure that Mr. Reeves did anything," she continues. Even *hearing* my English teacher's name said out loud nearly sends my stomach flying out of my butt.

I pause briefly. Then I mutter, "Right."

Lyla nods her head sternly at me like she's now concluding our morning business meeting. We get out of the car.

I don't have it in me to worry about what she's going to do about Jackson this morning. About who she's going to hang out with before the bell rings on the school steps. All I want to do is pretend like everything is fine. I want to find my friends and go to my classes, get cheerleading practice over with, then go home. Then I want to do it all over again tomorrow.

I start walking briskly as I normally do when I go places, but I slow down to where I'm nearly immobile when I see what has been put together on the lawn in front of the school.

It's a shrine.

For Sydney.

There are candles. Photos of her. Stuffed animals and flowers. Notes from classmates.

I almost can't even believe what I'm seeing. Nobody liked Sydney, as far as I knew. She was a new student at Blackfell High this year, and our junior year has barely even started.

But maybe I'm just projecting on these kids because I was actually someone who was more involved with her, yet I didn't bring anything.

"There were texts about it," Lyla says as she stands beside me. She must see the terrified look on my face as I stare at it all.

"I haven't checked any of my notifications," I admit. I don't want to look at my phone lately. It's too much.

Lyla doesn't say anything back to that. When I finally manage to tear my eyes away, the next thing I notice is the way everyone seems to be staring over in our direction. Not at the shrine and not at me, specifically. Most of them are looking at Lyla.

I keep walking towards the school entrance. Lyla trails after me until she stops at the steps and I don't.

I hear her behind me. "Oh, okay."

I stop at the door and turn back around her.

"Bye, then," she continues. She looks disappointed.

I feel bad for leaving her and I can tell she doesn't want me to, but I need to stick to my plan of acting like everything is normal. "I have to go find Sophia and them," I remind her. "You can come with?" I only say it like a question because I know the answer already.

"So I can listen to them pretending to be heartbroken about Sydney and watch them talk to everybody about how much they liked her when I know it's a load of crap? No thanks."

I wince because there is a very good chance all those things are going to happen. But they're my friends, regardless. They used to be her friends, too. When Trinity died, all of that changed.

I shrug. "Then I'll see you at lunch, okay?"

She just stares at me, saying nothing.

I groan dramatically and spin back around to go inside.

When I catch sight of Sophia's locker, I realize that she and the others aren't there. I search for them until the school bell rings, but I don't find them.

Not only are Sophia, Danielle, and Olive not in my first hour—Precalc—but it is one of the few classes where I don't have any friends to talk to. When I get to Government second period, however, I finally see Sophia and Olive. They are sitting together in the back of the classroom, but as I enter the classroom nearly late, there are no open seats by them.

They didn't save me one?

Trying to make eye contact with them but not succeeding, I sit down towards the front.

I'm irritated when I get to Fashion Merchandising in the third period. I also have this class with Sophia and Olive, and we have assigned seats at workstations around the classroom, so they can't avoid me this time.

"Um, *hello?*" I say to them in a bold voice as I slam my backpack down on top of the counter. They didn't even walk with me here just now. I had been alone in the hallway, frantically looking to make sure Warner wasn't close to approaching me.

"What?" Sophia snaps. I don't know why she has so much attitude with me or what their problem is, but I already have so much to deal with that I refuse to put up with this, too.

"What do you mean *what?*" I snap right back at her. "Why are you guys avoiding me and ignoring me?"

Sophia rolls her eyes. "Clearly, I'm not ignoring you. I'm talking to you right now, aren't I?"

I look at all Olive. It's so typical of her not to say anything and just sit there silently, like she is Sophia's puppet. I address her when I speak. "What did I do?"

Olive's face reddens. She's clearly uncomfortable with this. "You never showed up to Delilah's yesterday." She looks at Sophia as if worried she wasn't supposed to be the one to tell me why I'm in trouble.

Sophia crosses her arms. "You didn't even give us a text. You just completely stood us up. And you've been doing stuff like this ever since school started. We're starting to get really sick and tired of it."

I want to hit myself in the forehead. I forgot all about Delilah's. After cheer practice yesterday, I had told them I would meet them after I found my keys to my car. But then I had gone into the school and gotten chased by some masked freak.

My shoulders droop. "You guys..."

The bell rings and the class finishes taking their seats and quieting down. I have no choice but to do the same.

I think about passing them a note during the informational movie about Runway we have to watch, but what could I say? Should I tell them the truth about what happened to me? Could I even trust them? What if they had something to do with it?

That last thought is ridiculous, I know. But lately, everyone in my life has been lying to me. I'm beginning to find it very difficult to trust anything anyone says or does.

When class gets dismissed, I know I should try to resume resolving my fight with my friends, but instead, I throw my backpack over my shoulder and race out of there before the lights even come back on.

I should apologize. I know that. But they're going to want an explanation, and I'm just not ready to give that yet.

I sit with Lyla in the cafeteria. It's just the two of us at the table. Apparently, neither of us feels much like eating.

"Do you see Warner anywhere?" I ask as I scan the cafeteria, avoiding the table where my friends are currently sitting and glaring at me.

"No. But if he comes up to us, will just... pretend like I'm about to throw up or something. Then I'll run out of here and you follow me."

I nod my head, but I feel unsure. "And are we just going to do this the entire rest of the year until he graduates and hopefully moves away?"

"I don't know, Audrey," she says in an exasperated tone. "I am literally too tired to think about it right now."

"Fine." I change the subject. "How's today been so far?" I don't have any classes with my sister.

She speaks in a low voice so that she isn't overheard. "I don't know. I sort of feel like some of our classmates think I'm the one that drowned Sydney."

I tilt my head sympathetically. "I'm sure that's not true."

"I don't know. I *know* I didn't drown Sydney. And I know there's a chance nobody drowned her and that it really was an accident. But... Warner might've done it."

"Do you really think he would be capable of that?"

I have been wondering if Warner killed Sydney too. It just feels so unlikely because the boy I have gotten to know over the years doesn't seem like he'd ever want to hurt anyone. At least not on purpose.

"Anything is possible, Ree. Why else would he feel the need to lie about seeing her that night?"

I feel sick to my stomach.

And that feeling only worsens when, after lunch, I have my most dreaded class. Alone.

Lyla had given me a reassuring hug in the hallway before we parted ways, but I don't feel much better. I still don't want to face Mr. Reeves. Fine, maybe he hadn't been the one who terrorized me yesterday.

But maybe he had.

I approach the propped-open wooden classroom door. I linger in the doorway and am immediately faced with Mr. Reeves, standing at the whiteboard. He smiles at me in greeting, but I don't take another step.

All I can think about is yesterday. All I can see when I so much as blink my eyes is a man in a mask. It's the reason I barely even slept last night, but I caked on my concealer this morning hoping nobody would notice. I think I've done a good job so far acting like I'm fine.

I look at Mr. Reeves some more.

Did you do this to me?

"Are you coming in, Audrey?" Mr. Reeves asks. I try to figure out the way that he's looking at me. Does he know that I know about Warner? Does he want me to say something? "Audrey?" His face crinkles, showing his concern. Something about it doesn't feel very believable.

So, I change my mind.

Without a word, I turn on my heel and quickly walk back down the hallway. I have no idea where I will go, but I can't go in there.

The bell rings.

"Audrey, what's going on?" Mr. Reeves calls to me. I glance back and see that he has stepped outside of his classroom.

Seeing him standing there in the hallway, looking at me just as the masked man had done yesterday, is what makes me change from speed-walking to running.

CHAPTER 5

MADDY

I text Mia—or *Amelia*, since that's what she prefers to be called these days—and ask her if she can meet up again. I also add that it's kind of important.

She replies twenty minutes later and tells me that I can head to her office because she'll be alone there for a few hours.

Amelia Bailey Designs. I've driven past my old friend's place of work several times, but I've never been inside.

No doubt it will be just as clean, fashionable, and fancy as Mia is. So I dress in something a little nicer than a black shirt and black jeans like I normally do, then I get in my Hyundai and go to her work. She had texted me the address earlier, but I don't even need it.

Her suite is located on the ground floor of a small two-story complex. I pull up and park right in front of the courtyard, which is gorgeously bursting with flowers of all colors and has a beautiful modern waterfall right in the center. I don't even want to know what she pays per month to have a spot here. All the other businesses on the directories are mostly lawyers and therapists.

Her storefront is entirely glass, but it's tinted so that I cannot see inside. I smooth out my velvet maroon skirt and wonder if she can see me coming.

The inside is everything I imagined it would be, only girlier. Pinker. Her office furniture is white, but there are pink accent walls and decor. Even the chair behind the receptionist's desk is covered in pink fur. There's a neon sign on the wall behind it that says *Amelia Bailey Designs* in pink as well.

"I'm back here!" Mia's voice calls. I follow the sound of her and enter what must be her conference room. One of the walls is covered in pink and white floral wallpaper with a black backdrop. The curtains over the windows are velvet pink. The spiky modern light fixture hanging above the black marble conference table is gold, as are the legs on the table and chairs surrounding it.

Amelia is sitting at the head of the table in front of the TV mounted to the wall, her laptop open and a to-go cup of coffee on a coaster next to it.

She shoots me a smile when I walk in, but I can tell she's stressed out. We both are.

"Hey," I say with a pout. I walk over to the chair next to her and plop myself down in it. "Thanks for letting me come."

"Of course." We look at each other for a long, silent moment. I'm thinking about how strange it is to be friends with her again after so many years of hating her. I never thought I'd be in this situation, but I'm pleasantly surprised at how nice it is to have somebody to talk to again. I know I still have Nora, whom I try to stay in touch with and reach out to every once in a while and all, but something about my friendship with Amelia feels different than that. Deeper. More real.

Amelia doesn't exactly know that I've stayed friends with Nora over the years, but I don't plan on telling her about it. At least not anytime soon.

I clear my throat. "Your office... wow."

She smiles fondly. "It's girlier than I would have picked, but I let Lyla and Audrey have a say in the design when I remodeled it a couple of years ago."

I chuckle. "That makes more sense. I don't remember you being such a girly girl."

She puts her fingers gently on her chest. "Well, I was certainly more girly than you."

"You're making it out like I was some huge tomboy or something!" I wasn't a tomboy. I just preferred darker colors. I still do. And I preferred Aerosmith and Beastie Boys over Destiny's Child or Madonna.

She giggles with me. Then we fall into silence again. We know what it is we *should* be talking about, but I think we're both avoiding it.

"So, I know I said we should keep hanging out with Craig like we weren't on to him about whatever it is he's trying to do," I start. I'd so much rather talk about our old memories together. All the fun times we had. I'd so much rather gossip about all the kids in our graduating class who didn't age well. But we can't.

It still sucks to talk about Craig. I had been dating him for more than a few months. I have known him since high school. I've always thought he was cute, but I hadn't started crushing on him until we began frequenting the same dive bar about a year ago. I had actually really liked him, and I thought he liked me, too. I liked that he had a respectable job and that he seemed like he would be a guy that Warner wouldn't mind having around. And the main thing I want out of a relationship is someone Warner could potentially see as a father figure in his life. I just want Warner to have the best that I can possibly give him.

Amelia had been the one that confronted me at my work recently to tell me that Craig had been repeatedly going to her house and spending time with her. She told me that he never mentioned once that he and I were dating. She only found out because she had seen Craig and me together at a football game of Warner's that I dragged him to. She initially thought Craig and I were plotting against her, but what I'd be doing that for, I have no idea. I explained that I didn't know about any of it, and then we got to talking. And we talked for a long time. Even after I went back to work. We talked on the phone on my way home. We texted nonstop. Sent each other emails. We got all caught up on each other's lives, rekindled our friendship, and decided that we were going to keep spending time with Craig like nothing had changed because we wanted to know what he was up to.

I think I know what he's up to now.

"Yeah?" she asked me. "Did you find something?"

I grip my knees with both of my hands and nod my head. "Yes. Not only did I find him cornering my son and asking him about Sydney—that's a whole other thing—but he also came back over after you left yesterday to tell me that he wants to figure out what happened to Carson Price. And he thinks you and I might have had something to do with it."

I brace myself for her reaction.

Carson was Craig's best friend in high school. He disappeared without a trace on the night of my junior prom. Amelia's little sister, Nora, who had been dating him at the time, told the police and anyone that would listen that Carson was dead and that she had seen his body in the woods. The same woods where Sydney Hutton was found.

But *his* body was never found. He had been living in a foster home. He was labeled as a runaway.

Mia's body tensed in her chair. "He actually said that to you?"

"Yes. Things got sort of heated, even. I don't think I can go on pretending like I like him."

"Does he know that you and I are friends again?"

"I'm not sure. While it was a weird and heated conversation, it was also short."

She thinks for a moment. "Okay. We should still keep our friendship a secret, for now. Until we know for sure. And because..."

She's referring to our old classmates. The people around town. Everyone in Toxey knows we dislike each other. We agreed last night that it would be too strange to rekindle our friendship now. Especially with the Sydney situation. Because not only were Amelia and I at the prom the night Carson Price disappeared, but Amelia and I were also on that upperclassman camping trip together the night Sydney disappeared and then turned up dead. It didn't look good.

"I agree. I just wanted to let you know what Craig said."

"Have you talked to Warner much?" she asks, changing the subject.

"He doesn't want to talk to me right now, apparently." It sucks to admit it. I hate that our relationship has been so horrible and off lately.

"Neither do my kids."

"Maybe it's a good thing," I say in a lame attempt at a joke. "That way, at least they're not bugging us with questions about why we hate each other so much."

She nods her head enthusiastically. "I just don't even understand why they care so much. It's all ancient history."

I reach out, take her hand on top of the table, and give it a squeeze. I smile at her adoringly. She returns the look.

"I agree. Ancient history."

CHAPTER 6

WARNER

My car is fine. I'm fine. Sort of. After I was run off the road and scraped my jeep along the side of a fence before finally regaining control of it and putting it in Park, I peered through the settling dust around me and saw that I was alone. Whoever ran me off the road had disappeared.

Currently, my head still aches from hitting it against my car window during the collision and I have a slight limp because for some reason my leg is sore. I did some googling and learned that more than likely my body was too tense when the car hit the fence, which caused the soreness.

When I got to school and hopped out of my precious and badly dinged-up vintage Jeep this morning, I hobbled on over to the steps outside the entrance. I was a little late getting there, so the bell rang just a few short minutes later. I hadn't seen Audrey or Lyla at all. What I *had* seen, however, was the obnoxious shrine for Sydney sitting on the front lawn.

At least I didn't have to worry about running into Jackson today.

I know that it's all my fault and that I should feel terrible about it, but I'm grateful that Jackson has been suspended for three days. I've had so much other stuff going on that I don't even know where to start when it comes to apologizing to him. I know that I *should* apologize, I just don't know how.

He punched me because he received a text from me—even though I didn't send it, or at least I don't *remember* sending it—admitting that I am in love with his long-term girlfriend, Lyla Bailey.

The reason I am uncertain about how to make things right between us is that the text had been sort of true.

I don't think I'm in *love* with Lyla by any means. I just... I have an intense, ridiculous crush on her.

That's another thing I have to deal with. I haven't even had the opportunity to talk to Lyla about it since it happened yesterday.

But like I didn't see Audrey or Lyla this morning outside of school, nor did I run into them in the hallways. I didn't go into the cafeteria at lunch because I was sick of my classmates and friends coming up to me and asking me questions about Sydney's death and my fight with Jackson. Instead, I hid in the library amongst the stacks of shelves. I grabbed a Stephen King book from the shelf and sat there and read it to distract myself.

I spent my free period after lunch in the empty upstairs classroom, but now that that class is over, I am on a mission.

I hobble back down the stairs towards where Audrey and Lyla's lockers are. I'm determined to speak with them. I want to know what Audrey wanted to tell me earlier. I want to explain to Lyla that I never sent that text message. I also want to talk to them about what I discovered. About Carson Price. An easy Google search told me that their aunt, Nora Flynn, had been dating Carson Price when they were in high school. But then Carson disappeared. I am not sure if either of them even know that this ever happened. I just think it's weird that Carson and Sydney both "disappeared" in the same Boldosa Redwoods. And both times, my mom and Amelia Bailey had somehow been involved. Or around.

When I turn the corner, I see Audrey at her locker. I start heading in her direction and when our eyes lock, instead of waving to me or even smiling like she normally does, she turns, shuts her locker, and hurries away in the opposite direction.

I stop walking right there in the middle of the crowded hallway. *What the heck?*

Is Audrey avoiding me now? Does that mean that Lyla is, too?

I pull out my phone and compose a text to her.

Me: *Hey. Can we meet up?*

People walking past me shoot me dirty looks for blocking their path in the hall. But I don't care.

I stand there and stare at my phone for at least a good minute, hoping that I'll see Lyla starting to reply. Instead, my message stays unopened.

I continue to check my phone obsessively over my next classes, just hoping to see her four-letter name pop up on my screen. So then, by the time school gets out for the day, I am fully convinced that my—previously thought irrational—fears are true. The Bailey twins are avoiding me.

And—go figure—the cheerleaders aren't on the field when I get out there for practice later, so that means they decided to do their practice indoors today, Audrey included. I can't help but wonder if she had anything to do with that decision.

But what did I do? Before Sydney's body was found at the lake, the three of us had been on one team, trying to figure out what happened to Sydney, and trying to figure out why our mothers don't like each other. Now that we know that Sydney is dead, and they're suddenly avoiding me... does that mean they think—?

A body slams into me and sends me flying. I land on my back in the grass and look up at the dreary sky.

Dang it.

I have been so distracted thinking about them that I caught the football when it was passed to me, but didn't do anything about it. I didn't even move.

"Warner!" Coach Reeves calls. "What's going on with you, dude?"

Cody Lawson helps me up. He had been my attacker. The one who sacked me. "You good?" he asks me, his wide-set eyes giving me a concerned look through his football helmet.

A cool breeze blows over me. I'm finding that I am surprisingly cold right now. That football today isn't making me drenched in sweat and wishing I was in an ice bath like it usually is.

"Yeah, sorry." I take Cody's offer of a friendly handshake.

"You didn't even move."

"Yeah... I... I don't know."

Coach blows his whistle. It signals the end of practice. We all gather in a huddle over at the bench on the sidelines where we are drinking from our water bottles and using our sweat towels. At least, the *rest* of my team is. I'm just standing here aimlessly.

"We don't have the advantage of a home game this Friday," Coach says to us. He's wearing a black Nike hat low over his eyes, casting a dark shadow that makes him look intimidating. It's strange to see how different he looks inside of his classroom compared to when he's coaching. But I don't find Mr. Reeves intimidating. I'd be willing to bet that the newbies do, though.

"Yeah, Carpenter," Ryan Copeland mutters under his breath, getting a laugh from some of my teammates.

"Well, I wasn't going to point out specifics, but..." Coach Reeves meets my eyes, talking animatedly and waving his clipboard around. "What was that out there?"

"Sorry," I grumble yet again. "Just have... a lot on my mind. I'll be good before the game."

I glance around at everyone, see how unconvinced they seem, and decide I just won't look at them for the remainder of today. I am going to just keep my head down and lay low.

"He's missing his girlfriend," Austin Booth jokes. "Leave him alone, guys."

I could snap and say that I don't care that Sydney is dead. That she wasn't my girlfriend. I could tell them to shut up. But even talking about Sydney in a joking sense makes my stomach hurt so badly I can barely breathe.

This is why Jackson is my best friend. If he were at practice, he would be telling the guys to shut up. Even though most of my teammates are my friends too, Jackson is the only one that ever has my back. Like *really*, has my back.

Things are going south fast.

Coach Reeves tells everyone to stop with the laughing and the comments. Then he resumes his after-practice speech.

My goal for inside the locker room a simple: I'm going to just grab my stuff from my locker, switch out of my cleats, and then get out of there. I won't even give the guys a chance to mess with me anymore.

The first part of that plan works out okay. I get all my belongings, shut my locker harder than I mean to, and make it out of the locker room. Coach's office is just outside of it, and unfortunately, he must have seen me passing by because he called my name to stop me. Then he summoned me into his office.

I like Coach Reeves. He's my favorite teacher and he's an insanely good coach. But I don't really feel like doing this right now. Too bad I'm football captain and also don't really have a choice in the matter.

"Sup, coach?" I ask, giving him a head nod as I stay in the doorway, hinting that I hope this conversation is quick so that I can leave.

Every teammate that leaves the locker room is going to see me in here talking to him. I don't want to give them more material to use against me later.

"Warner, why don't you come in and sit down," Coach starts.

I hesitate, but then do as I'm told. "What's this about?" I ask. I'm sitting at the very edge of my seat, not letting myself get comfortable. Coach and I have had plenty of talks in his office. Mainly about football. Sometimes about life. I don't have a dad, so he's usually my go-to person when I need some advice from someone other than my mother.

"I just—"

He gets up and closes the door to his office. That is definitely not something he normally does while talking to me.

Am I getting kicked off the team? Removed as captain?

I cough, expecting more bad news. It's not like this day can get much worse.

Coach sits back down in his chair and continues. "I just wanted to talk to you about what happened."

"Coach," I start, the exasperation plain in my voice. "Like I said, I was just distracted by some stuff—"

"I'm not talking about what happened to practice. I'm talking about what happened to Sydney."

The annoyed rant I had just planned going on dies in my throat. "Oh," I say instead.

"Are you okay?"

I do my best to seem as unaffected as possible. "Yeah. I mean, why wouldn't I be?"

He bounces the clicky part of his pen on the desk slowly multiple times, swirling his chair slightly with his feet. "Well, you had been talking to me about her the first night of the class trip. Just a little more than twenty-four hours before she disappeared."

I forgot about that. During the upperclassman camping trip, Mr. Reeves had asked to talk to me after the campfires when we all had some free time before we had to be in our tents for bed. Sydney had pushed me off my kayak and into the water earlier that day, earning us both punishment and risking getting me in trouble with Mr. Reeves because as football captain I'm supposed to be setting a good example for the team.

Coach and I were talked about whether or not I liked her. If there was something going on between us. I had acted repulsed. *Honestly? I think she's into me. She sort of won't leave me alone.*

"Yeah. But it's like I said. She had a crush on me or something. I didn't like her back. We weren't even friends."

"I get that. But you said she liked you and that she wouldn't leave you alone. So I'm gathering that she tried to talk to you a lot."

"I don't know. I guess." I stare at the pen that he keeps clicking. It's one of those nicer ones that feels thicker in your hand. It's shiny and emerald green. There's a phone number written on it. I think he's using one of the pens from the nice Italian restaurant in the upscale part of town.

"So, do you know anything about how she had been acting before she went missing? Did she seem different?"

"I barely saw her that second day, Coach. Didn't she... drown? Wasn't her death an accident?"

"Yeah, that's what the police are thinking. I guess I just wonder why she was even out there alone in the first place. What was she doing near water if she didn't know how to swim? And if she was having a hard time at school..."

What exactly is he trying to get at?

"Yeah, I don't know the answer to any of those." I put my hands on the armrests, bracing myself to get out of the chair. I don't know how I can make it any clearer that I want to go.

He stops clicking the pen. "I just wanted to check in with you, Warner."

"I'm fine, Coach." There's no point in confiding in him about what I'm going through. He'd have no idea how to help me.

"If you're going through some stuff, if being captain is too much added stress and pressure, you—"

"I want to be captain." I've always wanted it.

"I know you do, Warner. I'm just trying to tell you that it would be okay if you stepped down. Nobody would be mad. And I'm not saying I want you to do it or that your teammates are complaining, because neither of that is true. I just don't want you to get to a point where everything just becomes... too much. There are more important things than being captain of a high school football team."

I shake my head. "No, there's not. Not to me. Not right now."

Coach Reeves nods his head. I slowly get to my feet to test whether or not he's going to try to keep talking to me. He says nothing, so I walk over to the door.

"I'll work on keeping focused," I say. Then I open the door and walk back out into the hall. I can still hear that some of my teammates are messing around in the locker room next to me, so I pick up the pace as I head to my Jeep.

When I'm completely alone inside of it, I finally let out the breath I've been holding and let the freaked-out expression I've been trying to refrain from showing on my face finally appear. I look at my phone again. No response from Lyla. I fling it onto the passenger seat aggressively. It bounces and hits my glove compartment before falling to the floor. I grip my steering wheel so hard that my knuckles are all white. I can't get my conversation with Mr. Reeves out of my head. I have a feeling he thinks I have something to do with Sydney's drowning.

I sit there and remember another thing he had said to me about Sydney during our conversation at the upperclassmen camping trip. *I suggest you do something about your friend. You can't have her dragging you down like that.*

CHAPTER 7

LYLA

I lay in my queen-size bed that I have pushed up against the wall in my bedroom and stare at my ceiling fan. We don't have the AC or the heat on in the house, so I've opened the window. I like hearing the sound of the rain, and the breeze gently blowing through the trees outside our house is causing my fan to rotate slowly. If I pretend like my window has been closed this entire time, it makes it seem as if the fan is moving on its own. Like it's haunted.

On my stomach, my phone begins vibrating again. I look at who's calling and sigh loudly. It's Jackson. *Again.* He's been calling me and texting me nonstop ever since the fight between him and Warner happened. I don't want to talk to Jackson. I don't want to have anything to do with him at all, actually. I know that I've spent practically all of my teenage life being his girlfriend, but I just can't do it anymore. It's too hard being with him. I changed after I got in my car accident and Trinity died. I exhaust myself wondering when I'm going to go back to being the old me. And Jackson exhausts me when he asks me the same question. As of late, I have noticed that going back to the old me is likely never going to happen.

I had been in the cafeteria with Jackson yesterday morning. He told me what Warner had texted him about me, then he said that he wanted to fight him. When I tried to stop him from being an idiot, he shoved me.

He shoved me, and he left the cafeteria anyway.

Part of me feels like I'm making a big deal over nothing about that last part. He only shoved me because he was trying to get me to let go while I was holding on to him when he didn't want me to be. It wasn't like he slapped me across the face or pushed me to the ground.

Still, he had made enough of a scene to where people around us actually gasped out loud.

I don't answer his call, just like I haven't answered any of his previous ones all day long. For some reason, he isn't getting the clue. My phone starts buzzing yet again.

"Why does your mother even let you have a phone?!" I yell at Jackson's stupid contact photo. It's one I took of him sitting across from me at Delilah's one night. It's a very old photo from back when we were our happiest. "You were suspended!"

I let it go to voicemail again. I don't even bother to decline, and send the call right to voicemail. I don't want to give him the satisfaction of thinking I'm even angry enough to hang around my phone all day waiting to decline him.

The reason I don't just pick up the phone and break up with him is simply that I am too tired. I am already dealing with so much other drama that I can't take on anything else right now.

My day today had been rough. I had been standing outside of the school on the steps by myself before the first bell. Without Audrey and Jackson—and without Sydney and Trinity, too, I guess—I had no friends at Blackfell High.

I was alone, and I had nobody to blame but myself.

But the second I caught a glimpse of Warner getting out of his jeep and limping—why was he limping?—over to Sydney's shrine, I decided I couldn't be out there any longer. I walked inside. There in the halls, I felt like everyone had just been talking about me, but stopped mid-sentence. I mean *everyone*. The hall was practically silent. I had no choice but to flee into the girl's restroom and hide in a stall until first period. I didn't leave until the final bell rang and the hallways were cleared. That helped me avoid the whispers and stares out there, but then when I went inside my first period classroom with Mr. Reeves, the scene of me coming in late gave everyone an excuse to stare me down all over again. When I sunk in my seat at my desk, I heard giggling behind me.

Maybe whoever it was wasn't giggling about me.

But I have a pretty big feeling that they were.

Then my day got worse.

After Mr. Reeves took attendance and went back to his desk and gave us all a couple of minutes to chat while he prepared for the day, none other than Wrigley Hall moved from his seat to come to sit at the empty one next to mine. The seat was usually reserved for Jackson.

"What's up?" he asked me with a head nod. I was practically mortified.

"What are you doing?" I asked him, avoiding eye contact. It hurt to so much as *look* at Wrigley Hall.

It sucked that after everything, Wrigley could still act so carefree. That he was still his same exact self. Still stirring up trouble, throwing parties, and acting completely unaffected.

"I'm checking in on you," he said. Normally, I had Jackson in this class with me. If he were here today, I would have guaranteed that Wrigley wouldn't have approached me like this.

Wrigley Hall doesn't play sports. He isn't the most liked person in all of Blackfell high. He isn't incredibly outgoing, and he doesn't always crack stupid jokes. Wrigley Hall is tall and gangly. He has curly, overgrown brown hair. There is no sign of scruff on his face. He has a rich dad who works a lot and unknowingly gives him plenty of opportunities to throw house parties.

So, in other words, Wrigley Hall is the complete opposite of Jackson Mullens.

I could hear one of my classmates, who Wrigley usually sat next to in first hour, calling out to him as he sat by me instead. "Oh my gosh, Wrigley!" She paused to giggle. "What are you *doing*?"

He turned around in his seat to tell her to be quiet. Then he looked back at me. "So... how—how are you, Lyla?"

"Fine."

He was turned all the way in his seat to face my desk. I stayed facing the front, hoping Mr. Reeves hurried up and started teaching.

"There's a lot of stuff going around about you," Wrigley informed me.

"Like what?"

Look at him. Brave enough to go directly to the source for the accurate gossip.

"I don't know. About you and Jackson. You and Warner Carpenter. How you were that chick's friend who died."

"Which one?" I challenged with a sarcastic laugh.

Now I'm the girl who had been friends with two chicks that died.

Wrigley didn't answer the question. "I am trying not to get involved in any of the rumors," he claimed. "It just seems like maybe you could use somebody to talk to. You know, like how we used to."

I tensed in my chair. "No, thanks." Still, I wasn't looking at him.

"Oh, come on, Ly." He was leaning in closer and lowering his voice. "Why not? What did I do wrong?"

"All right, you guys, let's bring it back in." Mr. Reeves was back to standing at the front of the class.

I was grateful. I wouldn't have been able to tell Wrigley the answer to his question, anyway.

Wrigley wasn't the only person who approached me today whom I don't normally talk to. It seemed like everybody wanted to know how I was doing. Only a few of them were brave enough to ask the questions they really wanted to.

Do you know what happened to Sydney?

Were you with her that night?

Did you two get in a fight or something?

I even heard some senior girls talking about me in the lunch line. Either they didn't know that I was within earshot, or they just didn't care.

"I am so sick of hearing about that girl," one of them had said. "She is clearly just desperate for attention—one of those girls who thrives on the drama. It's so pathetic."

I don't even want to know what kind of things Sophia, Olive, and Danielle said about me today. They probably told people they didn't want to be my friend anymore because they were too afraid they were going to be the next to die. I don't know who started this rumor, but it was even going around school that I was "The Cursed One."

Why does it seem to hurt more when people say bad things about you that are true?

Maybe it's because I feel like somebody has taken all of my deep, personal thoughts and posted them on fliers all around the school for everybody to read. The thoughts I wouldn't ever tell anybody I was thinking. The thoughts that I wouldn't want anybody else to know I had.

I get a text.

Jackson: *You can't ignore me forever.*

I wish I could somehow find a way to prove Jackson wrong.

CHAPTER 8

Amelia

I follow Mr. and Mrs. Barton from their dining room into their kitchen. They start talking about their wishes, ideas, and concerns about this room, but I feel like I don't remember anything they just told me when we had been in the dining room.

Would it be rude of me to ask them if we could go back?

"I want the drawers to have that soft-close feature. You know what I'm talking about?" Mrs. Barton says to me. She has curly-Q brown hair down around her shoulders and bright red lipstick that she pulls off well. Her husband is next to her, checking his Apple watch every couple of minutes and then stepping away to send out some sort of voice text on it. He had to leave work for this meeting, and it was apparently pretty inconvenient, given the amount of work he was still trying to get done now that he wasn't there.

The Bartons' house was built by an excellent architect. It has good bones, but some of the interior themes are outdated, so the couple is just looking to spruce it up.

"Most definitely," I say to them. "That's usually a top request." I jot it down anyway, but I would never spec out anything else.

"Would it be too hard to move the sink to the island? I'd like to be able to look out the window when I'm doing the dishes."

"I'll get the contractor in here to see what we can do. I'm the same exact way, though."

The Barton's were a lovely couple and we have a lot in common.

Unlike Maddy and me. In our late thirties, we are even more different than we had been when we were in high school. And I thought *that* had been a challenge enough.

Ugh, high school.

Shoot!

I'm doing it again. I can't stop thinking about what Maddy told me about Craig. About him suspecting Maddy and I had something to do with Carson's disappearance all those years ago. About Craig thinking our kids are somehow involved in their classmate's death, even though Sydney Hutton more than likely drowned accidentally.

"Amelia?"

I snap my head to Mr. Barton. I had completely just tuned him out. What had he been saying?

Come on, Amelia. Something about... the space above the cabinets?

"No, you're right," I blurt out; my training and experience taking over my mouth like an autopilot. "The space above the cabinets is really just one big dust trap. It's becoming more and more common to just build the cabinets all the way up to the ceiling, so we can definitely do that."

The way Mr. and Mrs. Barton smile at each other reassures me that I have said the right thing. *Phew.*

We discuss the kitchen for a few minutes more, then we move into the master bedroom. They want their headboard and end tables to all be some sort of connected built-in. I'm taking all the required notes on my tablet which I have connected to my cell phone. Then I receive an email notification at the top of the screen and get distracted again.

I regrettably interrupt Mrs. Barton mid-sentence. "I'm so sorry, you two. I need to step away for just a moment. My daughter is texting me." I hold up the tablet to show that the text came in on here.

"No worries at all!" Mrs. Barton tells me. "We get it." They have kids around the same age as mine.

I offer an appreciative smile and step away. Then I read the email from Dean Reeves—neither of my daughters had actually texted me—in private:

Mia,

I just wanted to see how you were doing with the news about Sydney Hutton's death. The school has been a mess. I hope your girls are doing all right. It's hard to know exactly how to talk to them about it. It's hard to know exactly how they feel and if anything we're telling them is helping or if we're just annoying them.

I was wondering if you would be interested in meeting up for coffee sometime. It might be good to talk about it together. And it would be really good to hear from you again.

Dean.

I can't believe he has resorted to email.

This isn't the first time he's reached out to me since we got back from the upperclassman trip. He had messaged me on Facebook as well. He doesn't have my phone number, but I know it would be easy for him to get his hands on it if he really wanted to take it that far. Dean *is* my daughter's English teacher, after all.

I don't reply to the email. Just like I didn't reply to his message on Facebook. I admit, there have been a few times I thought about it, though. It would be nice to see him again. To talk to him. We had a really good time together working as chaperones for the yellow team on the upperclassman trip. I hadn't giggled that much since I was a teenager.

I know it's a horrible idea to see Dean. Which is why I'm not going to. Besides, Dean is Maddy's ex—no matter how long ago it was. Maddy and I are friends again. I just can't go down that road.

I wait a little bit so that it seems like I was replying to my daughter, then I rejoin my clients. We go through the rest of the house and finish up the site visit. Then I don't get to leave immediately because we begin talking about unrelated work things and before I know it, an extra forty-five minutes has passed.

"Well, Gentry seems like my kind of guy," Mr. Barton says after I tell them a funny golf story about my husband. "It'd be great to meet him sometime."

Mrs. Barton hugs her husband from the side and presses a hand on his chest. "We should go on a double date!"

"Oh, we haven't done that in so long!" Mr. Barton agreed.

"Oh... you know, Gentry *does* have to go out of town often for work, so I'm not sure how much time he has, but... I agree! It *would* be fun." When I return their smiles, I can feel how strained and fake mine is. It's just that... Right now, a date with Gentry doesn't seem like a very good idea.

When I finally get out of the house, I see that the sun has nearly set. I hope Gentry at least got takeout from somewhere or food delivered, since I'm not going to be able to make it home to cook everyone dinner in time. I don't have any texts or missed calls from him or my kids asking me where I am or what the plan is, at least. So that's a good sign.

I go to set my phone in my cupholder so I can put the car in drive and get out of here, but a thought stops me. Instead, I go to my internet browser and Google Sydney Hutton.

The first few results talk about her death—news articles. But as I scroll further and load up the next results page, I can't unable to find any other information about her.

Who was Sydney Hutton? Why had she tried to insert herself into my girls' lives? What was it about her that made Craig think it *at all* possible that my daughters and Maddy's son could have had anything to do with what happened to her?

I decide right then and there that I need to find out everything I can about Sydney Hutton. If I am going to have to prove that Lyla and Audrey couldn't have possibly done anything involving the circumstances that led to Sydney's disappearance and death, then I'm going to need all the information I can get.

CHAPTER 9

AUDREY

"So, do you have any fun plans for this weekend?" I ask Lyla as we walk through the parking lot of school the next morning. The shrine for Sydney is still outside and I think it might have even doubled in size since yesterday. It still baffles me that people are pretending to care about her this much, but I walk up to it again and set my small bouquet of half a dozen pink roses near her photo. I am only doing it because of the peer pressure I feel that there is to partake in this. It is horrible what happened to that girl—but this way of honoring her feels so fake to me. There are so many ways I would rather do it.

"Absolutely not," Lyla tells me. "Why, do you?" She doesn't have anything to set in the pile of other flowers, notes, candles, and cheesy stuffed animals, probably won from crane machines and tossed under beds carelessly for years. Lyla probably thinks she can get away with it looking like the flowers are from both of us.

Whatever.

I glance at Sydney's picture one last time, noticing that it's a zoomed-in photo of her and a few girls from the purple team on the upper classmen camping trip—The Purple People Eaters. During the trip, teachers and chaperones had gone around incessantly, forcing us to stop what we were doing and pose so that we could be photographed. All the girls Sydney had been in this particular picture with are cropped out, but I have a feeling none of them even wanted to take the picture with her in the first place. I wonder why they wouldn't use a different photo of Sydney. One of her old school yearbook photos, or a picture of her that real parents or foster parents had captured at one point in time.

I turn away and keep walking with Lyla. "Thankfully, the football game is away tonight. So I have the night off from cheerleading. I'll probably just do something with the girls like usual."

"They're not mad at you anymore?" We stop at the school steps.

"They are, but not for long." I flip my hair over my shoulders and give her a casual shrug. I refuse to be afraid of Sophia any longer, and I refuse to let her and Danielle and Olive continue to be mad at me when it's not my fault that I couldn't show up to Delilah's the other night in the first place. I give Lyla a goodbye wave and waltz inside the school, right up to where my friends are standing in front of Sophia's locker.

"What are we doing tonight?" I ask them with a cheery smile. I have to sort of force my way into their circle, but now that I'm here, all of their eyes are on me.

"Oh! Hi, Audrey!" Danielle smiles at me happily. At least she's not mad at me. "We were thinking of going shopping after school and then either having a sleepover or seeing if anyone is throwing a party or doing something."

"That sounds perfect," I gush. "You guys can probably come to my house if you want."

Sophia looks offended that I'm here. "Is this your way of apologizing?" Her chin juts out as she speaks. "Because if so, it needs some work."

I drop the happy act. "I'm sorry I wasn't at Delilah's. My car keys mysteriously disappeared forever, so I had to wait for my parents to bring me the spare set. My parents are fighting. Then they were mad at me for losing the key, and it was just... a lot. I completely spaced. And I should've texted you guys later, but then I found out about Sydney..."

"When we found out about Sydney, we all texted in the group chat," Sophia points out.

"I know. I saw all the messages. I was going to reply, but I—Lyla was really upset. By the time I finally got to go to bed, I forgot that I had been about to text you guys. It's not an excuse, and I didn't mean to not text you, nor did I mean to forget about you. You guys are my best friends and I will try harder to show you that. I promise."

I know that most of what I just told them is a lie, but I just don't know if I can trust them enough to tell them the truth. I want to be able to tell them everything that's been going on with me, but something in my gut is telling me to just keep it to myself.

"Oh my gosh, Audrey!" Danielle gives me a sympathetic pout and throws her arms around me in a hug. I hug her back, and when I feel Olive and Sophia join the hug, warmth fills me. Finally.

One crisis averted.

When we break apart, Sophia is smiling slightly, seemingly back to her normal self. "We love you, Audrey. Always. If we do have a sleepover, it's going to be at my house. My mom just bought me a green screen to film TikToks in front of, and we're super excited to mess with it."

My eyes light up. "Oh my God, I've actually been wanting to—"

My jaw snaps shut when I see Warner walking through the double doors and right in my direction.

My brain enters panic mode.

"I just remembered. I have to..." I can't think of an excuse fast enough. He's almost reached me. So instead of saying anything, I turn away from my friends, keeping my eyes trained on Warner so that I can gauge how close he's getting. I walk away in the other direction so fast that it's practically a run, but I only make it a few steps before my entire body collides with another body. One that is much taller, stronger, and more masculine than mine.

I gasp out loud as the person catches me. At first, all I can see is chest. A muscular, broad chest underneath a football jersey. My eyes trail up and meet the eyes of Ryan Copeland. He looks surprised at first, but then he smiles at me. I giggle. Some of my hair has fallen in my face from the collision. Nervously, I move it away, then I realize one of my hands is still on Ryan's chest and I'm still standing much closer to him than I need to be. I step away and giggle some more.

"Uh, hello to you, too," Ryan jokes. His voice is so deep and his hair is so beautiful and his eyes are like warm pools of sunshine. I know all my friends are behind me right now, witnessing this. Ryan Copeland is a completely gorgeous senior. I guess I sort of set my sights on him after he complimented my boots at the upperclassman camping trip. Before that, I always thought he was hot, but I didn't think he even had any idea who I was.

"I-I am so sorry," I say to him with a wide, embarrassed smile. "I was trying to..." What had I been trying to do again?

Oh, my gosh.

I look over my shoulder. In the massive throng of students lingering in the halls before the bell, there is no longer any sign of Warner.

"Actually?" Ryan asks. I look back at him. "That kinda just made my morning."

Ryan Copeland is flirting with me. I can't believe it.

"No, it did not," I tell him with an eye roll.

He chuckles. "No, I'm serious. I've been trying to find an excuse to talk to you for a while now."

I could die right here and now. Ryan is the perfect distraction. One I didn't even realize I needed. But Ryan has just saved me from a potentially awkward and scary run-in with Warner. So whether Hottie Copeland knows it or not, he is my hero. My knight in shining... polyester cotton blend.

CHAPTER 10

MADDY

I refuse to sit at home all night feeling sorry for myself. I refuse to lounge around, thinking nonstop about stupid Craig and stupid Sydney—may she rest in peace—and worrying about what the future will bring. Warner won't be home until late because of his away football game. I'm already home from work. I don't have many girlfriends to hang out with, but Amelia and I just started being friends again—I don't want to bombard her with my constant urges to get together with her.

Normally on a free Friday night, I would go to my usual spot: The Mix. It's a total dive bar, but it's the perfect assortment of people my age, single lonely men older than my father, scantily clad and sassy bartenders, and bikers—usually from a gang. It has cheap drinks, good music, and pool tables, so there is really nothing more I could ask from it. But then Craig and I started dating, and we started going there on Fridays together. He liked it so much that he told me he had started to go without me, too, on nights when he got off a long shift in need of a cold one.

Now I feel like I shouldn't go to The Mix. I don't want to chance running into Craig. And even though he was incredibly rude and even slightly unsettling the last time I spoke with him, I still miss him, so I don't trust myself to even be in the same establishment as him yet.

Instead, I decide to step out of my comfort zone. I put on a little black dress. I pull out my strappy snake-skin heels. I touch up my hair and redo my makeup, putting more of it on than I normally do; it's been so long, I've almost forgotten how to wear eyeliner. And that, with the deep burgundy lipstick—I almost don't recognize myself when I look in the mirror.

I stare at myself in the mirror from different angles. "There. Perfectly classy."

When I am satisfied—which doesn't take long because I know I look gorgeous—I give myself a selfie-put and a wink in the mirror and make my way in my Hyundai to The Viper. It's a newer club-ish style bar and restaurant on the nicer side of Toxey.

I'm used to being on my own. So even though I've never been here before, I have no trouble going inside and walking up to the bar by myself. Besides, I know a lot of the people in Toxey. Chances are I'll run into somebody I know and I'll find people to make conversation with.

The wall underneath the bar top is glowing bright blue with a black lace-like pattern over the front of it made from metal. The interior of The Viper is sleek, yet dramatic and dark. It makes me feel like if vampires existed, they would exclusively drink at this place and this place only.

After I sit down, I scope out the others at the bar with me. I am pleased to see that while there are two couples in their 20s, there are also two couples that look to be in their 50s, and two girls sitting together that look closer to my age. I had only worried slightly before I got here if I was too old for this kind of scene. Now, I think I fit right in. It's still early, though. No one is even out on the dance floor yet.

I've only been here about half an hour before a scrumptious-looking man comes up beside me and shoots me a white, straight-teethed smile. He's dressed business casual, has dark blonde hair that could nearly pass for brown, and he has one of those dimples on his chin that I've always found attractive on a guy.

"How's your night going?" he asks me. He doesn't sit down. I wonder if he's trying to gauge whether or not I even want him talking to me before he does so. I've been feeling bored lately. And I am sad about Craig. And this guy is just so dang handsome that I can't resist myself.

I flash him a sultry smile and look at him under my lashes. "Well, I think it's about to get a lot better."

He chuckles. Even his laugh is attractive. How does someone get an attractive laugh, anyway?

"Nobody has used that one on me in a while," the man says.

"Oh, but don't worry—they were all definitely thinking it."

"Well, that is incredibly sweet of you. What are you drinking tonight?"

"A martini." He's already going to buy my next drink? Oh my goodness, this is too easy. Too perfect. Mr. Hot Stuff here is exactly the type of guy that can make me forget all about Craig and my complicated life.

"Did you try the Viper Martini?" he asks, nodding at the drink menu in front of me. "It's got this amazing smokiness in it. And we infuse the vodka here in house."

Wait a second.

"We?"

He grins. Then he holds out his hand for me to shake it. "My name is Steven. I'm the owner."

All I want to do now is go find a dark secluded booth, crawl under the table, and die of embarrassment. Steven hadn't come up to me to flirt. He's working.

I stutter as I try to find the words. "Wow, I—I'm so sorry. I thought you were..." I trail off and decide to give up. "I'm Maddy."

"Hey, Maddy. Don't even worry about it." We stop shaking hands, but for some reason, we are still holding them. Our eyes are locked onto each other. "After all, there's a reason I chose you as my first stop of the night."

I can finally feel my face again as relief floods me. So I hadn't been misreading the situation entirely, at least.

Steven and I end up talking for a lot longer than he is probably supposed to. I make him laugh. He makes me smile more than I have done in a while. Then, before he insists that he needs to get back to work, he asks for my phone number. Feeling giddy, I pull one of my business cards out of my clutch and hold it out to him. And he shoots me a wink that makes my knees weak and then finally walks away.

I'm still smiling to myself for a while as I sit at the bar, processing what has just happened. I'm really glad I decided to get myself out of the house tonight, and I'm really glad that, out of all the places I could have chosen to go, I decided to come here.

Maybe everything does happen for a reason.

I think about Craig and the situation I'm in. The smile leaves my face and I quickly change my mind.

Most things that happen don't have any reason.

A young female bartender hands me one of their black checkbooks. "Hi. Um, somebody wanted me to give this to you." She looks slightly confused.

I take the checkbook and mimic her expression. She shrugs and walks away.

My stomach dips with excitement. I have a few ideas about what Steven could have left for me inside of here.

I open up the checkbook, and my hopeful expression falls. It's replaced with more confusion at first. All that's in the checkbook is a photograph. I have to squint a little because it's dark in here, but as soon as I realize what it's a picture of and see the date and time-stamped at the bottom right-hand corner, I have to exert physical energy to prevent myself from crying out in disbelief.

I'm holding, in my hands, a photograph of my son and Sydney Hutton. It was taken during the upperclassman trip. It was taken in the dark, after curfew. And it was taken the night that Sydney died.

CHAPTER 11

LYLA

I don't care if my mom grounds me. I don't want to see anyone. I don't really feel like going anywhere but where I am right now. I don't care if she takes my phone away. There's nobody I want to talk to, and it honestly might help relieve some of my anxiety to not have it on me all the time. To not know if I'm getting any mysterious texts or being threatened by some creepy stalker.

Mom and Dad don't want Audrey or me staying out late. And if we do go somewhere, they want to know where we are at all times. But I don't want to tell them that I'm here. Here at the graveyard, late on a Friday night, sitting at Trinity's grave. I come here to talk to her often. But it's a secret. A secret that is just mine, when it feels like so little else is.

So Mom can get mad at me all she wants. I'm not telling her where I am, and I'm definitely not going to make it back home in time for curfew.

I plop down in the grass as soon as I reach her headstone. I could probably walk to it all the way from my house with my eyes closed now.

I let out a great deep sigh. I'm sitting hunched over and defeated, and I know it's bad for my posture, but I don't have any energy or apathy to do anything about it.

"Trin…" I don't even know where to start with this. If Trinity was here right now, she would tell me my life is like a movie. But then again, maybe if she had never died in the first place, nothing that has happened since our accident would have ever occurred at all. "I hope you're ready and have your listening ears on, because I have so much stuff that I need to get off my chest today."

The sun is just now starting to set. I dive in and talk to Trinity about everything I'm dealing with. About what has me worried. Then, I tell her things that I don't have anyone else to talk to about.

"I don't know what's wrong with me, Trinity. I can't stop thinking about... Warner." It feels strange to even say it out loud, but it's true. "I just don't know what to think about all of it. Why would he lie to me about seeing Sydney that night? What happened when he was with her, and how does it tie in with her ending up dead? I can't picture Warner doing anything to her. But... I don't know. Maybe there's more to it."

Audrey didn't even like to think about the possibility that Warner could have a reasonable explanation as to why he didn't tell us about Sydney. It's a closed discussion with her. Pointless to have. In the blink of an eye, my sister is always ready to change her mind about things. About people.

"And with the whole text message thing... did he really not send Jackson that text? Is he just regretting that he did send it and is trying to lie and say that it hadn't been him? Or had somebody actually taken his phone? And... I don't know. What if—what if it's true? What if Warner really does have feelings for me? He wouldn't, right? Since I'm Jackson's... girlfriend?" I groan. "Ugh, Jackson. Trin, I haven't been thinking about him at all. Is that weird?"

Every time he calls me, texts me, Snapchats me, or messages me on social media, I am able to either ignore it and not even open the message, or silence the call and then push it to the back of my mind. I know my issues with Jackson are big, but the other things I'm trying to deal with right now are bigger. At least, that's how I see it in my head.

"I'll just say it—I want to be wrong about Warner. I want him to be the good guy that I keep picturing him to be. And I want—if he has a crush on me or feels for me in some way—I want him to tell me. I just want to know the truth."

But one simple truth in a sea full of so many lies. It's like trying to find Waldo. Where would I even look?

I feel that I could never admit this stuff to anyone. Especially not to Audrey. I get the feeling she wouldn't be too pleased to find out I maybe have slight feelings for my boyfriend's best friend. I don't even like admitting it to myself because I know how messed up it is. I wish I could help it. I wish there was an OFF button. Some magical cure or remedy. But there's just not.

"I miss him."

I rest my chin on my knees and pout for a moment. Then I look at her name on the gravestone.

"And I miss you. I even miss Sydney, too, even though I never really got to know her that well. But at least she was someone I could talk to. Warner had been someone I could talk to, too. He didn't seem to mind that I had changed since you left. Unlike Jackson seems to mind."

I sit there forever in silence after that. I let my mind wander and play out scenarios that will most likely never happen. I pretend like everything is fixable. I imagine things easy and simple and back to the way they used to be.

When I finally jolt out of that toxic fantasy and go back to the reality I need to face, I look at my phone and see that it is much later than I thought. How is it that I've sat here thinking and talking to Trinity for so long?

I scramble to my feet and look around the cemetery. I'm alone here now. I'm surprised no one has come by to tell me that they're going to be closing the gates soon.

I rest my hand on top of Trinity's gravestone. The lump forms in my throat, but this time, I don't cry.

"Love you." I give it a gentle pat, and then I start walking back home.

I make it about ten steps away from the gravestone of my dead best friend when a noise spins me back around towards it. I don't see anything near me, but it had sounded like someone was calling my name. It sounded far away.

There is no way somebody knows I'm here and has come to see me, I tell myself. *You're imagining things.*

I turn back and keep walking. All the hairs on the back of my neck are standing straight up and goosebumps are rippling down my arms. Suddenly it feels as if the temperature around me has dropped forty degrees. I decide to pick up the pace a little, wanting to get out of here.

But then I hear it again. Louder this time.

"Lyla!"

Somebody is definitely calling my name. It sounds like they're crying out to me. They sound upset. Afraid.

I stop walking again and look back around. Before, it had sounded like the voice was coming more from the east. That time, it sounded like it was coming more from the west. Like the cry had been carried through the breeze. A ghostly whisper in the wind.

I can't believe I actually hallucinate stuff now. That has to be it—just hallucinations. No one is here trying to talk to me. Ghosts aren't real. My name isn't being said. Nobody needs my help.

I'm up to a slow jog now, my heart pounding in my chest. A twig snaps to my right, and I gasp in alarm.

I don't even look to see if anyone is there. I am too terrified now for that.

"Lyla!"

"No!" I hear myself shouting out loud. I picture what happened to Audrey in the hallways at school. The person who had been chasing her. What if they're here in the cemetery with me now? What if that person is Warner, and he wants to mess with me, just like he messed with my sister?

At the thought of someone in a mask trailing behind me, stalking me, I start sprinting. I can't get out of this cemetery fast enough.

CHAPTER 12

WARNER

Somehow, miraculously, we won the football game tonight. I didn't play my best, and neither did the rest of the team. Jackson hadn't been there and that hurt us, too. Yet, somehow, the other team did just enough bad of a job that we were able to scrape by.

I don't feel like celebrating the win. I don't want to go to any parties or kickbacks. I don't want to talk to any of my teammates. I'm not in any sort of mood to do any celebrating. Instead, I keep my headphones in my ears on the bus back to school, then I sneak away at the first possible chance once we're in the parking lot and get in my dinged-up Jeep to make my escape.

I know what I want to do tonight. It's time I finally clear the air. I need to talk to Jackson, and I need to talk to Lyla. I need to make things right so that I'm not mulling over all of this any longer. If I don't get my focus back on football and on school, I'm not going to be able to stay on the team. And I'm not going to be able to get into college and out of Toxey, either.

I decided that I will try to talk to Lyla first. I know Jackson is my best friend and I know he should hold more importance to me than Lyla does, but I choose Lyla first, anyway.

My palms are a sweaty mess on my steering wheel as I drive over to her house. Since she's not replying to my texts or calls, I'm going to do things the old-fashioned way. I need to know what she thinks about all of this. I need to know what she thinks about me and what she thinks about that text message Jackson received from "me." I need to know how she feels about Jackson. I need to know that she one-hundred percent doesn't have any feelings for me and that she is going to rekindle things with Jackson. That she's going to make everything go back to the way it used to be—at least, as much as she could.

I'm nervous to show up at the Bailey residence and knock on her door, but I don't let my emotions stop me. And I tell myself I don't care who might answer.

I pull up to the curb outside her house, put my Jeep in park, and make my way quickly up to their front door before I can chicken out. My hand hovers in front of the doorbell, then I decide that it's better to knock.

I rap on the door three times.

Then I back away from it slightly and stick my hands in my pocket as I wait. What feels like an eternity goes by, and then the door unlocks and opens. It's none of the Bailey women that I've ever met before. In fact, I'm pretty sure this is Nora Flynn—Lyla's aunt. She's got long, dark brown hair and thick eyebrows, and even though Lyla and Audrey are blondes, I can still see some similarities between them and her.

"Uh, hi," I start off, talking fast. "Is Lyla around? I just have to talk to her about something super-fast. I'm sorry it's late, but I just got done with the game." I'm still wearing my football uniform to make it plainly obvious.

"Oh...uh,"—Nora looks over her shoulder and then returns to smiling at me through the crack in the door— "I'm sorry, but Lyla isn't here, actually."

My heart falls. I had expected her to be home. I had assumed she wouldn't be in the mood to do anything social, given everything that has been going on. I hope she isn't with Jackson.

"Do you know where she is?"

"Who are you?" Nora asks, tilting her head at me as she completely ignores my question.

"Sorry," I say. "Warner. I'm Lyla's... friend."

She slowly nods. I wonder how much she knows about me. If Lyla's ever told her anything about me before.

"Nice to meet you, Warner."

I'd tell her that it's nice to meet her, too, but she hasn't introduced herself. So I stand there, awkwardly silent, as she continues to give me a strange, hard look until finally, she answers me.

"I wish I had an answer for you, but I have no idea where Lyla went."

The door opens wider suddenly, and then I find myself facing Amelia Bailey as she stands right next to her sister. "What's going on?" she asks in a slightly snippy voice.

I had anticipated talking to maybe one adult. Definitely not two. And Lyla's mom does not look happy to see me.

"I was just looking for Lyla," I explain, knowing Mrs. Bailey is not going to be happy about it. But what else could I say? That I was here selling Girl Scout cookies?

"Warner." She steps closer to the door, slightly knocking Nora to the side. "You need to go home, okay?"

"I'm sorry, I just—"

"I don't know how aware of this you are, but you and my daughters are related to what happened to Sydney, somehow. At least, that's what the police think. If you don't want to make yourself look any more suspicious, then you need to keep your distance from them. Both of them."

My mouth drops open, but no words are able to fall out. Think of something, quick! Apologize!

"Mrs. Bailey, I really—"

"Go home, Warner."

I can't get another word in. Amelia Bailey has already shut the door on me.

My feet drag as I trudge back to my Jeep and start it up. I think about going home like Mrs. Bailey told me to do, but I am already here. And I want to talk to Lyla. I wouldn't let my mom stop me from doing it, so I'm not going to let Lyla's mom stop me, either.

I move my car down the street slightly and then turn it off again. Then I turn off my lights, too.

"She has to come back eventually," I say to no one.

I get on the Snapchat app and go to the map. Most of the people at my school have their locations turned off because of their parents demanding they keep it private. Jackson, however, is one of the few who has his location visible. I can see that his avatar is at his house. It's a good thing he has his location on. Now I'll be able to tell if he's with Lyla whenever she finally gets back here.

The second I click my phone off and the screen darkens, removing the last source of light I had around me, I see movement in my side-door mirror. My heart nearly skips a beat as I realize that it's Lyla. But she's not casually walking back to her house or riding her bike.

She's sprinting.

Lyla is sprinting and repeatedly looking over her shoulder. It's easy to tell that something has her completely freaked out.

She has to run past my Jeep before she gets to her house, so I scramble to get out of my car before I miss my chance to stop her.

The second she sees me waiting there for her, she comes to a sudden halt. Her eyes widen even more than they already were as she stares at me.

"Lyla?" I ask, feeling nervous and slightly worried. She's not dressed for a jog. She's wearing jeans and a cropped hoodie. So why is she running? Or what is she running from? "Are you okay?"

She doesn't look relieved to be seeing me. She looks... more afraid.

Instead of answering my question, she lets out a small, pained whimper, then she turns around and starts running in the opposite direction.

"Lyla, wait!" I start jogging after her. "Lyla, what are you doing?!" I can't believe I'm doing this right now. I can't believe I'm chasing my crush through the streets of her neighborhood. Should I be doing this? Does this make me crazy? Desperate? "Lyla, I just want to talk to you!"

She doesn't even bother to look over her shoulder at me. She just keeps going. So I force myself to stop going after her.

I put my hands on my knees and pant, but I don't think I'm out of breath from running.

I have no idea what just happened.

CHAPTER 13

AMELIA

I t's the end of September. That means that, in my mind, it's officially autumn. That's why I'm spending my Saturday morning currently digging through the numerous boxes on their shelves inside of my garage. I'm getting all of my autumn supplies out so I can decorate the house—make it a little cheerier and lively in here in the hopes of manifesting a different environment for my kids.

Joey has a soccer game this morning, but Gentry is there cheering him on, so I decided that I would skip this one. I know Joey is disappointed that I'm not there, but at least he has one parent to show him support. I just... can't be around my husband right now. I'm still reeling over the conversation I had with him last night, and I can't seem to wrap my head around it. If I went to the soccer game today, I'm afraid that Gentry and I would end up continuing our fight, and I don't want to risk embarrassing Joey in front of his teammates.

It feels like I have the house to myself this morning, even though I don't. Nora is sleeping in, up in the guest room, like she normally does on the weekends. The girls are awake, I think, but they are both keeping to themselves in their bedrooms.

I'm carrying two large gray storage tubs with the word FALL labeled on them neatly from my label-maker out of the garage, through the mudroom, and into the kitchen, when I hear a knock on my front door.

What is it with people showing up unannounced all of a sudden? Have I gone back in time? Is this the nineties? Just last night, Warner had shown up here. I never told Lyla that he had, and I advised Nora to do the same. Lyla was dealing with a lot right now already—she didn't need Warner adding to the drama.

I set the boxes down with a grunt—they are very heavy and I'm starting to sweat slightly—and then I go check the peephole of my front door. I don't know why part of me expects it to be Warner at the door yet again, back to try to speak to Lyla despite my warning. I'm ready to draw a huffy, irritated breath and throw the door open to warn him some more, but instead of a teenager waiting out on my doorstep, I see Craig Fritz through the peephole.

I leap away from the door as if it has shocked me, then I slap a hand over my mouth, worried Craig can hear my breathing on the other side. I don't want him to know that I have seen him out there. I don't want to answer the door. I look towards the staircase to listen for sounds of either of my girls or Nora coming down to answer it. Thankfully, it's still quiet up there.

The knocking sounds again, sending my heart to my throat.

"Amelia, are you there?" Craig asks through the door. I realize the handle is unlocked. He could just twist it and push my door right open. "I need to talk to you. I just have some questions."

I decide I don't even care if he hears it; I step forward again, lock the door—which is loud enough that there's a very high chance that he heard it—and lean up against the back of it. I squeeze my eyes shut and hold my breath, waiting to see what he does next. Waiting for him to go away.

I bet he wants to talk about Carson.

But what happened to Carson Price was so long ago. Why is Craig trying to dig all of this back up now?

With my eyes still closed, images fly through my head from the night of my junior prom: a flash of the frilly metallic backdrop that pictures were taken in front of. The live band. Maddy and I causing a scene in the middle of the dance floor. Then blood. So much blood.

I have to open my eyes so that I don't see it anymore. I don't want to go back to that night. I thought all of this was behind me.

The other side of the door I'm still leaning against remains silent. When I'm finally brave enough to peek through the peephole again, I see Craig getting back in his old brown car.

I finally let out the breath I'd been holding. Then I look at my staircase again. That's when it dawns on me.

Nora.

If Craig is looking for answers from all those years ago, then maybe that's the reason why Nora is here, too.

I glide down the hallway towards my bedroom in a flurry. I get my anxiety medication out of the cabinet in my bathroom, and with shaking hands, I twist the bottle open and toss a pill back into my mouth.

CHAPTER 14

AUDREY

Lyla's room across the hall faces the backyard. My bedroom faces the street.

So when somebody knocks on the door while I'm sorting through my clothes to see what I want to donate to Goodwill, I walk over to the window and peek out to see who it could be. I don't recognize the strange, old brown car. Curious, I walk over to the staircase. At the top of it, I freeze when I realize Mom is already on her way to answering the door.

Only, she doesn't answer it.

Spying on her carefully, not wanting to be seen, I watch as Mom gets a freaked-out look on her face, locks the door, and stands there leaning against it.

It's definitely strange behavior, so I go back to my room quietly on my tiptoes, then I spy through my shutters and wait until whoever it is goes back to their car so I can see them.

It's Detective Fritz.

I dart across the hall to Lyla's room. I don't knock before entering, even though she's always complaining that I need to.

"Oh my God, what?" she snaps when she sees me. She's currently lying on her floor, her phone in her hand. I'm willing to bet she's spent the entire morning aimlessly watching TikTok videos on it.

I don't care that she's in a mood. "Uh,"—I step into her room and close the door behind me. Then I lock it, just in case Mom tries to come in unannounced. I don't want her to know what I've just seen — "Detective Fritz was just at our door again, and Mom saw it was him through the peephole, then she, like, freaked out and didn't answer it."

My sister had already had an irritated look on her face when I burst into her room without her permission, but now her eyes are narrowed even further, almost to slits. "I wonder why," she says.

"You don't think he was here about us, do you?" I ask. "I heard Mom and Dad talking the other night. They were mentioning something about wondering if they needed to call their lawyer."

Lyla, who had propped herself up on her elbows when I first entered, now sits herself up all the way. "Because of us? Because of Detective Fritz and Sydney?"

"Probably."

"But... we had nothing to do with what happened to Sydney."

I shrug. "Obviously. I wonder, though... how many people do you think get put in prison even when they're innocent?" It makes me feel slightly nauseated to think about it. But as far as I'm concerned, the person that the cops should be looking into is Warner. I don't know if I think he killed Sydney or not, but I am pretty certain he knows what happened to her. He's guilty of something. He wouldn't have lied to us about that night otherwise.

"Do you think Fritz has been back to Warner's house, too, then?"

"He'd at least be more on the right trail if he has."

I know Lyla snuck off to go see Sydney the night she died, too. I know there's a chance that Lyla could be lying to me about what happened after she snuck out of our tent during the upperclassman trip. But she's not only my sister, she's my twin. If she was lying to me, I get the feeling that I would be able to tell. I trust Lyla about this.

"Yeah," Lyla says, her eyes downcast. "Maybe." But Lyla doesn't look super convinced. She opens and shuts her mouth, and I can tell she's debating on whether or not she wants to tell me something. I walk over to the edge of her bed and take a seat. She looks up at me from down on the ground.

"What is it?" I ask.

"Something happened with Warner last night," she blurts out.

"What do you mean? With you?"

"Yeah. I was—well, I had a run-in with him. He—I think maybe he was following me. He showed up at the house, and I freaked out and ran away from him. And for a little bit, he sort of... chased after me."

My mouth drops open. "Oh my God, Lyla!"

"He told me he just wanted to talk. Do you think maybe he could have been the person in the mask who chased you at school?"

Ugh. That stupid incident I can't stop thinking about—the reason I had decided that I needed to clean out my entire closet today to keep my mind from wandering back to it. Could it have been Warner and not Mr. Reeves who chased me? Could Warner have been playing us this whole time? "I have no idea."

"What if he's dangerous, Ree? I keep thinking that maybe we should just show the police that photo."

I start to give her a look because we've talked about this already, but she holds up her finger to prevent me from speaking so that she can continue.

"It might help at least clear his name if he isn't the one behind it!"

"The police—or Detective Fritz, at least—already think we might have had something to do with Sydney's death. If we turn in that photo, he'll probably just think we're trying to pin the blame on somebody else. It could backfire and make us look even more guilty."

"Yeah...I feel like I wouldn't even want to go to Freaky Fritz about it, anyway," Lyla agrees. "He gives me the creeps."

"Yeah, and so does Warner," I say. "I can't believe he chased you. I can't believe he could've chased... me." What if Warner Carpenter just put on this sweet and innocent act so that no one would ever guess that he was behind something so horrible? He might have everybody fooled.

Lyla holds her head as if it hurts. Then she groans loudly. "I just don't know what to think!"

I start fuming inside. My blood boils thinking about Warner. I've been trying to lay low and stay away from him, but I don't want to be afraid of him anymore. I don't want to fall for any more of his tricks and land in any more of his traps.

Over the remainder of my weekend, my feelings about Warner fester. By the time Monday rolls around and I'm getting ready to go to school, I feel different, somehow. Braver. Almost like a loose cannon, too.

Lyla has been basically immobile on the couch all weekend because she had exerted too much effort with her bad leg while running away from Warner. I watched Mom and Dad take care of her and ask her what happened, and I had listened as Lyla came up with some ridiculous lie about why she had been running in the first place. She lied because she was scared. Of Warner. Of what would happen if she just told the truth.

Just like I am.

When we get to school, Lyla and I climb out of my Mini Cooper and notice right away that Warner has been waiting for us inside of his Jeep. I glare in his direction as I watch him jump out of it and storm toward us.

Lyla tugs on my lavender cardigan. "Let's go." Her voice is low and nervous. She tries to pull me along and away from Warner, but instead, I get out of her grasp and meet Warner in the middle of the parking lot.

"Audrey, what are you doing?" Lyla hisses after me.

Warner has a stone-set face, and he's squinting slightly from the rising sun behind me shining in his eyes. It's one of those rare bright and beautiful days here in Toxey, but my mood certainly isn't matching it.

Warner speaks first. "Hey." His voice is snippy. He's not yelling, but he doesn't sound friendly, either. "What is your guys' deal?"

"Ours?" I say in a threatening tone. I invade his personal space to show that I am not afraid of him. "What about you, Warner, huh?"

Warner looks over my shoulder at Lyla. I move my body so that I obstruct his view of her.

"No!" I snap, pointing a finger at his face. "Don't look at her. You don't get to go anywhere near her!" I didn't expect my voice to be as loud as is it. I didn't expect to feel this angry. I didn't plan for my entire body to be trembling with my confrontation.

Warner looks bewildered. "Are you kidding? I seriously don—"

"What's going on over here?"

I look to my right and see that a boy in my grade, Wrigley Hall, is quickly approaching us. He looks right at Lyla, then at Warner. When he reaches us, he inserts himself directly between Warner and me.

"What did I do?" Warner dares to ask, trying to look at me past Wrigley as if he's not even there.

Wrigley holds his arms out, acting as a peacekeeper between us. "Let's just calm down," he says to Warner, his body facing him, his back close to me. He's quite tall, and it feels a little bit like I suddenly have a bodyguard. But I hardly even know Wrigley, and I don't really know why he thinks he can insert himself in my business like this.

"Audrey," Warner says, like I hold the power to make Wrigley go away.

Wrigley gets quieter, addressing Warner, only. "Come on, dude."

Lyla snatches my hand from behind and drags me back away from the both of them. She doesn't look at me. She doesn't speak. She just holds me close to her, a safe distance away from the two boys, as she watches them wearily.

"I don't know what's happening," Warner mutters. This time, it seems like he might finally be addressing Wrigley instead of us.

Wrigley slowly shakes his head. "Just walk away, Warner. Just walk away."

Around us, an audience has formed. Warner doesn't move at first, looking conflicted. He looks over at us again, and Wrigley looks over his shoulder to do the same. There's something in Wrigley's expression when his eyes meet Lyla's. I don't really understand what it could be. Then he looks back at Warner. He's not being violent or aggressive, and neither is Warner. So I don't really know why everyone feels like watching this.

Warner finally shakes his head and walks away. The bell for first hour starts to ring and the crowd begins to disperse. Wrigley runs a hand through his hair, looks at Lyla again, nods his head at me, and then he leaves, too.

I know I'm not exactly sure what just happened and why Wrigley got involved, but I'm starting to wonder just how much I don't know about my sister.

CHAPTER 15

MADDY

I'm coming back from my lunch break—which didn't feel nearly as long as I needed it to be after the stressful weekend I had—and when I round the corner from the back of my hair salon, I see my coworkers lingering at the reception desk, eyeing something out the window and whispering to each other.

I begin approaching them, curious.

"What are you guys gossiping about now?" I joke, the chunky square heels of my boots clicking loudly on the linoleum tile as I walk in their direction.

Rochelle looks at me over her shoulder, an excited grin on her face. "We're just eyeing the cute police officer out front who's just sitting in his car."

"I'm trying to figure out what he's doing exactly," Mariah says. They part a little to let me in so I can get a look. Lunch threatens to come right back out the way it went when I see that they're referring to Craig.

Rochelle giggles some more. "I swear, he's been sitting there for over an hour. He keeps looking over here, too."

"Maybe some sort of drug bust is going to happen," Mariah muses.

"That coffee shop next door does sell donuts..." Rochelle jokes. The girls laugh. I don't.

"How long did you say he's been out there?" I ask, looking at Mariah since she's the receptionist who is by the window the most. Craig is indeed looking right towards the storefront of the salon, and he looks angry. His jaw is tight.

"Since I noticed him," Mariah informs me. "At least an hour. Maybe even longer."

You guys may not know why he's out there, but I sure do.

A memory hits me from all the way back in high school. My junior year. That year.

It was morning. I had just gone to school the weekend after the prom. It was right after Dean Reeves had come up to me to tell me that Nora Flynn had found Carson Price...dead.

"Dead?" I had whispered back to Dean. I could feel it in the air even though I hadn't even stepped foot inside of the high school yet—the news had spread around to everyone. Toxey had turned a couple of dials darker.

I stood there in shock, barely able to move as Dean looked at the ground with somber eyes.

Then Craig Fritz, a senior, approached us both. He looked wrecked that morning. His eyes were bloodshot and had dark circles underneath them. He had a serious case of bed head. His body language was slumped. His fists were clenched. "I can't believe this is happening," he said. He stood next to Dean and looked right at me. I thought it was because I wasn't that different from Carson. I had been the new kid in town, too. A misfit. I hadn't been like the other people at Blackfell High School.

But I was still alive.

It was as if Craig was silently saying, "This could've happened to you."

Dean had put a friendly, comforting hand on Craig's shoulder. Back then, they had been friends.

I didn't know what to say to Craig. Carson had been his friend. Sure, Craig had had lots of friends in high school. But I'm pretty sure with Carson, Craig was his only one.

"The police have been searching the woods all weekend," Craig went on to inform us. "They haven't found a... body... yet."

Dean must've sensed why I had an alarmed, confused stare. I didn't know how Craig had gotten his hands on that information. How he knew so much already. "Craig's uncle is a cop," he told me. "The town is trying to keep everything quiet because nobody wants to let out the story of a prom night death in a small town like this. It's not good for the tourism."

"Apparently that's all that matters." Craig's tone had changed from sad to angry in an instant. "Getting tourists to visit. Not finding out where Carson is and who did this to him!"

I had jumped backward, startled by how suddenly loud and violent Craig had become. It caught me completely off guard. I knew Craig could have a temper sometimes, but I hadn't ever seen a side of him like that.

"Maddy?"

I snap out of my thoughts and see that my coworker, Rochelle, is staring at me in concern. "You okay?"

I can't believe this is what Craig has been up to all these years. I can't believe he's sitting in his cop car, spying on me right now.

"Uh, headache," I lie. Then I pull out my phone and compose a text to Nora, whom I had made plans to see today.

Me: *I have to cancel tonight. I'm so sorry.*

I send the text, and mere seconds later, I look down and see that Nora is calling me. I walk away from the girls, towards my salon station where I am more alone since we have no guests currently. "Hey, Nor," I say when I answer.

"What changed?" she asks immediately, disappointment plain in her tone. I can practically see her pouting.

She has me on the spot now. I hadn't thought up a good excuse yet. I would tell her about Craig, but how could I possibly? How could she ever understand?

"Just an ear-splitting headache," I throw out, deciding I'll share the same lie I had used with my coworkers. It makes my growing pile of lies easier to keep track of.

"Aw. But it's still early. You might feel better in a couple of hours?"

"It, uh, started last night and hasn't gone away," I try. "If it does go away, though, I can call you?"

"Bummer," she says. Then she lets out a long sigh. "But fine. Fingers crossed."

When I hang up, the guilt stings my cheeks. I don't enjoy lying to the people that I care about. I never have.

I end up exaggerating the headache lie so much that I leave work early, using it as my excuse. I feel horrible about it as I drive home, not because I left my coworkers hanging, but because I really can't afford to be taking time off right now.

I lay on my couch and watch horrible garbage reality TV on Netflix until Warner gets home from school. I haven't talked to him hardly at all since I received that picture of him and Sydney in the checkbook at The Viper. Warner had kept himself busy and out of the house the whole weekend.

If I had told him I was going to be home when he got home today, he probably would have found another excuse to avoid me. But I can't let him do it for one more day. As scared as I am to know what's going on with him, I am more scared to be left in the dark about it.

"Hey, you," I say in a small voice when he walks into the house.

"Mom—I didn't expect you to be home already." He drops his backpack by the door and walks into the kitchen while I look at him from over the back of the couch.

"How was school?"

He gets out the gallon container of milk and pours the last of it into a glass. "Fine."

"So... that black eye you got there..." I might as well just get to the point with him before he can come up with a reason to dip out on me again.

"It's not a big deal." He tosses the empty jug into the recycling bin and begins chugging the glass of milk. But the way he tilts his head upwards to drink it only makes the overhead kitchen light illuminate his black eye more clearly. It's definitely not nothing.

I get to my feet. "I know it's from Jackson. What happened?" How did my son go from having a best friend to being punched by him? Why do I feel like everything changed when Sydney Hutton showed up at Blackfell High School? And why won't he just talk to me about it? All I want to do is show him my support and help him.

"Mom, please, can we not do this? It's fine. Nothing."

"Well, did you guys make up yet?" I want to know if the fight with Jackson had anything to do with what happened that night at the upperclassman trip. If it had anything to do with what Warner might or might not have done to Sydney. It scares me to my core, but I just keep waiting for Warner to look me dead in the eyes with a straight face and say, "I killed her, Mom."

If that is what happened, then I wish he would tell me. We would figure it out together. I'll do whatever it takes to protect him.

"Make up?" Warner asks in a disgusted voice. "We're not five. Just—we're working some stuff out."

"Was it about Sydney?" I hold my breath.

He pauses just before tilting the glass back to his mouth again. It's brief. Then he drains the rest of his milk in large gulps. He shakes his head like a father disappointed in his child, then he leaves down the hallway to his room.

I plop back down on the couch, feeling helpless. Amelia said we need to work together to get as much information on Sydney as possible so we can prove our kids didn't have anything to do with her drowning. But all the information I am finding out from my son is instead leading me to believe that he did.

CHAPTER 16

LYLA

It's been easy enough to avoid Jackson these past few days. I just ignore every call and text message he sends me, and he doesn't have a car, so he can't physically come out to try to see me, *and* he's been suspended from school. It's like I have gotten a three-day vacation from him.

But now, it's Tuesday. That means that Jackson's three-day suspension is finally over and that he's going to be at school.

"Are you nervous about seeing him?" Audrey asks when we pull into her parking spot at school.

Of course, I'm nervous. This is the first time I've had a sinking feeling in my stomach over something other than the shrine sitting on the front curb outside.

I look out the window at the school steps. Thankfully, Jackson isn't here yet.

I shrug at my sister. It's weird to talk to her about this because I have a feeling that she wants me to be with Jackson still. That she wants me to work it out with him. She thinks we're good together and that he brings out a good side of me. *I* think she's wrong. But I really don't feel like arguing with her right now.

Audrey senses that I don't want to talk. She gets out of the car and throws her backpack over her shoulder. I take a deep breath and do the same. My goal is to hang out in the bathroom until the bell rings. Then, since Jackson and I have first hour together, I'll just wait until he's already seated before I enter the class, and then I'll find a seat far away from him. I'm going to avoid him at all costs, just like I have been doing with Warner.

I pause at the steps and wave goodbye to my sister, but then we both notice how one of the front office women is staring at me and standing by the door.

"Which one of you is Lyla Bailey?" she asks, looking back and forth between Audrey and me. "I can't remember which one of you got the cute haircut."

"It's me," I say nervously.

Audrey has a hand on the other door, ready to go inside, but she doesn't move. I'm guessing she wants to know what this front office lady wants with me, and so do I.

"Of course you are," the woman says. "Would you mind coming with me?"

"Do you want both of us?" Audrey asks. The woman purses her large lips and shakes her head. "I'll just need Lyla this morning."

She opens the door to the left, so Audrey gives me one last confused look before opening the door to the right and going inside. I slowly trail after her, going up the steps and walking through the door that the front office woman is holding open for me. I'm rarely in the front office, so I can't remember her name, but I know she does some sort of administrative stuff.

"Come with me, Lyla." The woman steps ahead of me and carries on down the hallway. I stare straight at her blue blazer-covered back, afraid to eye everyone who's lingering around the hallways until the first bell rings. I have no idea what I did wrong or where we're going. Not until we reach the front office and I am brought directly to Principal Mathers's secluded office.

My stomach knots and my heart lurches when I see who's already in the principal's office with him.

Jackson Mullens.

I know it's only been three days, but something looks different about him already. Maybe I'm just seeing him differently after what happened. It's hard to tell.

He looks over his shoulder as he strokes his stubble, then when he realizes who has walked in, he sits up straighter and clears his throat. His expression goes from annoyed to alert.

Principal Mathers is already sitting behind his desk. "Hey, Lyla, come on in."

"Hey, Ly," Jackson says to me in a quiet voice. I purse my lips and look away from him. Principal Mathers watches the exchange.

"Jackson, why don't you wait out in the hall?"

Feeling uncomfortable, I wait until Jackson stands, slides past me, and steps out into the hall. Then I do as I'm told.

The front office lady nods her head at Principal Mathers and then closes the door as the bell telling us to get to first period rings. Principal Mathers and I are alone.

"Do you want to sit?" Principal Mathers asks me.

I chew on my bottom lip. "No... that's okay." What could he possibly want from me? And Jackson?

"So I just wanted to talk to you while I have Jackson waiting out there," he starts, sounding soft. "The thing is, Jackson was suspended for three days because he punched his classmate, Warner Carpenter."

"I'm aware," I say uneasily.

Principal Mathers nods his head. "Right. Well, I didn't get this new information until this morning. Lyla, some students have come up to me to tell me that they saw Jackson push you in the cafeteria that same day. I will not name those students, but it was clear they were nervous about you having to... put yourself in a position where you are forced to face Jackson again before you might be ready."

"Oh..."

I don't know what to say. I don't know what I am supposed to do.

Jackson has always been a people person. He has always followed the rules and has always been a charming, good listener. He's won over all the teachers at Blackfell High. I wonder what they think of him now.

"Anyway," Principal Mathers continues. "I wanted to talk to you personally about it, Lyla. I wanted to get your thoughts. Is everything okay between Jackson and you? Do you feel... safe, attending school and having classes with him? You can be honest. I want to get the air cleared right now before I readmit Jackson."

I don't like the situation that I've found myself in. Yes, Jackson did technically push me in the cafeteria that morning. But he's also technically still my boyfriend. We've been together for a long, long time, and he used to make me really happy. And who am I to be a tattletale? I didn't complain to anyone that Jackson pushed me. I had been able to brush it aside, even.

"Everything's fine," I say to the principal. My voice sounds weak and unbelievable, but I look Mathers directly in the eyes because maybe that will help.

Principal Mathers shifts in his seat. "And you're sure about that?"

"Mhm."

What would happen if I turned around and dashed out of here right now? Would that make it even less believable?

"All right, then. Thank you for taking the time to talk it over. You're free to go to first hour."

Since I'm already standing close to the door, I nod my head and get out of there as quickly as possible. Principal Mathers follows me out so that he can ask Jackson to come back into his office—probably so he can tell him the good news.

I walk as fast as possible without it looking ridiculous. I don't want Jackson to think that I want to walk to first hour with him. I don't want him to get the wrong idea about why I said I was fine with him coming back. Everything is not fine.

Seconds later, I can hear Jackson's feet jogging lightly on the vinyl flooring behind me, echoing through the empty halls. Everyone's already in first hour; we're alone out here.

"Lyla, wait up."

I can't ignore him or pretend I didn't hear him. So I stop walking and let him reach me. We're already late, so I might as well get this over with.

"Hey, I'm so sorry," he says right away when he gets in front of me. And he does look apologetic, too—the sincerity is clear in his eyes. He reaches out like he wants to touch my forearm, but then he puts his hand back. "I know I shouldn't have done it. I should've never put my hands on you like that. I hardly even remember doing it, and I know that's not an excuse. But I was just... I was seeing red. I was so... *angry* at Warner. I was confused and I didn't know what happened or when he started feeling that way or why he would send me a text like that. I'm just really... sorry."

The only reason it takes me so long to respond is because of the giant lump in my throat. I don't want to start crying the second I speak, so I take some time to try to make it go away. To try and push it all back.

"I don't really know what to say," I decide, tucking some hair behind my ear.

"I get it." Jackson shuffles his feet. "I had a lot of time to think the past three days. Nobody would talk to me. I felt like I had no one. With Warner... I know I shouldn't have punched him either. It sucks because now I feel like I'm losing you *and* my best friend."

That does suck. It sucks that the text that got sent to Jackson had to ruin the friendship they had built up over the years—whether or not Warner had sent that text.

"I think you just need to work it out with him."

I don't want them to stop being friends. I don't want to be the person that came between the two of them. I'm not worth it.

Jackson nods his head, but I can tell that he's gnawing on the inside of his cheek. He hates the idea of confronting Warner. But he needs to.

"And what about us?" he asks. "Are we going to... work it out?"

This is a conversation I'm not ready for yet. I did not come to school prepared to deal with him at *all*, let alone to have this talk.

"Jackson, I'm sorry. I just... I need some time still."

"But Lyla... you've been ignoring me for three days already."

"I... I'm sorry."

I know we're going to the same class, but I continue walking toward it anyway, and this time as I go, I don't hear his footsteps trailing after me.

CHAPTER 17

AMELIA

While I'm sitting at my desk at work the next Tuesday, I quickly come to the realization that I shouldn't have ignored Dean's email.

I had never replied to it when I had been at the site visit with the Bartons because even if I did want to have coffee with Dean; I knew it wasn't a good idea, so I felt too conflicted to say anything back at all.

I should've at least replied to let him know that I didn't know if meeting with him was a good idea or not. Because as I type on my computer, I look up and see that Dean Reeves is getting out of his car and stepping up onto the curb of the sidewalk, heading directly towards my office.

I freeze mid-sentence of the email I had been typing to a client of mine. I hear the small bell chime, signaling his entrance into my office at the receptionist's desk. My receptionist is a young twenty-one-year-old still pursuing her interior design degree. She's working here on an internship. She does a lot of administrative stuff but also some small design work when I need the help. Her name is Ivy.

The door to my personal office is propped open, so I can vaguely hear what is being said out in the lobby.

"Is Amelia Bailey in?" Dean asks Ivy.

I straighten up in my chair and flatten my hair. I look at the small mirror on my desk and make sure my makeup isn't smudged. I pretend to be invested in the email that I was trying to get written, even though as I start typing now, I'm typing absolutely nothing—I'm just pressing keys to sound like I'm busy.

I'll have to make sure I don't accidentally send this.

In mere seconds, Ivy is standing in the archway of my office. I turn to her and smile, minimizing the email. "What's up?"

"I have someone named Dean Reeves asking if you're free to talk? He has coffee."

Please don't ask questions please don't ask questions please don't ask questions.

"Oh. Well... send him in."

"Is he a new client?"

"Uh... no..."

"A vendor?"

"No. He is... well, it's complicated." I want to palm myself on the forehead. It's complicated? Why did I tell her that?

Ivy shrugs and goes to retrieve him. I look around my white and blush-pink office. The chairs on the other side of my desk are those chairs with white fuzzy cushions on the seat. Is Dean Reeves even going to want to sit down in an office this girly?

Dean's footsteps come down the hall. I don't know what to do with myself. Should I be standing when he walks in? Sitting? Should I pretend like I'm still working? Do I act surprised? Happy?

I don't have any time to think about it deeper before suddenly, he's entering my office.

I get up from my desk, banging my knee under it as I go. I wince at the pain but then offer Dean a smile.

"Dean!" I cry out louder than necessary. "What—what are you doing here?"

He is, indeed, holding two coffees in his hands. "Came to see you," he says.

"Well, that's... I guess I am just..."

I'm a mess. A complete mess!

"It's just coffee, Mia."

Mia. Hearing him say my nickname makes my stomach twist. It makes me feel like I want to sit back down again.

"Right. How thoughtful." I give him a tight-lipped smile and accept the coffee that he's handing out to me. Then I motion to the chair. "Do you want to take a seat?"

"No, actually, I shouldn't. I'm just swinging by."

"Oh?"

"Yeah. I don't know if you've been getting my messages and are ignoring me on purpose, or if I'm just not getting your replies—" He pauses to shoot me a look to see if I'm going to tell him which answer is right. I don't. So he continues. "But I need to talk to you."

"Is everything okay?"

"Probably," he says. "But I have to get back to school before lunch ends. I'm here to set up a time and place since technology isn't being effective."

"I'm sorry, I've just been kind of dealing with a lot, and I've been really busy, and—"

"I get it. It won't take long. What works best for you?"

Dean has practically backed me into a corner. This isn't another one of his online messages that I can simply ignore.

I swallow and consider it.

It's just coffee. He's the one who asked to talk to me about something—whatever that something is. I'm not doing anything wrong by hearing what he has to say.

"Alright then," I finally say. "Tomorrow, when school gets out?"

"Works for me. Swing by my classroom."

"I need to talk to you, too, anyway."

I don't know why I just said that. Again, I want to hit myself.

He raises an eyebrow. "Yeah? Well, then, I look forward to it, Mia."

"Me too." I smile and take a sip of coffee. He grins back at me before leaving.

I'm stunned by what I'm tasting—it's a hot, sugar-free, vanilla latte with soy milk.

So many years have gone by, and Dean Reeves still knows my favorite order.

CHAPTER 18

WARNER

J ackson is back.

I don't see him before school, but I learn during my first-hour physics class that he has officially returned. Still, I don't get a glimpse of him until he shows up to our weight training class in second period.

A few people have asked me how I feel about it. Tons of people want to know about the gossip between Jackson and me. They want to know if we are still friends, too. I don't know how to answer that question because I don't know myself. I haven't exactly made any attempt to try to remedy anything with him since he got suspended. Yeah, he got a text message stating that I was in love with his girlfriend, but he was the one who punched me in the face. It wasn't like I had actually tried to get with Lyla. And I know I didn't send that text, either. Does it really have to be me who is supposed to try and make things right?

We're all in the gym, getting ready to do our workout routines. Before our fight, Jackson had always been my spotter. But when he was gone, I had worked out with Cody.

"You want to spot me again today?" I ask Cody.

"Oh, are you and Jackson not... ?"

I like Cody enough. He's funny and we have a lot in common. But he can also be super oblivious and airheaded.

I try to sound unbothered. "No." But Jackson is already at the squat rack with Chance as his spotter. He hasn't even as much as looked in my direction. Not even to glare at me. I don't know if that's worse or not. What if he's simply just done with me? What if we're no longer friends? What if we never get past this?

Whatever. I have enough to deal with.

"Alright. Fine with me," Cody says. We go to the bench press. When it comes to the weights, I'm surprised at how much more I'm able to lift than yesterday. Even Cody is surprised by it. But more than likely it's because of how angry and stressed out I am about the Jackson and Lyla stuff.

As I lift, I keep waiting for Jackson to say something to me. To look in my direction. To bump his shoulder into mine. But all period long, nothing happens.

Since Jackson is a grade under me, the only classes we have together are our electives. But fourth hour is my other elective, free period, and it's only for seniors.

At lunch, I brave myself and go to the cafeteria and sit with all of our shared friends. Jackson sits at the table, too, but he sits away from me at the other end and pretends like I don't exist. He seems happy enough, joking around and laughing with the guys like usual. However, multiple times, I catch him looking over his shoulder in Lyla's direction. Lyla is sitting at a table alone. Her sister, Audrey, is sitting at her normal table with her posse—Olive, Sophia, and Danielle—but this time, Ryan, who is usually with us, is sitting over there with one of his friends as well. I think Ryan has a thing for Audrey. I always saw Ryan's type to be girls more like Sophia, the mean queen of the school. Audrey is popular and beautiful, but she's a little more understated. Nice.

The third and final time I have to deal with Jackson for the day is during football practice. Jackson has a talk with Mr. Reeves in his office before we all go out into the field, and to my dismay, I see that Coach Reeves has let Jackson resume his spot on the team.

Fifteen minutes into the practice is when I realize why Jackson has been ignoring me all day. He's been waiting until now. Waiting to take out all of his pent-up aggression and anger towards me on the field. Jackson is one heck of a football player, and we need him back on the team if we want to have any chance of making it to state this year, but he's exerting a little too much effort today. He's showing off a little too much. And he's knocking me to the ground a little too hard, to where the breath is knocked out of me and pain is searing through my body every single time he does it.

I've had enough when Jackson gives me an unsolicited shove simply because I am in his path to get the ball. I fall to the ground on my back, rage shooting through me in an instant.

"What is your problem, dude?!" I shout at him.

"Just playing the game, Carpenter." Jackson extends his arms out wide and gives me a shrug. I can see the smirk under his helmet.

I get back to my feet and shove him back. "I didn't send that text!"

The whistle blows. "Hey! Break it up!"

Coach Reeves appears out of nowhere and pushes the two of us apart, inserting himself between us. I am reminded of my confrontation with Audrey and Lyla. How Wrigley had inserted himself between us then. I should probably stop letting this happen. I should stop getting myself in positions where I am at risk of getting into trouble. I don't want to get expelled and end up having to live in Toxey for the rest of my life like Mom.

Jackson walks away and rolls his shoulders back. I stand there fuming, Coach glaring at me.

"What was that, huh?" he asks in irritation. He blows his whistle again, right in my ear, making me wince. "Everyone take five!"

I don't want to talk to Coach Reeves right now, so I turn and walk over to the sidelines. I grab my drawstring backpack and take my water bottle out of it. I spray some water over my face and into my mouth, then I shake it off.

"Jackson's got it out for you," one of my teammates says with a chuckle. I ignore him and look over at Jackson, who is in a semi-circle with some of the other guys, looking like the god of Blackfell High. Gone for three days, but he returns only stronger and better than ever.

I drink some more water, then pull my phone out of my bag. Normally I keep it in the locker, but I've been extra anxious, hoping that I'll hear from Lyla eventually, even if it's just a simple Snapchat that she also sent to ten other friends of hers. I just want to hear from her.

Although it's not from Lyla, I do have one new text message.

I put my thumbprint in, wait for it to unlock, and read the message from an unknown number. The anger I was feeling inside my body is quickly replaced with dread.

Unknown: *Murderer.*

CHAPTER 19

Audrey

Just like I know I can't avoid Mr. Reeves forever, I know I can't avoid going to cheerleading practice forever, either. When the final bell of the day rings and everyone is either leaving school or heading to their practices, I go to the bathroom and lock myself in a stall. I feel sweaty and clammy. My heart is racing and my hands are trembling. My chest hurts. It physically hurts. I wonder vaguely if I'm dying.

I know I'm having a panic attack, especially because I'm seeing small dots forming in my eyesight. But I wonder if a panic attack can be bad enough to actually kill someone.

You have to do this, Audrey. Nobody is going to try and attack you. There are still tons of people at school right now. You'll be okay. Coach Green isn't going to let some random guy in a mask anywhere near the locker rooms while practice is in session.

I manage to pull myself together, eventually. But I still don't go in the locker room. Instead, I change for practice right there in the bathroom and get out onto the field early.

It always takes the girls ten hours to get changed and outside whenever we have the practices on the field. The football team is usually already running some drills or doing whatever it is they do by the time we get out here.

On the track around the football field, I begin stretching, keeping a careful eye on Warner.

Was it you?

"You good?"

I look up to see who has suddenly blocked my view. It's Ryan Copeland. He is reaching into his Blackfell High drawstring bag and pulling out his Gatorade brand water bottle. He sat with us at lunch today. Uninvited. He and Brandt White just plopped down at our table and started making conversation. I could tell my friends were completely confused, but my stomach was full of excitement and butterflies. Ryan Copeland was there for me.

And now here he is again, pretending to take a water break just for the chance to talk to me. I can't believe this is actually happening.

"Oh, hi!" My voice is chipper, probably ten times more chipper than it needs to be. "I'm good. How are you?"

That was a dumb question, Audrey.

"You looked mad just now," Ryan points out. He turns to the field and then turns back to me. "Were you glaring at Warner? I heard there was some sort of situation in the parking lot between you two yesterday. What happened?"

I don't answer right away because I don't know how to. I don't know how to explain to Ryan the strange situation that I'm in. "It's nothing," I decide. I like Ryan, and I like talking to him. He offers me a good distraction, and he's incredibly sweet. But I don't know him that well. I don't trust him enough to let him in very far.

"Did you guys use to, like... have a thing or something?" Ryan presses, his voice sounding overly casual.

"Me and *Warner*?" I ask with an eyebrow raised. I get into my right splits, partially because I'm stretching, and partially because I want him to be impressed by how flexible I am.

"I don't know. Yeah. I saw you sitting with him during the camping trip. And now you look like you hate him."

"I've never had a thing with Warner Carpenter."

I just happen to know that his biological father is your football coach and that he, his father, and his mother might all be messing with my life.

I giggle and smile at Ryan. "Never."

He looks pleased, but I can tell that he's trying not to look pleased. It makes me laugh more.

"Why?" I ask, deciding to be bold.

"Just curious." He smiles, revealing straight, white teeth and premature crow's feet at the corners of his eyes. When he smiles genuinely, his entire face scrunches up and it's completely adorable.

"Audrey!"

We both look over my shoulder and see Sophia, Danielle, and Olive sauntering over to us. They're leading the rest of the cheerleaders like they're all in charge of them.

"Looks like you're being summoned by the queen."

I look back at Ryan to see him bowing at me.

"Come on," I complain. He chuckles and gets back out onto the field as my friends reach me.

"What are you doing out here?" Sophia asks.

"Why weren't you in the locker room?" Danielle joins, her head cocked to the side in concern. Sophia doesn't look concerned, though. She looks annoyed.

I think about that day again. When we had walked out of school together to my car and I had looked for my keys. I told them I would meet them at Delilah's when I realized I didn't have them.

Is it ridiculous of me to think that maybe they played a prank on me that day? That one of them had dressed up like that psychopath and chased me through the school just a mess with me? Sophia is model-like tall. Maybe the clothes she was wearing were super baggy to hide her shape and the fact that she was a girl.

"Well?" Sophia urges.

I snap out of my thoughts. "Why? Did you guys miss me?" I give them a playful smile. "Chill out. Geez." I don't want them to know what happened. I don't want to tell them the reason why I didn't go to the locker room. So I have to come up with a lie—my new specialty—instead. "I wanted to get out here early so that I could talk to Ryan," I say in a quiet voice with wide eyes, pointing with my head in Ryan's direction. "And I did."

"Oh my gosh, so are you guys a thing now?" Olive asks.

"I was wondering why he decided to sit with us at lunch today, but then I noticed the way that he kept flirting with you!" Danielle throws in. The three of us giggle while Sophia looks over at Ryan.

"Stop staring!" I hiss at her. Finally, she cracks a smile, too.

"Oh, we're so going to Delilah's after this and discussing."

"So you actually have a crush on somebody at school?"

We're in a booth at Delilah's, and we just placed our orders for our sweets. It's packed in here for Tuesday afternoon, and we only managed to snag this table because Sophia asked a lingering family if they were done because they were no longer eating and she had been waiting for a place to sit. Only she would be brave enough to do something like that.

Now that we have our privacy, it's time for their interrogation to start.

"It's so unheard of!" Danielle jokes. I playfully swat at her. Then I roll my eyes.

"I know, I know. It's so unlike me to crush on anyone." But I definitely am crushing on Ryan Copeland. He's easily the hottest guy in all of Toxey. He is a mature, handsome senior, and I think he has a crush on me, too.

"So, like, if he were to ask you out...?" Danielle trails off.

I bite my bottom lip, then I giggle ridiculously. They squeal in excitement for me.

"You'd totally say yes!" Sophia states. She grabs my arm on top of the table next to me. "We both have somebody that we're going after, then!"

I whip my head to look at her. "Wait, who do you have a crush on?" I feel so out of the loop.

"Well, I haven't told any of you guys yet," she informs us. I exchange glances with the other two, all of us eagerly waiting to hear what name is going to come out of Sophia's mouth. For some reason, I am worried that it's going to be Warner. I don't want her to have a crush on Warner.

"You guys can't tell a soul," Sophia says. She looks at each of us in turn, like she's seeing into our souls and will be able to tell if we plan on ratting out her secret or not.

"Swear we won't," Olive says. Danielle nods her head in agreement. So finally, Sophia leans in really close, and we all lean in over the table with her.

She speaks quietly. "I totally have a crush on Bryson Anthony."

Olive gasps and slaps her hand over her mouth. Danielle raises an eyebrow. I smile at Sophia.

"I had a feeling that you liked him!" I say excitedly. I'm happy for her. Guys would kill to date a girl like Sophia. I was just beginning to think that she thought she was too above them all. Maybe getting a boyfriend would be good for her.

"No you did not," Sophia argues.

"Yes huh!" I tease. "Ever since he cut off his dreadlocks and has that new military-style buzz-cut 'do. You haven't been able to keep your eyes off of him!"

We all giggle about it some more. Then we launch into a conversation over our crushes as my phone starts buzzing in my back pocket. My dad is calling.

"Hang on a sec," I say to my friends before answering. Then I turn my head and plug one of my ears as a waiter sets our desserts down, and I answer the phone.

"Dad?"

"Audrey, where are you?" He sounds strange.

"I'm just at Delilah's with the girls..." I trail off, confused.

"You need to come home."

"Now?"

"Yes, now. I mean it. "

"Oh—um...okay."

I hang up the phone and look at my friends in surprise. They all stop the conversation and give me confused looks, waiting for me to fill them in.

Slowly, I get to my feet. "Can I Venmo one of you guys for the dessert?" I ask, worry filling me and making me not even in the mood to take my sundae to go. "Uh, that was my dad. I—I have to go, I guess."

"Is everything okay?" Danielle asks. It's not like my dad to pull me away from my friends like this.

"I don't really know."

"Want us to go with you?" Sophia asks. I'm touched by the offer.

"No, I'm sure... I'm sure everything is fine." I start walking away. "I'll call you guys tonight and tell you what happens!"

We exchange goodbye waves, then I hurriedly go to my car.

CHAPTER 20

MADDY

Yesterday with Craig was weird, creepy, and uncomfortable. My first instinct had been to run. To avoid it and pretend like it wasn't an issue. To push it aside and forget about it. Or *try to,* at least.

But I'm not going to be able to forget about it. And I can't stand idly by and let Craig behave this way towards me. I didn't do anything wrong. And as far as I'm concerned, my son didn't do anything wrong, either.

I've been at work for hours already, but I haven't seen Craig outside like he had been yesterday. Still, I decide that I'm going to send him a text.

Me: *Leave me alone.*

I drop my phone in my purse and close the cabinet that it's inside of at my workstation. Then I wash up and get ready for my next client. He's a small toddler with a curly fro of hair. Cutting it and making him giggle puts a big smile on my face. That, paired with my bravery for texting Craig, has put me in a much better mood.

"I want to cut his hair every time from now on," I tell his mom afterward. The little boy's name is JJ, and his mother's name is Julia.

Julia smiles fondly at her son before they head up to the receptionist's desk to pay. "I think JJ would love that very much," she tells me. Then she tips me with a twenty-dollar bill.

Score.

I thank them, give JJ a high five goodbye, then I clean up my workstation. When I check my phone afterward, I see that Craig has, *unfortunately,* replied.

Craig: *I haven't talked to you in a few days, Maddy. Seems kind of strange that you would text me out of the blue to tell me to leave you alone.*

Me: *I'm not an idiot. I saw you outside of my hair salon yesterday. I don't appreciate you stalking me.*

Craig: *Don't consider it stalking. Consider it me just doing my job. The truth will be revealed. It always is.*

Usually, I'm pretty good at not letting things get to me. I'm pretty good about dusting myself off and getting back on my feet. But I've been feeling down these past few days. About Craig and Warner and all of that, yes. But it's more than that.

I'm still not entirely over Craig.

I know I should be because he is a huge jerk, but I don't even feel like the relationship ever got closure. One moment I was with him, happy as can be, and the next moment I both miss him *and* want him to stay as far away from me as possible. It doesn't make any sense.

I let out a frustrated grumble, loud enough that my coworker asks me if I'm okay.

"Fine," I bite out. "Just fine." I'm about to throw my phone harshly back into my bag, but then a new text stops me. It's from Steven this time.

Steven: *Is it too weird if we talk on the phone today? I'm not really much of the texting type.*

I smile despite my anger towards Craig. I've been waiting to hear from Steven ever since I met him at the bar that night. The same night that I was mysteriously handed that strange photo of Warner from his upperclassman camping trip.

"Girl, just a second ago you looked ready to punch someone. Now you're *smiling?*" Rochelle has no idea what to make of my behavior.

"That's men for you," I joke. Then I reply to Steven.

Me: *Leaving work soon. I would love to talk.*

"Hey, Maddy."

I'm in my car, driving home from work. It's not that I couldn't wait until I got home to talk to Steven on the phone—I don't want my son to overhear me having this conversation later.

"How's the restaurant?" I ask. I'm still slightly embarrassed that when we met, I had thought he was just a guy trying to pick me up at the bar. I hadn't realized he was the owner of the place.

"I think things are going well so far. I'm not in town at the moment because I'm at one of my other locations."

"Well, I'm impressed," I admit. "How many restaurants do you own?"

He chuckles lightly. "Just a few. I just wanted to tell you that I've been thinking about you a lot since we met."

His compliment fills me with excitement *and* dread. He's so sweet now, but how long will it last? When will he turn on me like everyone else has?

"Oh yeah?" I ask. The steering wheel is slippery under my grasp from my sweaty palms.

"It's just... I feel like it's fairly rare that I am able to meet a pretty, interesting woman like yourself organically."

"I don't know if I would call it *organic*."

We both laugh.

I am shocked when I find myself pulling into my driveway. Talking on the phone with Steven had only felt like a couple of minutes. He had a way of making time feel like it flew. Not only did he know all the right words, and not only was he full of great charm, wit, and good banter, but he was funny, too. *Normal.* Easy to talk to and great at listening—instead of trying to get me to know him, he kept asking me questions about *myself*.

I just finished telling him that I have a son.

"I have a boy, too," he replies. "What's yours like?"

"Oh, you do?" I ask, not answering his question. I feel like it's time to talk about *him* now a little bit. "Is he your only one?"

"Yep. He's a junior over at Blackfell High."

"My son might know him then," I say. "Warner is a senior."

"Warner? The name sounds familiar. He might've talked about him before. Small world."

I know I shouldn't be getting ahead of myself by thinking about this, but I picture things working out with Steven-the-restaurant-entrepreneur. I picture Warner and Steven's son being friends. All of us living under one roof together. I picture Warner feeling like he finally has a father figure, and I picture him being as close to Steven as a brother would be.

This is all just a fantasy—just an *idea* of how good I could have it. I'm realistic enough to know that it's highly unlikely.

I stay parked in my car as we continue speaking. A whole hour goes by without me even noticing it. The only thing that makes me look at the clock is when I see the blinds of my living room move. Warner must have checked outside to see if I'm home yet or not. I don't want him to know that I'm sitting in my car having a long phone conversation with my new crush—that's probably the last thing he wants to hear come out of my mouth.

"I should go," I finally say to Steven, but I don't want to hang up. I could talk to him all night. Easily.

"Yeah, I probably should, too. Can I... can I call you again?"

Apparently, Steven has to go out of town for work a lot. Most chicks would see this as a turnoff. They'd see it as too much strain on a relationship. The way *I* see it, the slower Steven and I take things, the better.

"I'd love that." I grin like an idiot. It's the kind of grin that I would be embarrassed to let anybody else see.

"Great. I'll... I'll have to ask Wrigley if he knows your son."

"Wrigley? I'll ask Warner if he knows him, too."

"Alright, then. Have a good night, Maddy."

"Bye, Steven."

Talking with Steven went a million times better than I ever thought it would. In fact, an entire two minutes go by and I'm still sitting in my car smiling about it.

Steven Hall.

Madeline Hall. I giggle. I can be *such* a loser. But it doesn't hurt to daydream.

Craig who?

CHAPTER 21

AMELIA

If someone were to ask me how I thought I would be spending Tuesday night, I wouldn't have said this.

Gentry, Audrey, Lyla, and I are currently sitting in the waiting room of the police station. We're here because we got called in for questioning in regards to Sydney Hutton's death during the upper-classmen camping trip.

I'm sitting between my two girls, composing a text to my father.

Me: *I need the contact info of our family's lawyer.*

"Lawyer?!" Audrey asks in a high-pitched tone, looking over my shoulder. I hold my phone to my chest and shoot her a look.

"It's a just-in-case thing," I say to her. "We probably don't even need one. You guys didn't do anything wrong, and we are just cooperating with the police investigation."

"Sydney's death was an accident," Lyla says on the other side of me. "She didn't know how to swim. She probably fell into the lake. Right?"

I don't have an answer for her.

"If the police ask you anything that makes you uncomfortable, decline to answer," I instruct, preparing them. "We're here of our own free will and we can leave when we want to. When you tell them the truth, all of this will be sorted out." I look back and forth between Audrey and Lyla, waiting for one of them to give me any sort of sign that maybe the truth is only about to make things worse. Instead, they both have identical strained expressions on their faces.

It's better to be safe than sorry.

No—I hate clichés.

It's better to be arranged than arraigned.

They call Audrey first.

Gentry and I both go with her, telling Lyla to stay put. We follow the officer to an interrogation room. I've always wondered if they look the same in real life as they do on movies and TV shows.

They do.

Metal chairs. Metal folding table. One single overhead dim ceiling light hanging down directly above the tabletop. Not all of them have the two-way mirror in movies and TV shows.

This one does.

The officer who led us back here, someone I don't recognize, tells us to take our seats and then leaves. It's unfortunate because I had been hoping that maybe it was going to be her doing the questioning.

It's a little cramped on our side of the table with three people.

"Where'd she go?" Audrey asks in a small voice.

I look at Gentry, who is staring around the room, probably wondering how his life came to this. Before I can even answer my daughter, the door opens again, and Craig strolls in. He has the audacity to offer us a smile, then he sits across from us and we start with the formalities. I keep my arms crossed; I already know that I am going to have a difficult time being civil with him.

"I tried to swing by the other day, but I guess nobody was home," Craig says to us. He looks right at me as if he knows that I had been standing right on the other side of the door that day.

"Our apologies," Gentry says.

"Well, no worries. Thanks for coming in on such short notice. How are you doing tonight, Audrey?"

"Fine, thank you."

"You're in cheer, right?"

"Yes."

"Is it true that Sydney Hutton tried out for the cheerleading team but did not make it?"

Audrey looks at me. I gave her an encouraging nod. This is all harmless information. So far.

She looks back at Craig, swallows, and nods her head. "That's correct."

"During the tryouts, did you ever hang out with her? Talk to her?"

"Um, I remember seeing her...but I don't think I ever talked to her."

"You don't think? Or you know for a fact?"

"I—I know for a fact."

Craig has papers in front of him, along with folders and a pen. He doesn't have any sort of recording device from the looks of it, and he isn't writing things down. His hands are clasped together on top of the table. I find it odd.

"So, when did you start being friends with her, then?" he continued.

"We weren't friends," Audrey says.

"Really? Interesting. I suppose I could have my facts wrong. Tell me, Audrey. Did you have any classes with Sydney?"

"No."

"Did you ever hang out outside of school together?"

"No, we did not."

"Did you ever talk to her at all?"

Audrey looked in her lap for a moment. "Um, yes. She told me she wanted to invite my friends and me to a party. She never threw it, but she said that she planned on throwing one when her parents went out of town—her foster parents, I mean."

"When was this?"

"The beginning of the school year. Before the trip. She came up to me in the hallway. I thought maybe she thought I was Lyla or something."

My stomach dips. I would've preferred her not to have said that. Stay calm, Mia.

"Lyla? Your sister?" Craig asks, glancing at me for a moment. I haven't seen him look at Gentry once. I wondered if he was pretending like the other man wasn't even in the room at all.

"Yeah," Audrey says. "Because they have—had—one class together or something. I don't know. I thought it was strange because I had never talked to her before."

"And did you say you would go to this party?"

"Uh... I don't remember, actually."

"That's all right. What else do you remember about the conversation?"

"I don't know. That's it, I think."

"Tell me, did she ask you for your phone number ever?"

Audrey looks towards me again. "Yeah. That's the other thing that happened during that conversation."

Oh, great.

I can tell she had been trying to avoid telling him that part. It makes her look suspicious.

Craig finally writes something down, and it makes me anxious.

"How many other kids from school are getting questioned about that night?" I decide to hop in and ask.

"Don't worry, Mia. This is just routine stuff," Craig assures me.

Gentry stiffens next to me. I have a feeling it's because of the casual way Craig used my nickname. I had generally gone by Mia in high school, though—it wasn't as if Craig was using it as some sort of pet name towards me. Nothing had happened between us when I had been spending all that time with him before. Gentry sometimes just looks for things to be mad about.

"Let's hurry it up then," Gentry says, waving a dismissive hand.

Craig nods. "Sure. Sure. Audrey, did Sydney ever call or text you?"

I wait for Audrey to answer the question. When I hear prolonged silence, I look at her. She seems conflicted about something. She won't look at anyone.

"You're not in any sort of trouble, Audrey," Craig tells her. "I'm just trying to get all of my ducks in a row. Do you understand?"

"Um, I don't think I want to answer any more questions."

Craig looks surprised by this news. "No?"

Audrey looks at her dad. "Can we go now?"

Gentry sighs. "Absolutely we can." He gets to his feet.

"All right then," Craig says, looking deeply disappointed. "If you're sure, Audrey. Parents can stay seated. We're just going to swap her for Lyla."

It only takes a few minutes for Lyla to be in the same spot Audrey had been in.

"Hello again, Lyla," Craig starts.

Again? Had I known these two have met before?

Lyla crosses her arms and doesn't reply. I can immediately tell that she doesn't like him. It might be him specifically, or maybe she feels this way about cops in general—like rebellious teenagers tend to do.

Craig goes over the formalities again, and then he dives right in.

"When did you meet Sydney Hutton?" he asks Lyla.

"History class."

"Were you friends?"

"I guess."

"What do you mean by that?"

"I didn't know her very long. We didn't hang out that often. I barely even got to learn much about her before she died."

"So the night she died, where were you?"

"In my tent with Audrey."

"The whole night?"

"Yes. The whole night."

Craig smirks at her. "Tell me, have you gone on any casual strolls through the cemetery lately?"

Instead of answering, Lyla glares at him.

"Cemetery?" I ask. "What is he talking about, Lyla?"

"What's the point of this?" Lyla asks, ignoring me and staring at Craig. "Do you really think Sydney drowning wasn't an accident?"

"What would Sydney have been doing out by herself that night?" Craig deadpans. "Wasn't it a rule that the kids were supposed to be in bed? Didn't you guys have a curfew?"

"She was my friend—barely that. I didn't know her whole life story or the reasoning behind her every decision or what she was doing every second of every day."

"Uh huh. Do you think she had been meeting somebody that night?"

"I literally just told you that I don't know."

Gentry gets to his feet again. "All right, I think we're done here."

Craig continues staring Lyla down. To my surprise, she doesn't break eye contact with him.

"I said we're done here," Gentry repeats.

I hope my father texts me back with our lawyer's contact info. I get the feeling I'm going to need it.

CHAPTER 22

MADDY

I knock on Warner's bedroom door. Then, instead of waiting for him to reply, I thrust it open.

He's sitting on his bed, his laptop open. Immediately, he looks annoyed when he sees that I have invaded his privacy. But there's no time for that now. He can be annoyed all he wants.

"Come on, Warner," I say, my voice demanding and a little bit shaky, but I hope he doesn't notice the latter. "We gotta go."

He cocks an eyebrow at me. "What do you mean? Go where?"

My stomach dips. He's not going to like my answer.

"We have to go to the police station. For questioning about what happened to Sydney Hutton."

I don't even wait around to see his reaction. I turn and decide I'll wait for him in the car.

It only takes him a couple of minutes to join me inside of my Hyundai. He gets in the passenger seat, looking slightly pale. Why does he look pale?

"It should just be a formality. You didn't do anything wrong." I look at him as I speak, trying to catch him sweating or narrowing his eyes at my words. It's not that I want to catch him in a lie. In fact, I'm terrified to catch him in a lie.

To my gratitude, Warner rolls his eyes, huffs loudly, and leans back into his seat while he puts his seatbelt on. I pull out of the driveway and zoom towards the station. I can't stop changing the radio channels as I go. Plenty of decent songs are playing, but I can't settle on one. And I can't stop moving. I feel like I need to keep myself busy doing something other than driving and thinking about how horrible this might be.

"Mom, what's your deal?" Warner swipes my hand away from the radio. I guess we're settling on an old Maroon 5 song, then.

"What do you mean?" I ask.

"Just—look at you! You're freaking out."

"No, I'm not."

I don't need him to know how nervous I feel. I don't need him to know that I am, in fact, freaking out.

I thought I was better at hiding my emotions than this.

"Look, I'm not afraid of any cops. Or any questions they may ask. Despite what people might be thinking, I did not do anything to Sydney. So can you just chill?"

I take a deep breath, but my grip on the steering wheel does not loosen.

We pull into the parking lot of the station, and the sight of the first officer in uniform makes me feel sick.

Warner wants me to chill. I need to just chill.

"Are we going to get out?" Warner asks.

"Yes," I say, not looking at him. "Just try to remember that we are here to help. That you're not a suspect. Don't let them treat you like you are one. Just answer the questions as best you can and as honestly as you can. You know nothing, so they should suspect nothing. It's going to be fine. I love you."

Something about this still feels so wrong, though. I get the feeling that Warner knows more than he lets on. I get the feeling that he knows more than maybe anybody else knows. Anybody besides the person who gave me the photo of him talking to Sydney the night she died.

"Warner?" I turn and look at him. I want to ask him about the photo. I want to tell him that it was given to me and that I know something is up. I want to give him a chance to come clean about it himself and tell me what really happened that night.

But I'm so afraid.

"What?" he snaps. His voice has this permanent tone of attitude whenever he talks to me now. I'm almost used to it.

I gnaw on the inside of my cheek for a few moments more. Then the question leaves my mouth. I just can't do it. For now, the fact that I know about him meeting with Sydney that night is going to stay a secret. Even if the police ask me about it when we're inside of the station.

"Nothing," I say.

"Okay..." he trails off. "This better not take long. I have a crap-ton of homework and I need to go over some plays for the team." He hops out of the car and starts heading inside before even checking to see if I've gotten out of my seat yet.

I don't know why he's not more nervous.

Maybe it's because I'm nervous enough for the both of us.

Audrey

Lyla overslept today. I don't realize it until I'm banging on her door telling her that we need to leave. When she finally unlocks it and opens it up, I see that she looks very much like she has just rolled out of bed.

"Lyla!" I complain. She looks like she doesn't even care that we're running behind.

"I'll hurry," she says in a tired, slow voice that makes me feel like she isn't going to hurry at all.

I end up being late to first hour. That means that I couldn't meet up with Sophia, Olive, and Danielle before school to tell them about why I had to leave Delilah's so abruptly last night. I know I could've texted them when I got home—or called them even, but I was too stressed out about everything. My mind is still racing. We had been at the police station to help Detective Craig Fritz answer questions about what happened to Sydney. So how come I feel like we had been there to be questioned as suspects—like I've been accused of being the one who killed her?

I barely even sit down in my seat in Government second hour before Olive is practically in my lap, scooting her desk so that it's pressed against mine. Her wide, excited hazel eyes are staring me down. I know why she's excited. For the gossip. And for the chance to get to hear said gossip before anyone else. Danielle isn't in this class with us, but Sophia should be arriving at any moment.

"So?" Olive asks. Her auburn hair is glistening in the streams of light shining in through the closed blinds of the windows. It's surprisingly sunny again outside. Toxey always has a way of checking what my mood is and making the weather reflect exactly the opposite of it.

"So what?" I ask, feigning ignorance. "What's wrong with you? Why are you sitting so close to me?"

She rolls her eyes. "Yesterday! When your dad made you leave Delilah's... We texted you. You didn't reply. What happened?"

I pretend I have something in my eye so that I can look away from her and try to figure out a story in my head. Do I want to tell them that I got questioned by the police? Do I want to give them something to pass around the school? They might be my best friends, but I know them well enough to not trust that they will keep any of my secrets.

Sophia pops down on the other side of me, making me jump slightly. "There you are!" she says. Then, at seeing the way Olive has placed her desk closer to mine, Sophia moves hers, too. "Way to text us back last night."

I have to tell them something. I don't want to start another fight with them. I don't want them to be mad at me for not replying to them last night. I don't want to be like Lyla, who, now that she doesn't know what she's doing with her relationship with Jackson, wanders around the school alone, no friends to talk to at all.

I'm just not good at making up lies.

I sigh and run a stressed-out hand through my hair. I didn't even do anything with it today. It sits on my head, stick-straight, hanging down to the middle of my waist. It feels slightly frizzy, too; I hadn't even used any gloss serum on it.

"I couldn't reply because I didn't get home until super late," I lie. But this lie at least ties into the truth.

"Where were you?" Olive asks.

I make sure that our peers around us aren't eavesdropping as they walk through the open doorway and settle into their seats before the bell rings and Mr. Guillen speaks in his loud, booming voice. He sounds like a sports announcer or talk show host, so he's often the one that does the rallying during spirit week assemblies.

I motion for Olive and Sophia to lean in closer. "I had to go to the police station yesterday," I whisper.

They both gasp—just as I was expecting.

"Yeah," I continue. "About Sydney Hutton. I'm sure you guys are going to get called to answer questions eventually, too."

"Are you kidding me?" Sophia asks.

"Why just you?"

"Not just me," I clarify. "Lyla had to go, too. I don't know what order they're calling people in to talk, but we just had to answer questions about how well we knew Sydney and what we saw and heard that night. "

"Okay, but nobody else has mentioned that they were questioned," Sophia says, drawing a conclusion in her mind—I can see the gears turning.

Crud.

Sophia is smarter than I give her credit for.

I wait for her to come to the realization.

"Wait a second—do they think you did something to her?" she finally asks, her eyes the size of saucers.

Even at the question, a gasp is elicited from Olive all over again.

"I-I don't know," I say truthfully. I can't believe I've even given them this much information. But if the word got out and they found out where I had been last night from somebody else, it would probably be the end of our friendship, so it's probably for the best that I tell them anyway.

Sophia slowly raises a hand over her mouth. She does it glamorously, though, and I feel like if I took a photo of her like this, it would easily win some sort of beauty contest or—at the least—get her thousands of likes on Instagram.

"Hang on, did you get highlights again?" I ask, just now noticing them. She had been blonde last year, but started off this school year as a brunette. Then once Lyla started getting all the attention put on her, Sophia slowly started going back to blonde, adding some highlights in every couple of weeks. She had smiled at us and told us, "Blondes do have more fun," when we asked her why she had changed her mind. She would never admit that she likes to be the center of attention. But she doesn't have to admit it—it's painfully obvious.

Sophia smiles and lifts her right shoulder as if to say, Perhaps I might have.

"She did, and they look great," Olive says. "But do not try to change the subject, Audrey. What kind of questions did they ask you? Which police officer was it? My dad knows a few of them. This is literally so crazy!"

"Shush!" I hiss. When I glance over my shoulder, I can see that Olive and Sophia are drawing attention to us.

The bell rings to signal the start of the period.

"I'll tell you more about it later," I tell them.

When I don't hear Mr. Guillen's loud voice starting up the class, I look to see why. It's because he is currently on the phone at his desk. My stomach dips when I see that his eyes are trained right on me as he nods his head to whatever it is the person on the other line is saying to him.

I swallow.

Mr. Guillen says goodbye to them and hangs up the phone. I quickly look away even though he still staring at me.

"Audrey," he calls.

I pretend like I didn't hear him.

"Audrey Bailey."

His voice is too loud to ignore. I turn my head back to him. He's motioning for me to go to his desk.

"What's happening?" Olive asks.

"Are you about to get arrested?" Sophia jokes. I shoot her a glare as I get out of my desk and go to my teacher.

"You have to go and see Principal Mathers," Mr. Guillen informs me. I can tell he's trying to talk quieter so that the desks closest to his don't overhear. But immediately, I hear whispers behind me, signaling that he has failed.

Great.

"Why?" I ask.

"I'm sure you'll find out once you get up there."

He grabs his stack of hall passes from a tray on his desk and fills one out for me. He tears it off and hands it over and then shoos me out of the class.

I drag my feet practically the entire way to the front office. When I get inside, I don't know if I should tell the receptionist that I'm here to see the principal or if I'm supposed to just go straight to his office—this isn't something that I typically do. In fact, I don't even know that I've ever been to the principal's office.

"Oh, hello, Audrey!" Principal Mathers says in a bright, cheery tone, appearing around the corner with a cup of what I assume is coffee in one hand and a stack of papers in the other.

"Um, hi," I say in a shy voice.

"Why don't you come right this way?" Principal Mathers waves me along, then he leads the way down a hallway into the office behind a fogged glass door with thick gold blocked letters painted right onto it, spelling Principal.

As we step inside, Principal Mathers closes the door behind him.

His office is exactly what I pictured. The brick walls have been painted a sickly green color. There is a small table with two chairs on either side of it in between the door to the hall and the door to a closet. The commercial carpet is flat and dull, and a glaringly bright geometric rug sits in front of his desk, two more chairs placed on top of that. Principal Mathers's desk is L-shaped and made of mahogany. His rolling chair is one of those ergonomic ones. His desktop looks ancient and dusty. He has some memorabilia, awards, and accomplishments hanging on the wall behind his desk.

What I didn't picture was the unfamiliar uniformed officer standing in front of the desk.

"Take a seat, Audrey." He motions to a chair by the man. I'm glad he isn't Craig Fritz. I so don't need that right now. I do as I'm told, my heart pounding. I don't even know why I'm so nervous right now. I don't know why I'm in here. Mom is always telling me that I shouldn't stress out unless I have a reason to. That I can't stress out about the unknown.

"So, Officer Wilde, here, works at the precinct," Principal Mathers starts. "He told me he saw you and your sister there last night."

It's exactly what I thought it would be about.

"Okay..." I trail off, not meeting his gaze.

"Well, I guess it sort of got me thinking. Nobody really seems to know how Sydney drowned in the lake that night. I believe it was an accident. Or at least—I want to believe. But Officer Wilde is here to just gather any information he can on the incident. Any help you want to or are able to give is voluntary. And the rest and the staff would like to be informed so we can get to the bottom of this as well. So that brings me to now. Don't worry, you aren't the only one being called into my office. We're going to be calling everyone up, actually. Everyone that went on the trip. Nobody is in trouble. We just want to be able to confirm that Sydney's death was indeed an accident."

Principal Mathers has a bald, shiny head. With the fluorescent lighting in the ceiling glistening down on it, I can see beads of sweat appearing on top of it. To me, it feels like the North Pole in here—Principal Mathers must be worried about something.

"Do you think there's a chance that you'll find out it wasn't an accident?" I can't help but ask. "That somebody maybe did this on purpose?"

He sits down in his own chair and puts his papers and coffee down. "I..." he trails off, looking at Officer Wilde, a man of average height with a classic, dark police mustache.

Maybe Principal Mathers is worried the school is going to get sued over this. Sued by Sydney's foster parents or something. Maybe he's worried the upperclassman trips are going to get canceled from now on since a student died at one of them. I wouldn't want to be Principal Mathers at all, if that were the case. A lot of the underclassmen students, and even those in junior high who have heard about the upperclassman trip, were going to be very angry if that was the case.

"I know you already had to do this yesterday," Officer Wilde says in a friendly, polite voice, "so I won't take much of your time. I know that we police officers can sometimes be ... intimidating. If there's something you want to tell me that you did not want to tell the detective you spoke to last night, you can."

"Or you can write it on a piece of paper and give it to us, if that makes it easier," Principal Mathers adds.

Principal Mathers has always seemed like a good enough guy to me. He seems a little bit like he doesn't offer the school much and that he doesn't work very hard, but he always appears to be in a good mood and acts friendly towards his students. The look on his face right now is incredibly sincere and honest. He doesn't look like he wants to incriminate me for anything. He just seems like he wants to get to the bottom of this so that it can be over with and never talked about again.

"I don't know how Sydney died..." I tell them, but the way I trail off insinuates that a 'but' is coming.

"Have you heard any of your peers talking about how it might've happened?" Officer Wilde asks. "Any strange rumors being spread?"

I'm debating on telling him about Warner. About the photo. I am inches away from letting it slip.

But I can't do it.

All I saw was that photo. I don't know the whole truth behind it—yet. I don't know why Warner met with Sydney that night, and I don't know why he lied about it. But I can't be the one who spreads the rumor that I think he did it.

"I just heard that she snuck out of her tent," I decide to say to them instead. "That maybe she wasn't a good swimmer. I didn't hear anything else."

CHAPTER 24

LYLA

I don't know why I'm getting called out of my chemistry class second hour to go to the principal's office, but I'm annoyed.

After the front office lady gives me a look like I did something wrong and points towards Principal Mathers's office, I am let inside of it and told to sit down in a chair. Principal Mathers sits across from me at his desk, giving me a friendly smile. Next to him is a cop.

"What is this about?" I demand. It's not that I'm upset that I was pulled from Chemistry when I had a lot of learning that I wanted to do—I just don't want to be here. I've been in here enough recently. I don't want to talk to him about Jackson anymore. I don't want to talk to any adults at all.

Heck.

I don't even want to talk.

"You have no reason to be worried about anything, Lyla," Principal Mathers starts off. "We're just calling every student in who was at the upperclassman camping trip, one-by-one, to have a quick chat with them."

The camping trip? So this is about Sydney then?

"Why?"

He stares at me for a moment, like the answer should be obvious. Then the officer clears his throat and chuckles, leaning back in his seat. "We just want to get everybody's story straight about that night. That's all."

"Okay... I don't know anything." I could probably lessen the attitude in my voice, but in all honesty, I just don't want to.

"Are you sure?" the officer asks.

"Excuse me?"

"It's just that... I've talked to several students already, Miss Bailey. A lot of them are saying that you were friends with Sydney. I feel like maybe you could help us."

I look around the room. Who is the 'us' he's referring to? And why am I getting called to talk about this two days in a row?

"Um, I don't know if you know this or not, but I already talked to you guys last night. You should just ask Detective Fritz for the answers I gave to the questions he asked me. I really don't want to do this again."

I move to get out of my seat.

"Not just yet, Miss Bailey," Principal Mathers interjects when he sees me doing it. I freeze, my butt raised from the chair. He motions for me to sit back down, so I do—bitterly.

"You don't need to act so defensively about this. I promise you, you're not in trouble. We just want to know what happened."

"But I don't know what happened," I say, feeling like I've said it a million times.

"At all?" the officer asks. There's something about the way he's looking at me. It's as if he's asked me a question he already knows the answer to. But whatever answer it is he thinks he has, he's wrong.

"I have no reason to lie to you, Principal Mathers and Officer... whoever you are."

"I'm Officer Wilde."

"I know you have no reason to lie, Lyla," Principal Mathers says. "However... it's come to our attention that Sydney was not the only person out of their tent that night."

A knot tightens in my stomach. "I don't..." I try to think of a way to get myself out of here.

"I'll cut to the chase, then," Wilde hops in. "It's come to our attention that you were out of your tent that night. I just want to know why."

I don't know who told him. I don't know how he got the information. I don't know if he knows that Warner was out of his tent, too. All I know is that I've had enough of this.

I leap from my chair. "You know what? Yes, I was out of my tent. There were probably lots of kids out of their tents. It was pretty easy to do. I couldn't spot a teacher, supervisor, or chaperone anywhere around me for miles. Instead of sitting here talking to us like we're the ones that did something wrong, maybe you should be talking to the ones that were supposed to be in charge of us. The ones that were supposed to be keeping a closer eye on us. Maybe if they had been doing their job, Sydney would have never drowned in the first place!"

I turn and go to the door.

"Now, Lyla, just you wait a minute!"

I don't think I've ever heard Principal Mathers raise his voice. But it doesn't scare me enough to stop me from leaving.

CHAPTER 25

WARNER

I knew it was coming even before I get called to take my turn. There has been word spreading around the school—talk that people are getting called up to Principal Mather's office, one-by-one, to talk with him and some police officer about what they think happened to Sydney Hutton during the upperclassmen trip.

Everyone is gossiping about it like it's something exciting and dramatic they saw happen on a TV show last night. But I doubt any of them have been texted by someone from an unknown number calling them a murderer. I doubt any of them have been sent an incriminating photo of themselves talking to Sydney the night she drowned that could easily be used against them in so many ways.

Last night at the police station had been weird enough. Craig Fritz had been the one who questioned me with my mom sitting next to me in the interrogation room. That had been a first for me. Apparently, I was only there to help with the investigation, but nothing about the way Craig Fritz talked to me or my mom made me feel like I was anything less than a criminal. Like I was anything less than the word that had been texted to me during practice earlier that day.

The door is already open to Principal Mathers's room when I arrive. I step inside and find him sitting silently with the officer, checking his phone. I wonder if he was warned about me by Craig Fritz.

"Hey Warner," Principal Mathers says in a tired voice. He nods towards the door with his head. "You can shut that."

What if I don't want to?

I do as he says anyway.

"This is Officer Wilde. I'm assisting him in asking students from the upperclassman camping trip about what happened during it.

This is just a very casual setting, and any information you give us is completely voluntary."

When I sit across from my principal, I can see the creases of worry on his forehead. Principal Mathers has always been a laid-back sort of dude. He probably hates all this confrontation stuff. Or maybe he's simply preparing to do whatever it takes to make sure he doesn't lose his job.

Wilde's opening sentence sounds totally rehearsed. "We're calling each student in, one-by-one, to ask them about what happened to Sydney Hutton the night she died during the upperclassman camping trip." He's used it with several students already, I can tell.

"I heard."

"I assumed you guys would all start to talk about it pretty quickly," Principal Mathers says with a sigh.

I nod.

The officer continues. "Well, why don't you go ahead and tell me what you think happened that night? Anything you saw or heard? Anything out of place or strange?"

"I think... Sydney drowned in Lake Oshwana, didn't she?"

"Well... yes. But what do you know about it?"

"What does anybody know about it? I thought nobody saw."

"So you didn't see anything that night, then?"

I've suddenly become very aware of the way my tongue moves around inside of my mouth. I sit there for a moment and wiggle it about behind my closed lips.

"Warner?" Principal Mathers urges.

"I didn't see anything."

"Are you sure?" Wilde asks.

"It was curfew, was it not? I was in my tent, asleep. So yes, I'm sure."

"So you're saying you didn't leave your tent at all that night?"

I want to scream, but I refrain. "I mean—unless I have some sort of sleepwalking disorder that I was never told about or informed of, I am pretty sure I didn't."

"I see."

"What happened to Sydney; it was an accident. I don't get why you and the other officers and detectives and everyone else seem like you're trying to make it out to be something more than that. She shouldn't have snuck out of her tent past curfew. She shouldn't have been at Lake Oshwana if she didn't know how to swim. It's messed up that it happened, and it sucks. But why can't we just move on from it already?"

I think about Audrey and Lyla and how they're ignoring me.

What if they sent me the photo? What if they have known all along that I did see Sydney that night, and they've been trying to pin her death on me ever since? What if they're the ones that have been messing with me? What if they had been a part of some sort of elaborate scheme with Sydney that night to draw me out to talk to her?

"I do hope we can move on from it, soon," Principal Mathers agrees.

"I'm just sick of all of the drama. It's not worth it."

Officer Wilde looks like he's about to ask me another question. I can't let it happen.

"Look, can I go? I told you what I know. She drowned. End of story. You questioning all of us is pointless and it's wasting everybody's day."

"Mr. Carpenter, I am just trying to help," he says.

I roll my eyes and get out of the chair. I test the waters to see if he's going to say something to stop me. However, he stays silent.

The day passes in a blur as I replay my talks with Detective Fritz, Principal Mathers, and Officer Wilde in my head. As I think of Audrey and Lyla and what they could be trying to do to me. I think about my mom and how angry she's been making me lately. About how everyone seems to have some sort of secret and some sort of need to manipulate and control everybody around them. It makes me realize that I cannot wait to get out of Toxey.

When school gets out, I race to see Coach Reeves in his classroom. We don't have practice today, but I still need to talk to him about something.

Mr. Reeves is erasing his whiteboard when I knock on the door frame of his classroom. I felt like a salmon trying to swim upstream as I moved against the throng of students trying to get out of the school so that I could come here.

He gives me a friendly smile, and I see that there's nobody else inside the room.

"What's up, Warner?" Mr. Reeves asks.

"Got a minute?"

He sets down the whiteboard eraser. "I do."

He stays standing, so I do, too.

"Cool. Um... I was just wondering if maybe you could help me with my college applications."

Coach raises both of his eyebrows. I don't doubt that he had been expecting me to want to talk football. He's not my teacher anymore., but I've always felt like I can talk to Coach about things.

"You want my help?"

"Well, you aren't just a football coach, right?" I look around the room dramatically to point out the fact that we are inside his English classroom.

He chuckles. "Sure, sure. That's great that you want to go to college. Where are you thinking?"

"Florida."

I don't think his eyebrows can raise any higher. It's giving him tons of lines on his forehead and making him look slightly like a mad scientist. "Florida," he repeats.

I shrug. "Yeah. I don't know. Maybe the University of Miami. Or the University of South Florida."

"Particular reason?"

Because I'm desperate to get out of this place. I'm desperate to be somewhere where it's sunny all the time and where not a single person knows who I am, and I don't know anything about anyone else.

"I don't know."

"Huh." Coach Reeves stands there and thinks for a moment. "Has your mom not been able to help you?"

There's the question I had really been hoping he wouldn't ask.

"I, uh, didn't ask her to help me," I admit. "I sort of don't want her to know where I'm applying."

He leans against his desk and crosses his arms. Surprisingly, he doesn't look judgmental or concerned. He strokes his scruff and nods at me. "I see. I'm sure I can help," he tells me. For what feels like the first time in years, a bit of warmth spreads through me. Hope. I have no idea what I'm doing when it comes to college, but with Coach Reeves's help, I might finally get my ticket out of here.

"Seriously?" I ask.

"Sure, Warner. Whatever you need."

"Oh, man," I say, unable to stop the smile spreading across my face. "You rock. You have no idea."

He laughs. "I'll shoot you an email through the school's portal when I look through my schedule to see when I can help."

"Thank you so much," I say. "I'm serious." I turn to leave.

"Oh, by the way," Coach says, causing me to spin back around. Maybe he'll tell me he has some old college essay saved that he can give me.

One can dream.

"I noticed the damage on your usually shiny, perfect red Jeep out there. I know a guy that can get the side of it fixed up for you. Dirt cheap, too."

"Oh yeah?" I had planned on just using YouTube to figure out how I could fix it myself and to figure out where to buy the parts and the paint. But having somebody else do it for dirt cheap does sound enticing.

"Yeah, I'll send that through the school's portal, too. What happened?"

What happened?

It's the first time somebody's asked me that question where I haven't felt sick to my stomach trying to come up with a way to cover up the truth. For the first time, I'm finding that I want to tell Mr. Reeves what really happened. Maybe he could give me some advice. He's given me lots of great advice before.

"Uh... actually, Coach—"

I stop talking mid-sentence when somebody breezes in through the open door.

Amelia Bailey.

Amelia freezes when she sees me.

"Oh!" she cries out softly before looking at Coach Reeves. "Am I interrupting? Should I come back another time?"

What reason can Amelia Bailey possibly have for needing to talk to Coach Reeves? And why can't she just talk to him over email or the phone if it's something student-related?

I don't know why, but I have a bad feeling about why Amelia is here.

Coach glances in my direction. "I was just about to talk to Warner about something, actually--"

"No, no!" I blurt out. "I'm good, actually. Thanks again, Coach."

I can't get out of there fast enough.

CHAPTER 26

AMELIA

It immediately strikes me as odd when I go to see Dean Reeves inside of his classroom and find him and Warner Carpenter having a casual conversation. Or what appeared to be one, anyway.

For one, Warner is no longer in his junior year, so I know that Dean is no longer his English teacher. Two, the last I heard about it, Maddy was pretending she had no idea who Warner's father was. I know I haven't been friends with Maddy again for that long, but as far as I thought I knew, she had absolutely zero intentions to come clean. To anyone.

I also find it strange when Warner looks at me as if I am some sort of ghoul or demon that has shown up in his nightmares to torture him. And the way he ran out of the classroom in a rush after Dean told me that he had been about to talk to him about something...

I give Dean a quizzical look, and then I turn to peer out the doorway. When Warner is a far enough distance away, I close the classroom door and turn to Dean again.

"What?" Dean asks about the look I'm giving him.

"N-nothing," I stutter. I'm not a woman who typically stutters. Nor am I usually a woman who spends fifteen minutes too long picking out a simple outfit to go visit her daughter's teacher inside his classroom.

"Just say it," Dean says in sarcastic annoyance. He's still leaning against his desk. His dress shirt is rolled up at the sleeves to his elbows and his arms are crossed in front of him. My eyes wander down to his exposed forearms. I clear my throat.

"It's just that—Warner still doesn't... know, ri—?"

Dean interrupts me. "No," he says in a loud voice, stepping away from his desk. When he speaks again, he's calmer. "No, he doesn't."

I purse my lips and nod, looking at the floor under my designer slip-on sneakers. I went for a more casual, yet still business-like, look today. I suppose I want Dean to think that I'm not always so uptight and prissy all the time. To think that I'm the kind of girl that does enjoy being out in nature, despite how I might have seemed during some parts of the upperclassman camping trip.

Dean shakes his head and sits down behind his desk. "Warner was just... It doesn't matter." He motions to the desk closest to it. One that's for students.

"You want me to sit in that?"

I stare at it, memories flooding me from back when I attended Blackfell High. I might have sat in that very same desk at one point.

"Or you can stand if you want," he tells me, a glimmer in his eye. He finds this amusing.

I smirk at him and take my seat. It's just as uncomfortable as I remember it being. I never understood how anyone was able to lay their heads down on the desk and take a nap. I could never.

It's weird to see Dean on the other side of things. The last time we were in this school together, apart from the meetings we had attended in regards to the upperclassman camping trip preparations, we had both been sitting in these desks.

"So why was it so important that we meet?" I ask.

"It's about one of your daughters, actually."

Of course it is.

"What is she doing now?"

"Which she are you referring to?" he asks.

"Lyla?"

He presses his lips tightly together and pulls them into a wide, straight line as he slowly shakes his head.

This surprises me. "This is about... Audrey?"

My daughter has never had school issues in her life. Not even in pre-K. She has always been a perfect angel. Lyla is usually a perfect angel, too, for the most part. But if anyone is more prone to outbursts and incidents, it's she.

"She's been skipping my class," Dean says.

What?

"I'm sorry?"

I have to be mishearing him.

"I'm not sure what's going on with her. I checked her attendance records and she hasn't been missing any other classes. Just mine."

"H-how long has this been going on for?"

"If she doesn't show up tomorrow, that makes it one full week."

I put a hand on my heart. "And you're just telling me about this now?" I'm nearly speechless. My daughter, skipping class? Skipping Dean's class? What could be the reason for this? It's English—her favorite subject, as far as I know.

"You automatically get sent a message when a student is marked absent from one of her classes," Dean reminds me. "Have you not gotten any of those messages?"

"I haven't." Why haven't I been getting these calls? Has the school been calling Gentry instead? Does Gentry know about this and just isn't doing anything about it? I wouldn't put it past him.

I can feel myself starting to get irritated.

"I had a feeling," Dean says. "I tried to reach out to you a few times, Mia."

"I know, but I didn't think it was..." I trail off. What was I about to tell him? That I thought he was only messaging me because he wanted to see me?

What is wrong with me?

Dean doesn't look too offended. "Don't worry, I get why you didn't reply."

I don't try to explain myself.

So he continues. "Uh, so, is Audrey... okay?"

"I thought so," I tell him. I can't meet his eyes. I'm disappointed in myself and worried about Audrey. I'm more worried than angry, in fact. "I wonder why it's your class."

"I never noticed any issues with her before last week. The first time she did it, she walked in, and... she gave me the strangest look... Then she just... turned around and left. I haven't seen her since."

I open my mouth, willing words to come out, but none do. I don't know what to say or what to do. I think I might be in shock. Which is incredibly dramatic because it's not like Audrey has committed a crime.

"All of the students are getting questioned about what happened to Sydney Hutton during the upperclassman camping trip," Dean informs me. "I think Audrey and Lyla were both called to the principal's office today."

I groan audibly. "Those poor girls. They just had to talk to the police about it last night."

Maybe I shouldn't have just disclosed that information to the English teacher, though.

Sensing my discomfort, Dean sighs and changes the subject back to what we had been discussing before the Sydney thing was brought up. "I don't know what's going on with Audrey. I just thought you should know. If there's anything I can do to help, just tell me, okay? I can try to talk to her if you'd like—get to the bottom of why it's happening."

Is it just me, or is his desk chair slowly rolling closer to my seat?

"No, it's okay," I say. "I'll talk to her. She will be back in your class ASAP."

"Have you ever considered how weird it is?" he suddenly asks.

"How weird what is?"

"The situation that's happened. Doesn't it just sort of feel kind of...?"

"Familiar?" My stomach dips.

"Yeah. I keep having these weird flashbacks to when I was in high school. I've been thinking about it more than I have in years."

"Tell me about it," I agree. "I hardly ever see Nora, and now she won't leave my house."

"How is Nora?"

"I'm surprised you care."

I can tell I've struck a nerve. I've hit him where it hurts.

"I'm sorry, I didn't mean it like that," I try.

"No, you did," he disagrees. "But it's fine. I do care about your sister. I'll always care about her. I don't know what she's told you or what you may think, but Nora pushed me away."

Dean Reeves had lived next door to me and Nora growing up. He's the same age as my little sister, and the two of them had been best friends since diapers. I always had a feeling that Nora was in love with him. But Dean never returned those feelings, and I think it really hurt my sister. Then, the first guy she ever met who made her forget about her crush on Dean disappeared or died... and that was when she shut off. Dean and Nora didn't speak anymore.

"I think it's a little bit of both of our faults," I admit. Before the upperclassman camping trip, I hadn't talked to Dean in years, and we've never discussed our past before. It's been hinted at between each other, but never brought out into the open.

"You know," Dean says, his eyes looking puzzled. "I never did find out how Parker Fritz found out that you and I..."

I feel myself blushing. Dean and I had kissed. I was fourteen and he was thirteen. We were on the swing on his back porch. The kiss had meant everything to me. But I lied to him and told him that I didn't like him. My reasoning was that I knew Nora was in love with him. I didn't want to hurt her that way. When I gave my fake explanation to Dean, he seemed like he believed me and backed off.

Then that day happened my senior year of high school. It was a day I would never forget.

I could see my then boyfriend, Parker Fritz—Craig's younger brother—putting books in his locker between classes. I had turned the corner and was smiling happily as I made my way towards him. I wouldn't say I was crazy obsessed and in love with Parker by any means. But he did make me happy. And I liked having a boyfriend. With Maddy no longer my friend and Nora gone, Parker was the closest thing I had to a best friend, too.

I remember how I had frozen in my step when Dean came passing by Parker in the hall. Parker turned at his locker swiftly, his broad jaw clenched.

"Reeves!" he had yelled. It was loud enough that I was pretty sure it echoed through every hall of the school.

Dean stopped moving and turned to Parker, a confused expression on his face.

Then, out of nowhere, Parker lunged at him. His fist hit him square in the cheek, and then they slammed into the lockers opposite of Parker's. Dean sunk to the floor and Parker stayed on top of him, continuing to bring the blows down on him.

"I know—you kissed—my girlfriend!" he shouted between his punches. "You've been lying to me for years!"

I had felt petrified, but I ran over to them anyway to try and stop it. They were much stronger than me and I barely helped break them apart. It took four other senior guys to pry Parker off of Dean.

Other than a busted lip, Parker had looked completely fine as he turned and glared at me, trying to get out of the four boys' grasps. "You!" he bellowed. I wanted to shrink into a ball and disappear. Everyone was staring at us. I had no idea how this had happened or how Parker found out about Dean and me. "How could you not tell me? He's my best friend!"

"Parker, I—" I looked back and forth between Dean and Parker. Dean was getting helped off the ground by some other guys. He was bleeding pretty heavily and his eyes were already swelling shut.

"She didn't do anything!" Dean still tried to yell at Parker.

"Shut up!" Parker shouted again, turning back to Dean and trying to get his hands freed so that he could keep hitting him.

I hadn't known what else to do—I turned and dashed into the girl's room, and I hid in there until the end of the day. My mom had to physically come into the school and escort me out of the bathroom after everybody else had left.

Then, later on, Parker had confronted me and asked if I still had feelings for Dean. I told him I didn't, but for obvious reasons, he didn't believe me and ended up dumping me.

Nora was already gone when that happened. I had already started distancing myself from her. We never talked about the fact that Dean and I had kissed. I never knew if she ever found out about it or how it made her feel if she had. It would seem silly for me to try to bring it up to her now. And Nora is usually the type who reacts loudly and violently when things happen that she doesn't like. So something tells me she might not have any idea about Dean and me.

"Oh, please," I say to Dean, back inside of his English classroom.

He laughs incredulously. "What? I don't!"

"Well, I can promise you that I never told a soul."

"And neither did I. You were right—I didn't want to hurt Nora."

"Uh huh."

Dean had to have accidentally let the secret about our kiss slip to somebody before. That was how it got out. Because I never told anyone. Not even Maddy. Maddy, who had dated Dean while Nora was dating Carson Price. Nora had seemed completely fine with it.

"I guess there's no use lingering over the possibilities of what happened now," Dean points out.

"I agree," I say. "Anyway. Nora is still visiting. I think she's made herself a permanent resident inside my house. So... she's there if you want to talk to her."

Dean doesn't look at me as he slowly nods his head. I can tell he is deeply considering it. "I know it made things a little messy," he says, "but I still don't regret it."

My stomach tumbles down to my feet.

He's not thinking about Nora at all! He's still thinking about the kiss we shared when we were kids!

"I—oh," I say nervously, sliding out of the desk and getting to my feet.

"Chill, Mia," Dean says, getting to his feet as well. "I'm not saying I'm dying to kiss you now, or anything. I'm just saying that I'm proud of myself for going after what I wanted, even if I ended up getting shot down by you. It was a good life lesson."

I giggle nervously, then I put one hand on the door and turn to look at him. "I'm going to talk to Audrey. Thank you for meeting me and telling me about that."

He doesn't answer me right away. I can tell by the way he's looking at me that he doesn't want me to leave.

But then he sighs. "You're welcome, Mia. Have a good night."

I give him a lame attempt at a smile and go back home to my family.

CHAPTER 27

WARNER

There are just too many coincidences. I have to talk to my mom.

Amelia Bailey showing up at my coach's classroom threw me off for some reason, and I can't stop thinking about it. I can't stop thinking about how strange it is that Amelia Bailey and my mother stopped being friends at their prom the night when Carson Price went missing. Carson Price had been Nora Flynn's boyfriend. Nora is Amelia Bailey's sister. Carson Price and Sydney Hutton both died—or disappeared—in the same Boldosa Redwood forest.

It could just be that—a string of strange coincidences.

Or it could be something else. Something tying all those strings together into some big knot... or maybe like a spider web.

I have work today, coaching the little league soccer team. So when I get home from that, around the same time my mom gets home from work, I sit at the small rickety kitchen table working on homework until Mom walks in through the door. She's smiling at her phone and looking like she's typing a message to somebody.

Barf. I don't want to know who.

"Hey, Ma."

She snaps her head up, startled. Then she raises an eyebrow sky high.

"Hi, Warner." She puts her phone in her back pocket and steps towards me, placing her purse on the counter where she always does. "What's going on?"

"Nothing's going on," I lie. But she knows me too well. I don't normally hang out at the dining table lately. I've become more of a recluse at our house, trying to avoid Mom as much as possible.

"Oh, okay..." she trails off. But she still slowly steps towards me with her eyes fixed on mine.

I suppose I might as well just come out with it.

"I have to talk to you about Amelia Bailey."

She looks taken aback. "Amelia Bailey? What about her?"

"What happened between you guys?"

"Wh-what's bringing this on all of a sudden?" She crosses her arms and juts one of her hips out.

"It doesn't matter. Just tell me."

Why does she seem so reluctant to do so?

"I don't see why you need to know, though. We were friends, and then we stopped being friends. Simple as that."

I can feel myself growing angry. Like I'm going to have an outburst. I grip my pencil hard, trying to stay calm. "Mom. Just tell me why you stopped being friends."

"Why do you care?" she asks, her voice rising in pitch as she grows defensive. I get my inability to keep my anger in from her, one hundred percent.

"Because! You don't want me to keep things from you, yet you're always harboring secrets from me. How can you expect me to want to tell you anything when you don't return the decency?"

"Is this about one of those girls? Lyla or Audrey?"

My stomach sinks at the mention of them. "Mom!"

She groans dramatically, her shoulders slumping.

I'm not going to let it go, though. "Why is it such a secret? Why did you guys stop being friends the same time Amelia's little sister's boyfriend went missing?"

Her mouth opens and closes like a fish. "How did you—where did you even—who is telling you these things?"

"Stop answering my questions with questions," I say, surprising myself at how even I'm able to keep my voice even.

"The reason Mia and I stopped being friends has nothing to do with that!"

"Then what was it?!"

Whoops. There goes the tone.

"We were just getting sick of each other, okay?! We were too different. She was always focused on being perfect and getting into the best college and following her parents' orders. I wasn't that way. I liked to rebel. I liked to go to parties. I wasn't as focused on getting an education after high school. We were just getting on each other's nerves all the time and it built up so much that we just exploded on each other. That's it." She storms into the kitchen and gets herself a glass out of the cabinet and fills it with water from the sink. "You need to drop this, Warner. I'm not kidding. That's all that happened. Leave it alone and stop asking me about it."

She chugs the water.

"But I—"

She stops drinking just to interrupt me. "No, Warner. Enough. I'm serious." She puts the glass down and walks over to the front door. "I'm taking the trash to the curb."

I sit there dumbfounded and stare at the screen door after she leaves.

If that was all that happened between Amelia and Mom that night, then why was it such a big deal for her to tell me about it? And why does she seem so desperate to get me to drop it?

CHAPTER 28

MADDY

I am flustered and huffing when I clumsily grab the trash bin and drag it to the road for pick-up in the morning.

My heart is pounding. My lips are quivering, and I'm trying not to start crying right now. I have to walk back into that house, and if Warner is still sitting at the kitchen table, he's going to see me.

That means I have to keep it together.

I stand there on the side of the road with my hands on my hips as I take deep, soothing breaths. There is a technique I found out about that I am supposed to use when I have anxiety this bad. The three-three-three rule. I need to name three things I see, then I name three sounds I hear, and then I move three different parts of my body. Apparently it will help center me and bring me back to the present moment—something I want to do seeing as my mind keeps trying to fly into darkness.

Three things I see.

"The dumpster." I scan my front yard. "My small, stupid house." My eyes fall on Warner's red Jeep. I'm about to name that next, but then I notice something.

The side of his Jeep—it's dented and scraped. He has it parked so the damaged side isn't visible when I get out of my car and head inside. I only see it now because I had to bring the trash bin out around the other side of it to get it to the street.

I forget about the soothing technique and dash back inside the house. Like I thought, Warner is still at the table, but he's just sitting there staring at nothing instead of doing his homework.

"What happened to your Jeep?" I ask.

He rolls his eyes. "I don't know."

"What do you mean you don't know?"

"It was a hit-and-run or something. It was parked in the lot at the soccer fields and when I got back to it, it was all messed up."

At least he hadn't been in the car when this happened. It makes me feel the slightest bit better. I would feel absolutely horrible if he had gotten hurt, and I didn't even know about it.

"And you didn't think to tell me?" I ask. "Did you call the police or report it?"

"I—no, I didn't bother. There are no cameras around that parking lot. Whoever did it, the police are never going to be able to find them."

I press my fingers to my forehead and temple. "Warner, are you kidding me? It doesn't matter if there are no cameras and you don't think there's a chance of the police finding who did it. It needs to be reported to the police. Especially when it comes to your insurance!"

"Sorry!" he hisses. "I didn't know!"

"When did this even happen?"

"I don't know. Like a week ago."

"Ugh. Do you have any idea how irresponsible that is?"

"Hold on," Warner snaps, turning in his chair aggressively. "You are seriously not about to lecture me about responsibility right now."

"Excuse me?"

"Look in the mirror, Ma! You calling me irresponsible is being hypocritical! I am the most responsible one in this house, like always!"

I am angry, but really more at myself than at him.

I want to keep arguing with him. I want to tell him he can't talk to me like that.

But the truth is, Warner is right.

Before he can be the one to storm off, I decide to do it first. I go straight to my room and close and lock the door. I flop down on my bed with my shoes and my work clothes still on and stare at the ceiling.

I'm irresponsible with the house chores. I'm irresponsible with Warner and the typical things a mother is supposed to keep up with. His conferences, his games, and even his health and dentist checkups. I am irresponsible with money, too. I used to have a massive trust fund from my disgustingly rich parents. I no longer talk to my parents. And I no longer have the fund, either. Not having the fund is the main reason why I don't talk to them. After I told them

I gambled it all away on a road trip to Las Vegas for my eighteenth birthday, they had just about had it with me.

That part doesn't bother me so much, though. I had had it with them a long time before that.

CHAPTER 29

AUDREY

I'm in the parking lot at school. It's dark and cloudy out like it always is. I'm alone. My car is the only one in the lot.

I go to dig for my car keys out of my gym bag. I'm in my cheerleading uniform. Did we have a game today? I can't remember any earlier events that led up to now.

And I can't find my car keys.

I drop my bag to the floor and turn around. My heart flies to my throat when I see, across the lot, a man in a shiny mask. The mask is cartoon, yet human-like, with a wide smile and big eyes. With harsh facial lines. Narrowed eyebrows that look crazy. Crazy like the person under the mask must be. They're just standing there, a knife in their right hand, staring at me.

I don't have anywhere to run this time. My feet are cemented into the ground.

He takes a step toward me.

My eyes snap open.

I am in my bed. At home.

I bolt upright, my heart pounding.

I don't get how I can have dreams like this nearly every night and feel equally terrified every time I wake from them. Shouldn't I be used to it by now?

I pull at my hair. I don't want to go to cheer practice. I don't want to be inside the school after hours. But I also don't want Sophia, Danielle, and Olive to know that something is up with me.

I decide to put the act on at lunch since it is the only time I will see my friends again until the end of the school day. I have Art History next, followed by AP Chemistry, and I'm hardly friends with anyone in those classes.

Instead of going to the lunch line, I wait for Sophia, Danielle, and Olive at the table. They arrive together with their lunch trays. All of them have healthy options, except Danielle has a banana nut muffin with her veggie wrap.

All of them look concerned and confused when they sit down with me.

"Are you not eating?" Danielle asks, immediately trying to slide the banana nut muffin my way.

I shake my head and try to look disgusted. "I don't feel well," I lie. "I'm super nauseous."

"Nauseated," Sophia corrects.

"Whatever," I snap. I need to sound irritable because I'm always irritable when I'm sick. I put one hand on my stomach and one hand over my face.

"Do you have food poisoning or something?" Olive asks, drenching her salad in Caesar dressing.

I shrug.

"Are you going to make it to practice today?" Sophia asks. I should have known that's what she'd be most concerned about—me making it to practice. Not about my well-being.

"I don't know if I can," I tell them. "Just smelling your guys' lunches is making me feel worse."

"Well, go to the nurse or something," Sophia instructs. "Stuff yourself with some ginger ale and saltine crackers. We have a big practice today."

I know we do. We are practicing some big lifts and throws. I'm usually a flyer.

"We'll see."

"I hope you feel better," Danielle tells me. "I'll keep this muffin in my locker in case you change your mind and need something to snack on."

I give her an appreciative smile. The others fall silent.

Lunch is weird for a little while, but then the girls start talking about some gossip going on around the school. Little stuff about who is dating whom and what couples are in a fight or about to break up. I'm not a part of the conversation. I'm also getting the feeling that Sophia and Olive don't quite buy my act. And they seem a little annoyed, too.

But that's just how it goes now, I guess. I constantly try to fix our friendship and hold it together, but then I immediately do something else to disappoint them again.

CHAPTER 30

MADDY

Nora and I ended up rescheduling our meet-up. We decide to get together at a bar outside of town. Somewhere where we won't be recognized. I would have just invited her over to my house because Warner is at school and I have Thursday off this week, but Nora said she needs to get out of the house.

We get there at the same time and hug in the parking lot. Nora looks beautiful. She has always been beautiful. Back in high school, I used to think that she and I passed more for sisters than Amelia and she did. Amelia always stayed blonde. Nora always colored her hair dark brown—the color of the thick, goopy mud in the woods after it rains. Her grass-green eyes are bright and happy at the sight of me. She has some circles under her eyes like she hadn't gotten a very good night's sleep, but if I remember correctly, she looks like this every time I see her. She's dressed in hippie fashion with a long sleeve paisley maxi dress and super strappy sandals, a leather faded and scratched bag around her shoulder.

Everything about her seems to be in slightly poor condition. Like her beat-up old gray Toyota Corolla that she arrived in. The bag she's wearing. Even her dress looks slightly faded, like she's washed it a million times or like she plucked it out of a Goodwill bin.

"I'm so happy you could make it this time!" Nora says to me when we pull away from our hug. We walk inside the bar together, the both of us smiling. It is nice when I get to see Nora. But I dread it, too.

We find a high-top table in the back corner by the dartboards of the bar. I've never been here before. It's not nearly as nice as The Viper, the new bar I tried out the other night when I met Steven. This bar is more my speed. It's divey and uncrowded.

"I needed this," Nora tells me. She scans the drink menu. "I'm pretending like I want a fancy cocktail, but let's be honest—I just want a double shot of whiskey."

My eyes widen. "Wow, you must be having some week."

She shrugs. "Not really. Why?"

"Oh, I don't know. Maybe I will have some whiskey, too." I don't ever drink whiskey. I don't know why I am even suggesting this. But when the server comes over to take our drink order, Nora orders us both a fancy brand of whiskey I've never heard of before—both of them doubles on the rocks.

"So, what's been going on with you?" I ask when the waiter walks away.

"Honestly? Absolutely nothing. I'm still crashing at Mia's house, in case you couldn't guess that."

Amelia doesn't know that I am meeting up with Nora. Nor does she know that Nora and I have stayed in contact all of these years.

But I'm keeping a secret from Nora, too—she doesn't know that I've become friends with Amelia again.

"How is that going?" I ask.

"I don't really talk to her that much. It's nice spending time with my nieces and nephew, but... I don't know. Being around Mia, you know how it is. It's a lot."

"I remember that, yeah."

When the drinks come, I'm quick to sip from mine. We continue catching up, but neither of us has much to talk about. However, the deeper we get into our double shot of whiskey, the more that starts to change.

I also find myself growing bolder. More daring. I have a question I've wanted to ask her for a long time but never had the courage to before. It's not even that big of a deal, so I don't know why I struggle with it so much. I don't know why it's hard for me to talk about. It's not like I'm about to talk to her about Carson Price. I never want to do that.

"So..." I say after we finish talking about a show on HBO Max that we are both obsessed with. "Why don't you stay at a hotel or something instead of Mia's house?"

"I don't want to spend the money. I can stay at Mia's for free."

"Right..."

So that means that she must not have the money to do it. Obviously she doesn't, seeing as she drives a god-awful car and never has new clothes.

"I feel like you want to ask me something," she says, staring me down hard. I glance at her glass and see that her whiskey is empty. I finished mine, too.

"I don't know," I say, unable to look back up at her.

"Just ask me, I don't bite."

I scratch the back of my neck. I'm going to do it.

"Okay, then. I was just wondering... what did you spend all the money on?"

I'm assuming she wasted it all. Wasted it just like I told my parents that I did.

"What do you mean?" Nora asks. Her expression is hardening, which is exactly what I didn't want.

"I just—"

"Do you think I spent it all?"

"Did you not?"

"Wow."

"I'm sorry," I correct. "I didn't mean to assume. I just thought... You know, with you staying with Mia, and your car..."

Oh Gosh. None of this is coming outright. Why don't I just say exactly what it is I'm thinking. You seem really poor even though I gave you hundreds of thousands of dollars, so I'm guessing you spent it all already.

"Well, you know what happens when you assume, Mads. I don't like to live a lavish lifestyle. I'm smart with my money. And I have a lot of things that I'm saving it for."

I feel like a complete jerk. Nora is just frugal.

"I'm sorry I said anything," I say, wishing we could just forget this ever happened. Maybe I should order more whiskey.

She sits there looking offended for a few moments more, then finally, her face relaxes. "No, it's okay," she says. "If I saw it from your point of you, I probably think the same thing. But I promise you I wouldn't waste the gift you gave me. It has helped me with, uh... bills and when—when I needed it."

I reach across the table and squeeze her hand. I feel warm inside and relaxed now. Nora isn't mad at me. She still appreciates that I gave her most of my entire trust fund and she's using it wisely. That's all I had wanted to know. Because every day when I think about how I don't have that money anymore, I've been growing resentment towards Nora, thinking that she hadn't put it to good use. But Nora deserves that money. I do not.

CHAPTER 31

AMELIA

I've been feeling off already all day as it is, but now that I'm home, I feel even worse.

The main reason is probably that I had told Dean yesterday that I would talk to Audrey, but I didn't. I didn't even tell Gentry about how she hasn't been going to her English class.

I just wanted more time to plan out exactly what I was going to say to her. But I had plenty of downtime at work to do it today, and I still haven't come up with anything.

I get changed out of my work clothes and start cooking dinner. When I open the trashcan to toss some scraps inside it from my cutting board, I noticed shards of ceramic glass inside of it. It makes me freeze in my step. Then I slowly reach in and take a sliver of it out. I see a small bit of red and blue swirly paint and a floral design.

This is from the baking dish that Mom had given me. Somebody broke it.

I finish cooking in a little bit of a mood after that. Whoever broke my dish failed to tell me about it. I had liked that dish, but it wasn't that big of a deal that somebody broke it. It's that they didn't come clean about it that is frustrating to me.

When we all sit down for dinner, the six of us all here for a change, I decide to ask about it.

But nobody comes clean.

I raised my children better than this. Which leads me to believe that none of them broke it. I think it was Nora. I think Nora is acting more like a child than any of my own are. But I don't want to confront her in front of everyone. I will just have to do it privately at some point.

After dinner, I finish up some of Joey's laundry. I take it into his bedroom, where I find myself alone. He must be downstairs, either working on his homework or watching YouTube in the office.

I set the pile of clean clothes on top of his dresser and then start sorting them and putting them where they go. When I open the top drawer of the dresser, however, I see a sliver of the baking dish—the piece that had the main portion of the floral design on it.

Joey broke it?

I feel hurt. I feel guilty for thinking it had been Nora.

I march back downstairs to find my son in the living room. He has the TV on, but he is also watching YouTube on his phone.

"Joey, are you sure you did not break the dish?" I ask, giving him another chance to come clean while talking in a calm voice. "You can tell me if you did. I won't be mad at you, but only if you tell me the truth."

Joey clicks his phone off and sits upright. "Why are you asking me again?" he asks, looking over at Lyla, who's in the living room as well. I don't know where anyone else in the house is. It's just the three of us here. Lyla has her eyes narrowed at me, her focus no longer on the TV.

I know it looks bad. Joey is my foster son. Me blaming him over my biological children makes me look like a terrible mother. But a piece of the dish had literally been in his room.

"Joey, please just answer the question."

"I didn't break it!" His voice is high and upset.

I pull the sliver I found from my back pocket and hold it up in the air. "Then why did I find this hidden in your dresser drawer, Joey?"

"What? I don't know! I didn't break it."

"We don't lie in this house," I remind him.

Lyla barks out a sarcastic, loud laugh. I shoot her a glare.

"Are you kidding me?" she snaps. "Don't blame him for lying—if he even is. Where do you think he learned it from? He has to watch you and dad do it all the time!"

"Lyla!"

She gets up from the couch, rolls her eyes, and marches up the staircase. Joey trails off after her, not even looking at me.

I sit down on the couch, staring at the stupid piece of ceramic.

What is going on?

I feel like I'm losing control of my kids. Of my family. And I'm never not in control. I've always had a good relationship with all three of them. Now I feel like those relationships are beginning to fall apart.

I can fix this. I always fix things.

I just need to talk to them.

Lyla first.

I give it some time for her to cool off after snapping at me, then I gently go to her room and knock on her door.

"Come in."

This is a good sign.

I open the door and close it behind.

"What's going on?" she asks from the floor. She's sitting in the middle of her room, criss-cross-applesauce and on her phone. Normally, I only close the door if she's in trouble or if she wants to talk to me alone.

I sit down on her bed. "Lyla, I just want to know what's been going on with you." She's been snappy and full of attitude with pretty much every interaction we've had over the past couple of weeks. She's been acting out and getting into trouble, too.

"Nothing," she lies blatantly.

I sigh.

"It doesn't seem like nothing. You seem to be in a constant state of distress. I know I let you stop going to therapy... but maybe you need to go back."

Maybe she isn't over the death of Trinity. Especially not with Sydney Hutton dying. It probably brought up all of those horrible memories and feelings and had caused her to fall back on her progress.

Lyla looks like I've personally offended her. "No," she says quickly.

"Honey, I think it might help you more than you realize."

"It didn't help me at all the last time," she snaps. "I don't want to do it."

"Lyla, you—"

I stop when Lyla abruptly gets to her feet.

"I need to go somewhere," she tells me, fixing her socks and stuffing her feet inside her slip-on vans.

"Right now?"

I look at the time on my watch. It's nearly nine. On a school night.

Lyla ignores me and goes towards her bedroom door.

"Lyla, you can't just leave."

When she whips her head around to me, her eyes are full of fire. I've never seen her look at me with such disdain before. It breaks a dam inside of my heart. I can physically feel the pain of it.

"Watch me," she says. Then she's gone.

I run out of her bedroom. "Lyla!"

But then I hear the front door open and shut.

Across the hall, Audrey opens her bedroom door and pokes her head out. We look at each other. I need to make a decision. Talk to Audrey or go chase after Lyla.

I can't let Audrey go another day skipping school.

"Can I talk to you?" I decide to ask her.

She looks ready to be defensive. "Me?"

I nod my head and let myself into her room. I sit on her bed, thinking she will sit next to me. Instead, she sits at her desk.

I am too worked up about what happened with Lyla just now that I don't even gently go about this. "You need to stop skipping your first-period class, Audrey."

She looks caught red-handed.

I wait until she finally says something.

"Did... something happen between you and Mr. Reeves?" she asks, taking me by surprise. I don't even know what could've possibly led her to think that. Is that why she has been skipping?

"Of course not," I lie. Then I'm painfully reminded of the harsh words Lyla had said to me down in the living room. She's right. I am a hypocrite. It seems like all anyone does in this house is lie.

"Okay..." Audrey trails off. I can tell she doesn't believe me. Why would she?

"But please—do not try to change the subject," I say to her. "Since when do you ditch class? What's going on with you?"

"I don't know," she whines, looking away from me. "I'm just really stressed out right now. A lot is going on and I'm dealing with so much. School seems like the last thing on my mind lately. That's why I've been ditching."

"I understand that things are complicated right now, honey, but ditching is not okay. It can get you expelled. Mr. Reeves was nice enough to talk to me about it, and you aren't in any trouble. Probably because the school has never seen any behavior like this from you before. You need to start going. I'm going to be checking with Mr. Reeves to make sure that you attended tomorrow. Understood?"

She clenches her jaw. "Fine."

It's not fair that she's acting mad at me. She is the one who is in the wrong here.

"If you're so stressed out, then maybe I should pull you from cheer. It'll be one less thing you have to deal with," I say.

I might as well have just slapped her.

"No!" she gasps. "Don't do that! You can't! I'll go to English. You can't take me out of cheer!" She practically has tears in her eyes.

I don't know why all of my conversations are going so poorly. I'm just trying to help them. Lyla didn't want to be in cheer anymore, so I just figured if maybe Audrey wasn't in it, either, she would feel better.

I am totally failing at being a parent. Since when did that start happening?

CHAPTER 32

LYLA

I get a text shortly after I yell at my mom about Joey and storm up to my bedroom. It's from a number I don't recognize.

Unknown: *If you want your secrets safe, come to Delilah's at nine PM.*

I reply immediately.

Me: *Who is this?*

What secrets are they referring to?

I sit there staring at my phone screen, hoping they'll reply, and that's when my mom walks in to tell me I need to go back to therapy.

I didn't even want to go to Delilah's. But after talking to Mom, I didn't want to be in the house with her any longer, either.

So I get on my bike in the sprinkling rain and make my way to the diner. I'm probably going to be grounded for leaving my house like this. But really, it doesn't matter to me. Nothing does.

I'm thinking that the person who has been messing with us is going to be waiting for me at Delilah's. They're going to want something from me. They're going to make me do something. Or they're going to tell everyone about how killing Trinity was all my fault. And about how Sydney's death was probably all my fault, too.

I am a shaking, anxious mess when I pull up outside at the bike rack. It's around the corner from the front of the store, so I can't see inside through the windows. I have no idea who's going to be waiting for me, or why they would want to meet out in the open like this. Are they going to be wearing a mask? Are they going to speak with a voice changer so that I don't figure them out?

I check my phone one last time. I still have no response from when I asked about the identity of the messenger.

I can't believe this is actually happening. I can't believe I might finally be about to get some questions answered about this giant mystery.

I turn the corner of Delilah's and go in through the glass front door. The bell jingles, signaling my entrance.

It's brightly lit inside, but surprisingly quiet. I glance around the small ice cream parlor.

My heart sinks.

I have spotted the tormentor. He is sitting in a booth, facing the entrance and waving me over to him.

It's Warner.

CHAPTER 33

WARNER

Lyla looks ghostly pale when she slides into the booth across from me. Her short blonde hair is slightly damp from the rain outside. She smells like garden-fresh laundry detergent.

She places her hands on top of the table slowly. Every movement she makes is slow. Like when she moves her eyes to meet my gaze.

I've finally done it. I'm finally alone with Lyla.

"Why are you doing this, Warner?" she asks in a low voice.

Oh, right—she thinks I'm the one who's been messing with her.

"It's not me," I explain.

Naturally, she doesn't look like she believes me. She looks like she wants to get up and run out of here.

"I'm serious," I say. I hold up my phone. "I downloaded one of those texting apps and messaged you from that. So yeah, I did text you just now to get you to come here. But I'm not the one doing... all of this."

She stares at my phone screen. I have the text app pulled up to the message thread between us.

Still, she looks weary. "You tricked me into coming here to talk to you?"

"What else was I supposed to do, Lyla? I've been trying to talk to you for days. Every time, you run away like you think I'm going to try and hurt you or something. I swear to you, I'm not doing this."

"You're insane."

"Am I, Lyla? Or are you and your sister the crazy ones that are trying to get me thrown in jail over something that you did?"

"What?" she asks loudly.

"Why have you been running away from me? You and Audrey. Why are you suddenly not talking to me?"

I think I'm doing a pretty good job at looking calm and acting calm. But I can hear my heart pounding in my ears. If I showed Lyla my palms, we would both be able to see the sweat glistening in the overhead lighting above us.

"You..." She leans in closer. "You lied to us, Warner."

"About what?"

"About that night! You did see Sydney! You told us you hadn't."

I can't help but look over my shoulder. I didn't do anything to Sydney, but I don't need anyone overhearing our conversation and thinking that I did. Luckily, no one seems to be paying any attention, and I think we're keeping our voices quiet enough.

"What are you talking about?" I demand. I know exactly what she's talking about, though. I just need to hear her explain it. Explain how she knows. How she found out.

"I was sent a picture of you from that night. It's of you and Sydney together." She starts pulling her phone out of her back pocket, but I hold out my hand to stop her. I already know exactly what photo she's referring to.

Somebody had told them.

"I didn't do anything to Sydney, Lyla."

But now it makes so much more sense as to why they've been avoiding me. They weren't ever supposed to see that photo. No one was ever supposed to know.

She leans back in the booth and crosses her arms. "I don't know how you expect me to believe you."

"You just have to!" I hiss. "I didn't tell you and Audrey that I did see her that night exactly for this reason! I knew you'd react this way and think I did something! I was just scared. I promise you, I didn't do anything to her. I met with her, we talked, then I went back to my tent and that's all."

"You just talked?"

I exasperatedly nod my head.

"What was the conversation about?"

"She asked me to meet her. Just like she asked you guys to meet her. I don't know what her plan was and why she wanted us all together. Maybe she considered us all friends. I don't know. I didn't know that she had texted you, too. When she asked me to meet with her, I decided I would, only because I wanted to confront her. She got me in trouble when she pushed me into the lake from the kayak. I am the captain of the football team and I'm supposed to be setting a good example. She wouldn't stop bothering me, too. She couldn't take the hint that I didn't like her. Which, in her defense, I understand because I suck at telling people how I feel. So I met up with her to tell her to leave me alone."

I remember the conversation painfully clearly. I had been lying awake in my tent beside Jackson, who was dead asleep and snoring loudly. I was scrolling through Instagram, my eyes locked on a picture a girl in our grade had posted that had Lyla in it. It was from earlier that day. Lyla looked uncomfortable in her smile, and I could tell she hadn't wanted to be a part of the photo.

Then the text from Sydney appeared on my screen.

Sydney: *Sneak out of your tent and meet me. On the trail to the lake. After everyone is asleep.*

I had thought she was crazy.

Me: *I'm not gonna do that.*
Sydney: *Please? I just need to talk to you about something. It's important.*

I highly doubted it was anything important. She just wanted an excuse to hang out with me again. To throw herself at me. And I needed it to stop.

I didn't reply to her. So she texted me again.

Sydney: *I really hope you'll come.*

And I did.

I snuck out of the tent, careful not to wake Jackson. I delve through the bushes and tried to crouch low so that anyone else sneaking around or keeping an eye on us wouldn't catch me. I not only did not want to get caught sneaking out of my tent and breaking the rules of the upperclassman trip, but I also didn't want to get caught talking to Sydney in the dead of night. It would only allow for more rumors to be spread about our relationship.

I didn't know exactly where on the trail between the lake and the campsite Sydney would be waiting. So when a hand reached out of the darkness and clamped onto my forearm, I had jumped.

"Geez, Sydney!" I hissed. She didn't smile at me, though. In fact, she looked sort of troubled about something.

But I had to stand my ground.

"I can't believe you actually came," she had told me.

"I need to talk to you," I blurted out. I didn't want to lose my courage.

"Okay, then," she said. "Shoot." She had looked over my shoulder in the distance. I looked behind me, too, but didn't see anything.

So, I turned back to her and lick my lips. "You gotta leave me alone, Sydney."

"What do you mean?"

"What do you mean, what do I mean?" I snapped. "Sydney, you got me in trouble yesterday! You keep acting like we are good friends or something, and I hardly know you. I don't know if you're into me or whatever, but I don't feel the same way, okay?"

"Oh."

For some reason, it seemed like she was barely even listening to me.

"I only came to meet you to tell you that I don't want to talk to you anymore."

Her eyes snapped back to mine. She looked irritated for a moment, but then her lips turned downwards, and sadness crept into her expression.

"Harsh much?" she snapped. "I'm sorry I pushed you into the lake yesterday. I shouldn't have done it. But Warner, you are the only one who's been nice to me since I started here. I honestly thought we were friends."

"I'm only nice to you because I feel bad for you."

She bit her bottom lip and nodded.

I took a step back. I think I had said everything I wanted to. "I'm going to go. But this,"—I motioned between the two of us— "This is not happening again. We're done here."

I turned around to leave, but she gripped the back of my shirt. "Warner, wait!"

I stared at her with bewildered eyes, then I yanked myself out of her tight grasp. "No, Sydney!"

"But I meant what I said in that text, I do have something to tell you!"

"Whatever it is, I don't care."

"Warner, please!"

I ignored her.

Then I left.

At Delilah's, I tell the whole story to Lyla. Then I say, "You have to believe me," when I finish.

She has a glass of water in front of her now, brought over by one of the workers. I have a vanilla and chocolate fudge sundae sitting in front of me that I am unable to take a bite of. Not until I know that she's on my side again.

"I..." Lyla trails off. She's thinking.

Please believe me.

"Fine, Warner. I believe you."

Relief floods me and a smile plays at my lips even though this still isn't the time to smile.

"Thank you," I tell her. "Will you get your sister to believe me, too?"

"I'll try." There's a hint of a smile on her face, too.

"So, can we go back to being friends again, then?" I ask.

"Friends?"

My stomach sinks. The text.

"Just friends," I assure her, but only because that's the vibe I'm getting from her. Would I like to be more? Yes. Does she seem like she wants that? Not so much. "It might be a longshot trying to get you to believe me again, but I promise you when I say I never sent that text message to Jackson."

"Right, don't worry. I believe that, too."

"Oh. Good."

There are a few moments of awkward silence. Then she sighs before she speaks. "Thank God you didn't send that text. It would be super wrong for us to go down that road... you know—because of Jackson."

"Yeah, I agree one hundred percent."

Her words don't make me feel better enough to want any of my dessert because I think she's just insinuated that she would go down that road with me if it wouldn't hurt Jackson to do it.

CHAPTER 34

LYLA

When I leave Delilah's, I have multiple missed calls and texts from my parents. They're furious. I bike home without even bothering to call or text them back. But just like I'm expecting, when I walked through the front door of my house, they are both waiting for me in the living room. They scold me for being disrespectful to Mom, then they lecture me about not replying to their calls and texts. Then they tell me that I am being forced to go back to therapy whether I like it or not, and then they ground me.

I'm shunned to my room, my phone taken away from me. But it doesn't stop Audrey from bursting her way inside as I grab clothes to go take a shower.

Normally, I'd be annoyed at her for bursting her way in, but I'm glad to see her.

"Shut and lock it!" I whisper-yell at her. She quickly does as instructed, looking alarmed.

"What happened?" she demands. "Where were you?"

I tell her everything. Everything that just happened between Warner and me at Delilah's. I don't know if she's going to believe that Warner was telling the truth or not. But I hope she does because I really miss us all being on the same team about this.

She looks angry when I finish speaking.

"What?" I ask, confused as to why.

"Are you kidding me?" she snaps. "Are you trying to get yourself killed? Or kidnapped? That was seriously so stupid of you, Lyla!"

"What are you talking about?!"

"You went alone to go meet with the person that's been messing with us for weeks! Emphasis on alone! Are you crazy? How reckless can you be?"

I roll my eyes. "I'm fine."

It takes a lot of back-and-forth arguing for her to not be annoyed at me anymore. And it takes a lot more convincing and talking through it to get her to believe Warner, too. But eventually, she caves.

"Somebody out there wants to get all three of us. It has to be the same person," she says. We're both on my bed, sitting crisscross and facing each other.

"And they're dangerous," I remind her. "Warner could've gotten killed in that jeep incident."

Warner had filled me in about how the tormentor had chased him down in his car last week.

"Yeah, and they literally chased me with a giant, sharp, shiny knife!" Audrey whined.

"And I get the feeling they've been following me," I add. I think about when I had been at the cemetery, and how I felt like somebody was calling my name or that I was being watched.

"So weird," Audrey says. "Especially with what Warner said about Mom and Maddy."

"I do think it's weird that Warner and us were drawn together when our parents hate each other. But maybe there are more people getting messed with than just us. Maybe we are just the only ones that have been talking to each other about it."

"Hmm, I don't know, Ly. My mental capacity has maxed out for the night. I need to go to bed."

"Fine. But we're going to keep talking about this. With Warner."

"Whatever." She flips her hair and goes to her room.

CHAPTER 35

AUDREY

I have no choice but to finally face Mr. Reeves today—not after being scolded by Mom and threatened by her to be pulled from cheer. I can't lose cheer. I know I am afraid to go to practice right now, but it really is the only thing that makes me feel better. That makes me feel normal.

I suppose I do feel a little better today knowing that Warner has always been on our side this whole time. At least I have him and Lyla with me through this. If it is Mr. Reeves that is tormenting me, they'll be right there by my side to protect me.

School hasn't even been in session that long, so I didn't think anyone would notice that I have kept skipping my fourth-hour class. I figured my classmates might just think that I transferred classes or something.

But I had been wrong. Just last night, I got a Snapchat from a guy that has English with me—Kyron. He had sent me a random selfie of him in his room, the caption asking me why I kept ditching English. So I guess it's being talked about.

After lunch today, I hug Danielle, Sophia, and Olive in the hallway and then separate from them to go to class. The class.

I walk in, avoid Mr. Reeves's gaze at all possible costs, and slide into my desk. I sink down low in hopes of nobody noticing me or saying anything to me.

Naturally, it doesn't happen that easily.

"There she is!" Kyron calls from a few rows of desks over, pointing to me with a mischievous smile on his face. We're far enough in the back of the classroom that Mr. Reeves isn't paying attention to us over the chatter of the rest of the class.

"So you are still in this class!" Lindsey Weaver jokes.

"Guys, cut it out," I say. "It's not a big deal."

"Coming from you," Jeremy Garcia says.

"No wonder Ryan has a thing for you," Kyron teases. "You have a secret rebellious side to you."

"Stop," I say again, my cheeks turning pink.

"Welcome to the dark side," Tommy Moore says. He's a notorious class ditcher.

I can't believe they're making such a big deal out of this. It's only a matter of time before it gets back to my friends that I've been skipping out on fourth hour. It's going to be another thing they're going to get mad about for not telling them. At this point, I'm wondering why I don't just give up.

The bell rings, and Mr. Reeves starts calling everyone's name to do attendance.

"Audrey Bailey?"

"Here," I say in a small voice. I feel like everyone is staring at me, including Mr. Reeves. I sneak a peek at him. Yep. His eyes are glued to me.

"Thank you, Audrey," he says, even though he hasn't thanked anyone else.

Mr. Reeves seems so normal. He seems like the cool teacher that all the kids love to talk to and joke around with. He doesn't seem evil. Calculated. I don't want to think of him as the man in the mask. I don't want it to be him. But I'm terrified because I have no idea who else it could possibly be.

CHAPTER 36

Maddy

Warner has a football game tonight at Blackfell High School, and I have decided to go to it. The main reason is to support my son, of course, but I do have another motive behind it.

I go alone.

I'd invite someone, but my only friends are Nora and Mia, and I can't be seen with either of them. I'd ask Steven, but he hasn't even asked me out on a date yet. He splits his time between the multiple restaurants he owns in different states, so he's out of town a lot. We've been texting back-and-forth here and there, and he has called to talk to me on the phone a few times since Monday. He is a lot of fun to talk to, but I have a guard up. I don't want him to turn out to be just like Craig. To be just like all the other losers I've dated in the past.

I sit alone on the bleachers towards the front. The kick-off has already started and I'm running late, per usual.

But there on the sidelines with the other cheerleaders is Audrey Bailey.

My other motive.

She's cheering and smiling and appears bright and happy. She looks like the kind of girl that spills everyone's secrets.

How on earth am I supposed to trust her?

"Let's go, Warner!" I cheer for my son as he runs down the field with the ball. He gets tackled, and I wince. It's not enjoyable to watch that part of his games. I've heard too many horror stories about high school boys getting brain damage from hard tackles on the field, and about it affecting them long-term down the line. I don't know why I even let Warner play this sport.

I almost miss a lot of the game because I'm too distracted by the cheerleaders as I wait for the perfect moment to do what I came here to.

Eventually, Audrey takes her water bottle off of the bench where the cheerleaders keep their stuff, and I watch as she waves to the rest of her cheer team and walks away. She's probably off to go to the fountain to refill her bottle.

I step over the legs of high schoolers and parents beside me to get to the stairs of the bleachers, then I go after her.

I don't want to corner her in front of her peers and other teachers and parents, so I find a good secluded spot where she will have to pass by. When she makes her way back from the fountain, I swiftly grab her wrist and pull her around the corner so that we're hidden on the other side of the building where they sell snacks and drinks for the game.

Audrey looks terrified at first, but when she realizes it's me, her fear diminishes, but only slightly. Good. She should be scared of me.

"Hey," I start off, crossing my arms in front of me. I try to look as intimidating as possible.

"I need to get back to my team," Audrey Bailey tells me in a quiet voice.

"This won't take long," I inform her. "I'm just checking in."

"Checking in?"

I squint at her. "You know what I'm talking about. I am making sure that you've been holding up your end of the deal." I don't want to physically say the words out loud about my son and Coach Reeves. There might not be anybody around us at the moment, but I still can't take the chance that somebody might be listening where I can't see.

"I haven't told anyone."

I want to believe her, but Audrey won't meet my eyes. She's looking down at the ground, fiddling with her water bottle lid.

"I hope that's true, Audrey," I tell her. "Because if I find out otherwise, you're not going to like what happens."

"Wait a second..." She stares at me like she's trying to remember something. "Are you—?"

"Audrey?"

We turn. Amelia Bailey has spotted us.

Crap.

"Hi, Mom!" Audrey says in a bright voice.

Amelia stares at me. I stare back. We have to put the act on.

"What are you doing talking to my daughter?" Mia snaps at me.

"I was giving her tips on her middle leap," I say, making it up on the spot. I glance at Audrey and dare her to tell her mother otherwise. Then as I brush past Mia, I slam my shoulder into her harder than I needed to.

"My daughter is a better cheerleader than you ever could have hoped to be when you were in high school," Mia says as I walk away. Ouch.

I know she's only pretending, but it still stings a little.

I consider giving Mia an obscene hand jester, but thinking that might be a little too immature—even for me—I instead pretend like I didn't even hear her and walk back to my seat.

CHAPTER 37

AUDREY

I feel like a bit of a mess inside when Warner comes up to talk to me for a drink break during the game.

"Did Lyla talk to you?" he asks, removing his helmet and revealing his sweaty face, his wet hair plastered to his forehead. Still, he looks cute. Like he couldn't hurt a fly. Just like I sort of always expected he couldn't.

"Oh!" I say, a little too enthusiastically. I'm still shaken up from my conversation with Warner's mom, and I don't know how to act. "Yeah, she did."

He looks like he's still waiting for me to say something.

"I-I believe you," I say, looking around to see if anyone's paying attention to us.

His blue eyes glisten in the blinding spotlights of the field. He smiles big, and it makes my stomach flutter.

"Great," he says. "Thank you. Seriously."

"Yeah. I'm sorry that it took a little bit."

He nudges me lightly with his elbow. I don't even care that he's gotten a bit of sweat on me. "Don't worry about it. We're all confused and freaked out about whatever is going on. No more secrets. No more hiding things from each other. Yeah?"

This makes me feel like crap. "Definitely," I say, my voice cracking. I wish there was some other way he could find out about his father. Someway that wasn't from me that Maddy knew wasn't from me, too. I don't know what Maddy will do if I confess, but I don't want to find out. Especially if she is the one that's been tormenting us.

"Cool."

I smile at him. It dawns on me that I've actually missed talking to him these past couple of days. That I like when we team up together and talk about our situation. I like that we've formed this friendship, even if the circumstances surrounding it aren't ideal.

But what does this mean?
Do I have a crush on Warner Carpenter?

***

When the game ends and my voice is hoarse from cheering on our team is so hard, Ryan Copeland jogs over to me with a beaming smile on his face.

"You did so good!" I say to him with a grin. Then, to my surprise, he picks me up and twirls me around in front of everybody. I giggle ridiculously. He sets me down, looking like he is still on a high that's not going to go away for a while because of the win. The team needed this.

"And I saw your halftime show," he says. "You can really fly."

I blush. "Thanks."

"Seriously. It takes guts to do what you do. I don't know how you trust those other chicks to catch you."

"After you just did that with me in front of them, I wonder if maybe I even should," I joke. Every girl is obsessed with Ran Copeland. He's basically the king of the senior grade.

Ryan shrugs modestly. "Are you going to Wrigley's party after this?" he asks. "You should."

I glance up in the stands and see Mom and Dad waiting for me. They're definitely not going to want me to do that. It's already close to nine o'clock and they've been extra strict lately.

But then I look back at Ryan. He looks so excited and happy, and he practically showed the entire school that he likes me by picking me up and spinning me around. This is like a fairytale moment. How do I say no to that face?

"Well, if you want me there, then I am in."

He shoots me a wink. "Good."

I'll find a way to convince my parents to let me go. I've hardly done anything fun lately. I need this.

CHAPTER 38

LYLA

My parents suck at grounding.

I've been lying around at home all night, my family at the football game and Nora doing who knows what. Jackson messaged me not long and asked me to go to Wrigley Hall's party with him. I told him I can't because I'm grounded.

But then Audrey calls me when the football game ends.

"You have to come to Wrigley Hall's party with me."

"What?" I ask, astonished. "I'm grounded."

"Not tonight, you aren't," she says.

"What are you talking about?"

"I asked Mom and Dad if I can go, and they said only if you come with me. They want me to use the buddy system."

I laugh. Unbelievable.

"So hurry up and get changed!" she snaps.

"But, Audrey, I don't want—"

"You're going! Love you bye!"

The call ends.

I go back to the messaging thread between me and Jackson.

Jackson: *Are you really grounded or are you just saying that to get out of it? I just really want to make it up to you, Lyla. I want to make things better. I miss you so much.*

I suppose he has been doing a pretty good job lately. At school, he has been giving me the space I need. He still messages me and tries to catch my eye and give me waves across the hall, but he's been very respectful of my wishes.

And now I am supposed to go to Wrigley's party.

I guess I don't really have a choice. I press on Jackson's name with my thumb and give him a call.

———

Jackson and I arrive at Wrigley's mansion together. It's a giant gabled-roof house built in the eighties. It has a lush green front garden with tall old trees and immaculate landscaping. There's a three-car garage with another two-car garage on the other side of it. Inside, the house has been remodeled to match current interior design trends. The cabinets are white. The tile flooring is made to look like wood planks. There's a massive marble island in the center of the kitchen. The light fixtures are sleek and sophisticated. The foyer has one of those entrances where two staircases wrap around to the top floor. The house is already bustling full of teenagers by the time Jackson and I show up.

We walk into the house.

"Can I hold your hand?" Jackson asks in my ear.

I'm flattered that he would ask instead of just going for it, so I nod my head. He takes it. It feels familiar, yet foreign at the same time. This was probably the longest I had ever gone without holding his hand. I'm just now realizing it.

We go to the kitchen first to get some drinks. Wrigley is there, of course—just the person I was hoping to avoid the entire time I'm here—and he smiles at me when he sees me. But then he looks down at my hand linked through Jackson's.

"What's up, you two?!" he says in a friendly voice. "Help yourself to whatever is in the fridge."

"Have you seen Audrey?" I ask him. I haven't spotted her yet, and if she bailed on the party that she demanded I come to, I'm going to kill her.

"Just a few minutes ago, actually," Wrigley says. "I think she went out back."

Jackson gets me my drink, then he gets one for himself after. We walk around the house and say hi to people for a bit, then he pulls me aside in a hallway.

"Thank you for doing this," he tells me. He has a hopeful, friendly smile on his face. He's being the Jackson I remember him being. He looks handsome in his V-neck and jeans. He smells good, too. I think he used the body wash I got for him last Christmas.

"Sure," I say, feeling awkward. I feel like I owe him an apology. He is my boyfriend, and I have been ignoring him completely. I've been uncertain about whether or not I even want to be with him. I still am uncertain. But a high school house party is not the best place for us to have that conversation.

Jackson runs a hand through his jet-black hair, messing it up in a way that still makes him look good.

"I'm really sorry," he says.

I put a hand on his chest. "We don't have to talk about it now."

He grins. "All right. Let's just have a good time tonight, okay?"

I offer a smile and nod my head. He takes my hand again and we re-join the party.

***

I hope Audrey is having the time of her life at this party tonight because I don't know how much more I can take. Jackson has been super nice—it's true. But I'm currently standing by the staircase by myself, watching him off in the distance. He's being goofy and loud like he always is. He's everyone's favorite guy. The class clown. The friendly face. It seems like everyone has forgotten about the rumors going around that he pushed me. I haven't seen Warner anywhere, but it seems like the entire school has forgotten that they have beef between each other, too.

A lump forms in my throat as I watch Jackson. I used to love Jackson's goofiness. I used to join him in it, even. We would laugh so hard until our drinks came out of our noses.

It's too much for me now. He's too extroverted. I am not the same. I am not the perfect party date like I used to be. I'm sure he misses that. I'm sure he wants it back. But he will never get it.

I told myself I wouldn't do this here. But for some reason, now I can't think about anything else. It's like I'm suffocating, and I won't be able to breathe again until I get it over with.

"Jackson," I say in his ear, interrupting him as he chats with some of our classmates. He smiles at me and swings an arm over my shoulder.

"What's up, beautiful?"

"Can I talk to you?"

His smile fades. I go up the stairs with him, and we find a quiet, empty bedroom. It looks like a guest room based on the lack of decor and the hard mattress. We sit on the bed and look at each other.

Already, tears are streaming down my cheeks. He senses something is wrong.

"Lyla..."

I shake my head and don't look at him. "I'm sorry, Jackson."

"I just... I don't understand." But he does understand. He knows what's coming.

"I can't be who you want me to be," I tell him.

"What are you talking about? You're exactly what I want."

"No, I'm not. I used to be. But I'm not that anymore. I've been trying to figure out if I'll go back to the old me. I know you've been waiting for me to, as well. And you've been super patient and I really appreciate it. But I've come to the realization that it's just not going to happen."

He takes my hand and squeezes it. I let him, and I keep crying.

"I don't care," he tries. "Lyla. I don't. You went through something awful. I have been there for you through it. I want to continue to be there for you."

"We've grown apart, Jackson."

I know I'm doing the right thing. But hurting Jackson hurts me too. So, so much. More than I could have ever anticipated. I have physical chest pains and I feel like I'm about to faint.

When I meet his eyes again, I see that he's crying, too.

WARNER

Talking to Audrey again and knowing I have her friendship back feels amazing. Winning the football game a little while after that feels even more amazing. Then, when Coach Reeves pulls me aside and says that scouts had been in attendance and introduces me to a couple of them, I feel nearly indescribable. I had crushed the game. And I hadn't even known scouts had been watching. Three different men talk to me and give me their cards. I am not quite sure football is something I want to go to college for, but it's amazing to know that I have a chance. Scholarship potential, even.

I feel less amazing when I get to the party and see that Lyla and Jackson are there together. They're holding hands, too.

I hadn't even realized they made up. Lyla never mentioned anything to me about it when we caught up at Delilah's that night.

I think about going up and saying hi to them, but I still haven't talked to Jackson since our fight and I don't think tonight is a good time to do that. Instead, I let them have their space.

I am moping on the back porch about Lyla when Jessica Vaccari approaches me from inside. Jessica is a cute, dark-haired girl in my grade, and Jackson told me once that she has a thing for me.

"You did seriously amazing out there tonight," she says to me with a smile.

Part of me feels like Jessica is not even my caliber. She is ridiculously hot. Could-be-on-the-cover-of-magazines hot. She's tall and confident and never seems afraid to talk to anybody.

"Oh, thanks," I say, my mood lightening a little. I need to stop pouting about Lyla. There have to be other options out there for me that aren't my best friend's girlfriend.

I stay out on the porch and talk to Jessica for a good chunk of the night. When her friends demand that they go on a rescue mission to save one of their other friends from some geeky guy who won't stop talking to her, I go back inside and unfortunately come face-to-face with Jackson.

"Oh," I say stupidly.

His eyes are bloodshot.

"Lyla just dumped me."

My stomach sinks. I should feel happy about this news, but I feel completely awful. My best friend has just had his heart ripped out.

"Jackson... I'm so sorry."

He shrugs, but I can tell that he's wrecked.

"Did she say why?" I ask.

Please, please don't say because of me.

"We've grown apart. It makes sense, I guess. Just sucks." He looks like he might start crying again. I slap him on the shoulder. "Dude, let's go outside."

Looking like he doesn't know what else to do, he nods his head and follows me out.

"I have been meaning to talk to you, actually," I tell him. We walk out into the grass of Wrigley's massive backyard. It's so large that I can't even see where it ends before the darkness swallows it.

"Then why haven't you?" Jackson asks.

I scratch the back of my neck. "Because I suck, I guess."

He blows some air out of his nose in what I think might be a slight laugh.

"I just wanted to say that I don't know who sent that message to you. But I swear to you, it wasn't me."

He nods. "Yeah. Lyla told me."

"But I still feel like I messed everything up," I admit. "So I'm sorry."

"It was probably inevitable. I think she stopped wanting to be with me the moment Trinity died."

I can't imagine how he must be feeling.

We're silent a bit. Then he asks, "So you really don't feel anything for her, then?"

No more lies, Warner. No matter what happens.

"Jackson," I start. "I swear to you that nothing's going to happen between us. But... I do have feelings for Lyla. Somebody must have found out about it and that's why they sent you that message. I'm not going to act on those feelings, though, because I wouldn't do that to you. And Lyla isn't into me. I promise." It hurts my own feelings to say it out loud.

How much I wish things were different.

I stand there frozen as I stare at him, waiting for his reaction. I don't know if he's going to yell. Punch me again. Walk away. Tell me to stay away from him forever.

"I could kind of tell you maybe liked her."

I wince. "I'm sorry, dude."

For the first time in forever, Jackson gives me a smile.

I think we're going to be all right.

***

A little later into the party, I run into Lyla, who is cheering somebody on who's riding down the railing of the staircase. She smiles at me when she sees me.

"So what secret of yours drew you to Delilah's, anyway?" I ask.

She purses her lips and smirks at me. "Ha. Ha."

I chuckle to show that I'm just kidding. Any secrets she feels like keeping from me, she can. As long as they're not about me.

"I'm sorry about you and Jackson," I tell her, not meaning to change the subject so abruptly.

"How did you find out so quickly?"

"He told me himself, actually."

Her eyes widen. Her beautiful, sapphire blue eyes. "Wait... are you guys friends again?"

I shrug. But there's a smile on my face because I'm hopeful about it.

She nods slowly, but then her eyes glaze over. She looks sad. Worried.

I put a hand on her shoulder. "He's going to be okay," I reassure her. It couldn't have been easy ending their relationship. They had been together for a long, long time.

"Right."

"I mean, he's definitely going to pout for a long time, but—"

"Warner, you should know something."

I stop mid-sentence, my mouth still hanging open.

Lyla swallows audibly. She opens her mouth to continue, but then we're clouded in darkness. Complete, pitch-black darkness. The music has been cut, too.

My pulse quickens.

"All right, who is messing with the fuse box?!" a voice calls out in the darkness. Some of our peers laugh. Others groan in annoyance at the interruption.

I'm pretty sure all of them think it's a prank.

I, however, am not so sure about that.

CHAPTER 40

LYLA

It's almost as if the universe has given me a sign to not tell Warner about his father. I had been just about to when the power in the party suddenly shut off.

"Warner?" I ask, fumbling around in the dark for a hand to reach out to. Maybe I'm acting more afraid than the people around us, but I feel like I have a good reason as to why.

"Lyla," I hear Warner's voice say somewhere in the dark. My eyes are taking forever to adjust to the pitch blackness surrounding us. I reach out to him, but then a pounding starts in my ears and I feel like I'm getting further and further away.

"Somebody turn it back on!" a voice complains in the distance.

I don't like this one bit.

I walk away from Warner's fading voice, feeling around, bumping into things left and right, and accidentally clutching random body parts of my peers'. I want to find Audrey.

"What gives?!" another voice calls. Everyone thinks somebody did this as a prank. They're probably right, and I'm probably just overreacting.

I stop moving, my blood freezing to my core, when a high-pitched scream sounds out of nowhere. My heart skips a beat as I listen to the familiarity of it.

People gasp all around me. The scream is so loud that I cover my ears. I wonder if other people are covering theirs, too.

It continues.

Why have I heard this before?

"Lyla!" the screaming girl cries out. She's calling to me.

Me?

I don't say anything.

"Lyla!" it continues. "How could you do this to me?!" They keep screaming some more. I can feel myself beginning to have a panic attack. I try to push through more people, but it seems like I am walled in on all sides. My breathing quickens and I cover my ears tighter.

"No," I mutter. But the screaming continues.

"What's going on?!" somebody asks. I can feel the room around me beginning to realize this isn't just some dumb, harmless party prank. There is suddenly a heavy tension filling the air.

"Who is that?!" someone else cries. They sound almost as panicked as I feel.

The girl screams my name again. "Lyla, please!"

It sounds like Trinity's voice.

I sink to my knees. It's the panic attack taking over.

This is all just a hallucination.

No one's really screaming my name. This isn't a recording of my dead friend blaming me for her death.

People begin shining lights from their phones and looking around. "Somebody make it stop!" a voice yells.

"This is a seriously messed up thing to do, and whoever is doing it needs to knock it off!" someone else yells. They sound furious. Ready to hit someone over it.

Wait a second—so I'm not the only one that can hear it?

I want to yell back to the voice. I want to say I'm sorry. I want to make the screaming stop. But I can't. Someone is doing this to mess with me.

A light shines on my face. I can't see who's shining it on me because my eyes are blinded by it. But then a hand on my elbow pulls me back up.

"Lyla, come on," a shaky, yet stern voice says. It belongs to Wrigley.

The crowd around us won't stop talking as Wrigley drags me through the crowd and gets me to the front door, then the two of us escape out of the party together.

CHAPTER 41

WARNER

I try desperately not to let Lyla get too far away from me once the power goes out and the screaming starts. The sound makes my blood freeze and the hairs on the back of my neck stand at attention.

"Lyla?!" I call, fumbling around in the darkness trying to get back to her. But she isn't replying. Every step I take, I slam into another body as people freak out about whoever is doing this. The screaming continues. It's a girl's voice begging Lyla to help her and asking her why she did what she did. It's clear somebody is messing with her. Probably the same person that's been messing with all of us. I can't tell who the voice belongs to. But it might be Trinity's. Or someone who sounds like her.

"Lyla!" I try again, louder this time, worried about her. She can't have gotten far, right?

"Is this Sydney's voice?" a voice asks nearby to somebody.

"I think it might be Trinity's," another person says.

"TURN IT OFF!" a girl's voice shrieks, nearly louder than the screaming.

This is so messed up. I can't imagine how Lyla must be feeling.

A light from someone's phone finally cuts through the darkness and I see Lyla. She is on her knees on the floor, nearly in the fetal position as she covers her ears and rocks back and forth. People have seemed to form a circle around her as they stare at her and each other in horror and confusion. I race to go to her aid, but quickly realize I'm too late.

Wrigley Hall carefully picks her up by her elbows. She looks at him, her eyes full of freight and her skin ghostly white. Before I can do it, Wrigley ushers her through the dense crowd of scared people and away from the screaming noise, outside.

I stand there, dumbfounded, my heart pounding. This is the second time Wrigley has come to Lyla and Audrey's aide. I didn't even know he was close with either of them.

But I guess now I do.

CHAPTER 42

Audrey

I'm surprisingly enjoying myself at the party, talking to Ryan Copeland and flirting and giggling with him, too. But then somebody boxes the power.

"What's going on?" I ask.

"Somebody must be playing a prank," Ryan says to me. I can hardly see him next to me anymore.

Instantly, I am in panic mode. I don't think this is a prank. I think it's the masked man, back to mess with me. He must be here at the party. Any second now, I'm going to see him standing before me, holding the bright shiny blade.

I don't wait around to face him. Instead, I feel around for the railing that Ryan and I were leaning against, then I stumble up the stairs, scraping my shin on the wooden staircase several times on my way up. I fumble with my phone and turn on the flashlight app, my hands shaking uncontrollably along with the rest of my body. I let the light guide me as I check every door until I find one open, then I throw myself inside, close the door behind me, and lock it—for good measure. I sink to the ground against the wall, keeping my eyes closed and trying to bring myself back to reality. If I just keep my eyes closed, it's like I can pretend the lights are on and I'm the one controlling the darkness.

"Please go away," I mutter, tears streaming down my cheeks that I can't control. "Please leave me alone. Just leave me alone."

I hit the back of my head against the wall. I'm angry because I can't even enjoy a Friday night with my friends without something horrible happening. Whoever is continuously messing with us is ruining my life. I just want it back.

I don't know how long I stay up there having my panic attack, crying, and throwing my head repeatedly against the wall with my eyes closed.

There's a soft knock. "Audrey?" It's Danielle.

Finally, I open my eyes again. It's pitch black in here, but I can see light shining through the crack at the bottom of the door. I reach up and unlock the bathroom door, and then I sit back on the ground. Danielle takes it as her cue to let herself in. She flips the light on and closes the door behind her, looking down at me with wide eyes. My friends don't usually see me looking as messy as I do right now.

"What's going on? Why are you sitting here in the dark? What happened?" she asks.

I shake my head and keep crying. Danielle kneels down in front of me and puts her hands on my knees.

"Is it... is it because of Trinity?" Danielle asks. When I meet her gaze, I see that she has suddenly started crying, too.

I'm confused. "What about Trinity?" I ask.

"The—the recording somebody played. Didn't you hear it? People are saying it sounded like Trinity's voice."

Danielle wipes her eyes on some toilet paper.

"I didn't hear any recording," I admit. But then I realize I don't feel like telling Danielle the real reason why I came up here. "Or... I guess I didn't realize it was just a recording," I add in at the end.

"I think somebody did it to mess with Lyla," Danielle says. "You should've seen her, Audrey. She looked horrified. Wrigley grabbed her and pulled her out of the party. I don't know where they went."

My heart sinks. The person messing with us is at the party, then. He just chose to torment Lyla tonight instead of me.

"It was awful," Danielle continues.

I clutch her hands, which are still on top of my knees. Then I give her a brave smile. "People are jerks," I say to her.

She nods her head.

"At least it's over now, right?"

"Right. Are you going to be okay?"

I giggle. "Are you?"

She giggles, too. We sit there for a while and calm ourselves down, then she pulls me to my feet and we fix our makeup in the mirror, standing side-by-side at the two-sink vanity.

After a few minutes of silence, minus the person that keeps pounding on the door complaining that he needs to go to the bathroom, I look at Danielle's reflection in the mirror. Her eyes are still bloodshot, but her face isn't puffy like mine is from all the crying. "Danny?" I ask in a timid voice.

She tilts her head at me and waits.

"Can we... can we keep this between us?"

"Keep what?"

"You finding me crying on the bathroom floor?" I gnaw on the inside of my cheek. "I just really don't want to hear it from Sophia and Olive."

Danielle reaches out and gives my hand a reassuring squeeze. "Your secret is safe with me."

CHAPTER 43

Lyla

I stand outside with Wrigley for a long while, trying to catch my breath. He rubs my upper back in a soothing manner, keeping me close to him.

"That was so messed up," he says. I nod my head, too embarrassed to even look at him. "Do you know who that was?"

"No," I mutter. I don't want to talk about it anymore.

Luckily for me, Wrigley seems to sense that. "Well, hey—let's get out of here. Want to?"

I sneak a peek at him. Everything still feels a little blurry and hazy, and I'm still swaying slightly on my feet, but I don't miss the friendly expression he's wearing. How willing he was to leave his own party just to help me out.

"Okay," I say in a small voice.

He smiles at me kindly. "We can go anywhere you want. Just tell me which direction to go."

I look around the street, trying to grab my bearings. I realize we're not far from the pond I like to sit at. Without explaining myself, I begin walking. Soundlessly, he walks with me. When we reach the pond, I walk over to the edge of it and sit down in the fading green summer grass. He pops down next to me.

"You really don't have to leave your own party for me," I tell him, feeling guilty. But I'm also incredibly grateful that he's here with me because I don't think I could stand to be alone right now. I hope that wherever Audrey is, she's okay.

Wrigley shrugs. "There wouldn't be any point in being there now. Not if you're not there."

The line is so corny and unexpected that I scoff and roll my eyes. I don't say anything as I keep my focus out on the pond. There are no ducks right now. It's quiet here at the park, and the water is still.

"I'm really sorry that happened," he tells me. I nod. "I'll try my hardest to figure out who is responsible."

"Don't," I say, quicker than I probably should have. "I just—I don't need you getting involved in any more of my predicaments."

"Okay... but I don't like seeing you get messed around with like that."

"It doesn't make it your job to fix it."

He falls silent. I lean back on my hands and extend my feet outwards. I can still hear an echo of the scream far back in my brain. It sounds like a broken record player. It sounds like it'll never go away. Like I went to a really loud concert and have a permanent ringing in my ears. But instead of a ringing, it's a high-pitched, desperate scream.

"Why did you stop texting me, Lyla?"

I snap my head to Wrigley, surprised at his sudden outburst. As I think about it, I don't know why I'm surprised. He's been wanting an explanation for months now. Instead of giving him any, I've just avoided him completely.

Nothing ever happened between Wrigley and me. Before I got into my car accident, he and I were actually good friends. But it was a weird type of friendship. We only ever texted and Snapchatted each other. We didn't talk much at school, and we didn't even wave at each other in the hallways. We made eye contact often, of course, but Wrigley Hall was that bad boy type of student who wouldn't be caught dead giving people friendly waves. He was slightly strange because he likes to throw parties at his house, but he doesn't seem very much like he likes being around people.

He texted me one day, having got my number from one of his friends, asking me for homework help in Biology. From there, the texting sort of just... never stopped. At least, not until that fateful night.

I look down and see that Wrigley is sitting the same way as me, and his hand in the grass is only centimeters away from touching mine.

"I stopped texting a lot of people," I say to him.

"But why was I one of them?"

I can tell that I've hurt him. I hadn't meant to, but continuing my friendship with Wrigley just seemed like it would be a constant reminder of the horrible thing I had done, and my head and my heart just couldn't take it. So I stopped.

"I'm sorry," I try. It's the best I can do right now.

"It's… it's okay."

That's when I feel it. His pinky brushing against mine in the grass. I gaze at him, surprised that he's making the move. I've never really looked at Wrigley in a romantic sort of light, but that was because I had been in love with Jackson for so long.

I like Wrigley's curly brown hair. I like his skater bad boy clothing attire. I like that he minds his own business—for the most part—and doesn't seem to care at all what people think about him. I like his angular, straight nose and the tiny mole underneath his right ear. I like his deep baritone voice and how it never seems to tell me lies.

Wrigley looks up at the stars, so I do, too. Then I brush my pinky against his.

CHAPTER 44

AMELIA

I continue my research on Sydney Hutton the next morning, but I don't get very far. It's almost as if this girl never really existed. I'm beginning to wonder if maybe she didn't. But then I sit there and think about how ridiculous that would be.

Gentry is out golfing. Nora is out—not that I know where—and Joey rode his bike to the park to hang out with the friend he met at the swimming hole not too long ago. The girls had a sleepover at Danielle's house after the party they went to last night. I didn't want to be one of those moms, but given everything going on, I felt like I had to be—I had texted Danielle's mother last night to confirm that this was true, and she replied and told me that it was.

It's not that I don't trust my daughters.

Or maybe it is.

I think I used to trust them, but I don't really know if I do anymore.

I'm about ready to punch my computer screen when my phone dings with a text message. I pick it up and see that it's from Joey.

Joey: *Is it OK if I go over to Blake's house for lunch?*

Me: *Sure sweetie.*

I smile at my phone, glad that Joey has made a good friend, and I'm about to click the screen off when it lights up with a phone call. From Maddy.

"Hey!" I say in a cheery tone. I always like getting to converse with her, and since nobody's home, I can do it without having to try to be secretive about it.

"What are you doing right now?" Maddy asks.

"Trying and failing miserably to dig up information on Sydney Hutton. Why do you ask?" It feels good to be able to talk to somebody about what's been going on in my life. To not have to hide things from someone. Most things.

"Do you want to meet up for a bite or coffee? I need to get out of the house."

I'm still in my pajamas. I planned on staying in them all day and having what I like to call a "lazy day." It's good to have one every once in a while for my mental health.

"Oh... I..."

"Please?"

I sigh. "I love you, but I really don't feel like getting ready."

"Is your family around? What if I came to you?"

I open my mouth to turn her down without even thinking almost, but then I realize that there is no reason this time for me to say no to her. I'm not expecting my kids home for a couple of hours at the earliest. I don't know where Nora is, but if she shows up, then I will just have Maddy hide and sneak out.

"You know what? Yeah. Why don't you come over?"

"Wait, you're serious?"

Maddy has never been over to my house before.

"Yeah. I have a little bit of time before I'm expecting anyone home. I can text you my address..."

"No need. I know where to go!"

Maddy abruptly hangs up the call, making me giggle.

When she arrives a short while later, I let her inside and give her a tour of the place. She keeps saying, "Wow!" and muttering swear words of amazement underneath her breath in every room I take her to. Then she tells me that it looks like my place has been plucked right out of an HGTV show. She opens cabinets and inspects things deeper than I feel a regular house guest would. When she gets to the closet full of family board games and other miscellaneous storage items, she gasps.

"You still have this?!" She reaches up high on the shelf and plucks out an old board game from our childhood. Goosebumps: Terror in the Graveyard. It had been one of my Christmas gifts one year, and as soon as Maddy spotted it, she made me play it with her over and over.

I chuckle, thinking fondly back to the memory. "I wonder if it even still has all of its pieces."

She brushes a hand over the front of the box. Then with a sigh, she puts it away. "Do you ever wish you could go back?"

"God no."

She looks slightly offended.

"Would you?" I ask.

"I don't know," she says, closing the door. Then we retreat into the kitchen together. "Sort of."

"Why?"

"Things were just... easier? Maybe? I don't think I realized when I was younger how much harder it gets to get older."

If I could go back to before Maddy entered my life, then maybe I would agree with her. Instead, I shrug and get us some Topo Chico waters from my fridge. She holds the glass bottle and stares at it curiously.

"Fancy."

I roll my eyes. "It's just soda water."

"Yeah, but only fancy, rich people drink soda water."

I go to argue some more, but Maddy simply sticks her tongue out at me, so I return the gesture.

"So... have you heard anything from Craig lately?" she asks, completely changing the subject.

"Not since the day he had us come in for questioning."

"I can't believe I ever liked him."

"Well, he was a much nicer dude in high school."

"Then why did you date his brother instead of him?"

"Are you kidding? Parker all but attached himself to my side! It was almost as if I decided to date him because I just couldn't get rid of him."

Maddy snickers. "I remember that."

I think about how she had been dating Dean at the time. And how their relationship lasted a lot longer than I expected it to. It used to make me so angry that Maddy had decided to date Dean when she knew that Nora had such a big crush on him. But Nora had never been Maddy's best friend. She was just Maddy's best friend's little sister. I think the real reason I was so angry was that I wanted Dean, but I couldn't have him.

"How has Warner been doing?" I decide to ask.

"Still hates me these days for reasons I can't figure out. How are your daughters doing?"

"I thought they were fine. But then I learned that Audrey's been skipping Dean's class. None of the other classes, either. Just Dean's."

"That's... strange." Her eyes dart from side to side, her brows lowering as she does so.

"Isn't it? That's exactly how her father reacted when I told him."

"Do you let him handle all the punishing? If Warner's dad was around, I'd let him deal with all of that stuff."

"Huh."

"What?" She sits at the counter. I remain standing on the other side of it.

"Nothing."

"I know that look, Mia. You want to ask me something. Just ask."

"What? No, I don't?"

She raises an eyebrow and challenges me.

My shoulders sag. "Fine. I was just wondering... Did you ever find out who Warner's father was?"

"Oh," she says. "No. I never did."

My heart falls. I was hoping she trusted me enough now to be honest with me about it. I don't know what the harm would be in me knowing that Dean is Warner's father. I won't tell anyone, and I'm not mad at her for it. I'm glad I have Maddy back as a friend and that we're getting the chance to make up for all the lost time, but I think I need to make sure I still keep my guard up around her. I don't know if I can fully trust Maddy.

Then again, maybe she will tell me about Warner's dad, but maybe it will just take a little more time.

I open my mouth to tell her that it's okay that she doesn't know that she's a great mom all on her own, but then the door to the garage suddenly slams shut. I jump, startled, and turn around. Gentry is standing between the archway of the mudroom and kitchen, staring at Maddy and me. He's dripping wet from head to toe, and his mouth is hanging slightly open. I glance out the window.

I hadn't even realized it had started raining.

CHAPTER 45

MADDY

After giving Gentry an awkward hello, one that isn't returned, I excuse myself from Amelia's house and hurry back out to my car. On my way out, I hear Amelia asking Gentry what he was doing home so soon. Gentry replied, "We got rained out," and then he muttered something else that I couldn't hear.

I am able to easily ignore the fact that I feel a little bit like I was some boyfriend Amelia has just been caught cheating on Gentry with because I have other things on my mind. Things that I want addressed right now.

I know I don't have a good excuse as to why I know where Amelia and Dean both live. I'm too stressed out to care much if I freak Dean out by showing up at his house.

I roll up to the curb ten minutes after leaving Amelia's house. I gussy up slightly in my rearview mirror then march up the pathway from the sidewalk to the front door of his surprisingly lovely, medium-sized two-story home. All of this on a teacher's salary?

I ring the doorbell, then I knock twice. Within seconds, Dean is answering the door. He's wearing a simple V-neck and a pair of gym shorts, and he still has Nikes on his feet. He doesn't look like he just finished a workout, though.

"Maddy," he says, looking taken aback. Naturally.

"Did I catch you at a bad time?" I ask. He opens his mouth to reply, but I shove my way inside his house saying, "Don't care." I turn right into what I gather is his living room. He has a cream sectional, cognac leather La-Z-Boy, and a TV that takes up nearly the entire wall. Other than some books, newspapers, and school supplies littered about, his house is surprisingly clean.

Dean closes the front door and steps into the living room after me. "Yeah, sure, come on in."

I turn sharply to him. My expression is fierce. "We need to talk."

"I gathered that much, yeah," Dean says. He motions to the sectional. "Do you want to sit?"

I shake my head. I'm too pent-up to sit still. "Did you tell Amelia Bailey that her daughter has been skipping your class?"

"Uh... how would you—?"

"It doesn't matter. You should know something, Dean."

"O-okay?"

"Audrey knows that you're Warner's father," I blurt out before I can change my mind. "So that's probably why she's been skipping. Clearly, holding in the secret is doing a lot to her."

His face turns stony. "How did she find out?"

I quickly fill him in on the events that transpired that night during the upperclassman trip. And about how I have been trying my best to get her to keep her mouth closed ever since.

"Audrey is a good kid," Dean says. "I'm sure she'll keep this information to herself."

"You expect the daughter of my arch enemy to keep this massive secret about me to herself?" I scoff. "Are you kidding me, Dean?"

"Maddy, I'm sorry," he begins.

"Why did you have to come back here? All you've done is make my life completely miserable every single day!"

"You know why I came back," he snaps. I'll admit, I wasn't expecting him to get defensive. Usually, he grovels about this kind of thing since he was the one that decided he wasn't ready to be in Warner's life from the get-go and all.

"Good for you, Dean, you finally became a real man! Where were you eighteen years ago, huh? You're the reason things are the way that they are. You can't just waltz back to Toxey years and years later and think that you're some sort of matured, responsible hero ready to come to my aid!"

"I know I messed up, Maddy, but I want to be there for our son!"

"No!" I jab a finger in his direction. "It's not even fair of you to call him that!"

"I'm worried about him! Aren't you? With this Sydney situation, he's been falling behind in school. He's not acting like himself during practice. Something's really wrong!"

"He's not your responsibility to worry about!"

"If he's not my responsibility to worry about as a father, he's at least my responsibility to worry about as his former teacher and his football coach!"

I fling one of the books off of his end table with the back of my hand, letting out a ferocious growl. "Ugh! why can't you just leave us alone? Go back to whatever hole you crawled out of, Dean!"

"I know that you're mad. No amount of apologies is ever going to make you not mad at me, and I get that. But Mads, he's not just a teenage boy anymore. He's damaged. In danger. He's in need of help and feels like he has no one to turn to. Don't you see that?"

"Warner barely knew that girl. He didn't do anything to her. He's a normal, hormonal teenage boy. I'm the one who needs him. He's all that I have, Dean. If this secret gets out, I'll... I'll lose him. Forever."

I can't let that happen.

CHAPTER 46

AMELIA

I follow Gentry down the hall to our bedroom. "Where are you going?" I ask.

"Oh, I'm sorry," he calls condescendingly over his shoulder. "Would you like me to stay in my soaking wet clothes while I have this fight with you, Mia?"

"There's nothing to fight about," I try.

He lets out a loud, sarcastic laugh. "Oh, sure. We have no reason to be upset with each other."

I follow him into our master bathroom as he rips off his shirt.

"You know," he continues. "I'm just not sure how much more of this I can take."

I fling my hands in the air exasperatedly. "How much more of what?!"

"This! You! All your lies. All your secrets. When did you get like this?"

"Like what?"

"When did you become the type of wife who has so many secrets?"

What a freaking hypocrite.

"You know what, Gentry?" I ask, my voice turning dark and deep. It's a voice reserved only for moments when I am at my angriest. I don't even recognize myself when I use it. "I'm not the one who's full of them."

"What's that supposed to mean?" he dares.

"I think you know exactly what I mean."

He stands there frozen, his hands hovering at his belt. The fact that I've rendered him unable to move says it all.

CHAPTER 47

LYLA

Jackson has been pouty and moody all day long. It started when I woke up at Sophia's house after Audrey dragged me to have a sleepover with her and the rest of my old friends—which I did *not* want to do, by the way. He had texted me asking me if I slept okay. I had been able to ignore him when the rest of the girls woke up and we went downstairs to a brunch made by Sophia's mom and stepdad. Her parents seemed super happy to see me and preoccupied my time all morning long asking me questions about what I had been up to. I didn't have the heart to tell them I was only here because Audrey forced me to be.

Now, I'm back home lying in bed, staring at the ceiling. I know I have homework I could do. Chores I could work on. It's super nice outside, so I could even lounge out by the pool and try to catch a little bit of a tan. But I have no energy to do anything. I think maybe I'm depressed.

My phone vibrates, and when I look at the screen, Jackson has sent me another message.

Jackson: *Do you want me to bring all your stuff back?*

When I don't reply quickly enough, he calls me.

"What, Jackson?" I say when I answer.

"You didn't text me back," he replies.

"We just broke up yesterday. Can we take a couple of days to... I don't know, let it sink in, or something?"

"I don't wanna take a few days to let it sink in, Lyla. I don't want to be broken up. I want you to forgive me and take me back."

"Jackson—"

"What, Lyla? Can you really sit there and tell me that you're okay with all of this? That after everything we've been through, you're totally fine just not being together anymore?"

"I don't know if I'm okay or not," I admit. "But I still think it needed to happen. Okay? I really can't do this right now."

"Why not?"

"Because I'm... busy."

"Busy? Doing what?"

"That's not your business anymore."

"Lyla!"

I end the call briefly. I can feel myself fuming inside. We broke up. That means he can't still treat me like he has control over me and has a right to know what I'm doing. He needs to figure that out.

When my phone buzzes again, I groan loudly. However, it's not a text from Jackson this time.

Wrigley: *How was the sleepover?*

I smile and send him a reply. We've been texting since I left the party last night—or more so, since I left Wrigley at the pond. I didn't return to the party. I made Audrey, Danielle, Sophia, and Olive meet me at the pond if they wanted me to go back to Sophia's house with them, since it was the only way Audrey would be allowed to spend the night with them. Wrigley had been bummed that I was leaving, but we exchanged a hug goodbye, and when I got in the car, all four of them asked me five hundred questions about what I was doing with Wrigley and if we were together or not. I wanted to tell them they're not my friends anymore and therefore it was none of their business, but I managed to play nice. For my sister's sake.

About an hour later, Dad calls my name from downstairs. I trudge down each step, feeling like I weigh five thousand pounds. All I want to do is be back in bed.

He is standing in front of the door. "You have a visitor."

I stare at Dad, then I stare at the door. Dad shrugs and walks down the hall to his office. When I open the door, Jackson is standing there looking desolate.

"What do you want?" I ask with a sigh.

"I thought you were busy."

"I am," I say.

"Doing what? Are you with somebody?"

I motion down to the leggings and oversize T-shirt I'm wearing. "Does it look like I'm hanging out with someone right now?"

His shoulders rise to under his ears. "I don't know!" he says in a shrill voice.

"Jackson, you're being crazy."

"I don't care."

My phone buzzes in my hand. Wrigley has texted me again. I quickly text him back, not caring if it's rude to text in front of Jackson. It was rude of him to show up at my house unannounced.

Me: *Save me.*

"Who are you texting?"

"No one."

Wrigley: *What do you mean?*

Me: *Jackson showed up at my house. He is not taking the breakup well.*

"Obviously it's someone, Lyla," Jackson snaps.

I glare at him. "It's just Danielle." I almost want to tell him the truth. But I don't need any more drama right now. Just because I'm angry doesn't mean I need to make Jackson angrier, too.

He clenches his jaw and looks away from me for a little bit.

"Can you please go?" I ask.

"I can't believe you're doing this."

"Jackson. I'm sorry."

He says nothing. He just stands there, staring at me. So I shake my head and close the door.

Too lazy to walk back up to my bedroom, I wander into the family room and sink into the sectional. I put on some insanely unrealistic teenage drama on HBO Max and check my phone every few minutes to see why it's taking Wrigley so long to reply to me. I don't know why I told him about Jackson showing up. Did I maybe want to make him a little bit jealous? Did I just want to point out that I am not with Jackson anymore, in case he was wondering?

For some reason, since my talk with Wrigley at the pond, it's been easier to text him. It's almost as if we've started over and I'm texting him as the new Lyla and not the old Lyla. I think it's the only thing that makes it feel a little more okay with the fact that texting him had been the reason I killed my best friend.

One and a half episodes of this ridiculous show later, the doorbell rings. I look around to see if anybody else is going to answer it, but it seems like I'm the only one nearby. Groaning, I get my butt off the couch and go answer the door again.

My heart catches in my throat when I see Wrigley standing on my doorstep. His reddish-brown hair is curly and frizzy and glistening in the sunlight. His smile is bright on his face. He's wearing a gray flannel and black jeans. He looks effortlessly cool. And here I am, in my oversized, stained old T-shirt.

"Oh my God," I can't help but say.

"Hi to you, too," he replies.

"What the heck are you doing here?" A smile begins to form on my face, but more because I'm embarrassed and less because I'm happy to see him. If I had known he was coming over, I would've gotten changed. I would've fixed my hair. Brushed my teeth, at least!

"You told me to save you. So here I am."

I don't even know what to say.

So he continues. "Feel like taking a drive?"

This is really happening. I'm really about to hang out on a Saturday afternoon with Wrigley Hall.

"Let me just go change."

I think, technically, I'm still grounded, but I don't see Mom or Dad around anywhere to tell me I can't go.

I leave Wrigley waiting, dashing up the stairs to get changed, brush my teeth, put on deodorant, and run a comb through my hair. When I meet Wrigley outside, his eyes noticeably check out my outfit: jeans and a black long sleeve mock neck.

He leads the way to his car, some sort of Honda from the mid-2000s. When he opens the passenger door for me, I feel butterflies in my stomach. Jackson never opened the door for me when we went places. Probably because he didn't have a car of his own to do so. But still.

"So, where are we driving to?" I ask as I buckle in. I'm nervous to be in a car with someone I've never driven with before, but I don't tell Wrigley. He doesn't need to know about my nearly crippling car anxiety. I don't want to scare him away.

"I was thinking maybe we could take a drive to Lake Oshwana?"

I tilt my head back. "Uh...oh."

"We don't have to," he tells me. "I was just kind of thinking about how sad you seemed last night. How that horrible, messed-up thing happened at my party. I don't know. I figured maybe going to the place where Sydney... you know, died, would help you possibly get a little bit of... closure?"

It's an incredibly thoughtful gesture of him to make. But I don't know if I can face that lake.

I give him something halfway between a smile and a grimace. "Let's do it," I say, despite myself.

"Yeah? Okay, cool."

I sit back and fidget with my hands on my lap. "So, where is your dad?"

Wrigley's dad is always going out of town.

Wrigley shrugs. "Honestly, at this point, I don't even keep track anymore. Maybe New York. Maybe Chicago?"

"For work?" I ask.

He nods. "Hey, do you like alternative music?"

Happiness warms my insides. "It's my favorite type of music," I gush.

"Ever heard of Backseat Muses?"

I shake my head.

He grins. "All right, check this out." He gets on his phone, which makes me a little nervous because he's in the driver's seat. But thankfully, we're at a stop sign. He does something on it, tapping his thumb across the screen. Then, over his Bluetooth, an upbeat sound starts playing through his car's speakers. Immediately, I can tell I'm going to like this band.

We spend the entire drive to Lake Oshwana listening to his music suggestions. I like them all so much that I begin to write them down in the notes app on my phone. We drive with the windows down, and I stick my head out every so often to feel the breeze through my hair and the sun kissing my cheeks. I'm nervous to go to the lake, but I'm having a good time during the drive. This might be exactly what I needed. Somebody to pull me out of my darkness.

Eventually, we pull into the parking lot near where our campsite had been during the upperclassman trip. I hop out of the car, noticing right away how much woodsier it smells up here. The humidity is thicker, too.

Wrigley walks around his car to stand by my side. "Are you sure you're okay to do this?"

I nod my head. I'm so nervous that I can't bring myself to speak. Wrigley leads the way, not seeming to mind that I am trailing behind a few steps the whole way down the pathway. This is the last place Sydney had ever been. It's so strange to think about.

We take the trail through the trees and then enter a clearing. The dock has none of the kayaks that had been tied up to it during our trip. Instead, families and groups of friends are littered about, enjoying the last warm weekend we're probably going to have for the rest of the year.

It looks different like this. With a family's here. The kayaks gone. No large groups of teenagers being forced to stay together by their chaperones.

My eyes go to the dock, where four young girls are giggling and taking turns jumping off of it together.

I wonder where she drowned. Where it happened. Had she been standing on that dock when a foot slipped in? Had something pulled her in?

Someone?

I don't take a step further.

Wrigley gets a good distance away from me before he realizes I've stopped moving, then he turns around and stretches his arms out wide. "You got this!"

I wonder if Wrigley knows much about loss.

I tuck some hair behind my ear and stare out at the water. How can people go swimming in the lake knowing a dead body had been pulled out of it not long ago? A small, dead body had been rotting just underneath the surface. Those small children's feet could've been grazing Sydney's long blonde hair without them even realizing it.

A shudder ripples through me, and I turn away. This isn't helping like I thought it would.

I can hear Wrigley running back up to me. "Hey hey hey," he says in his soothing voice. He wraps his arms around me and pulls me into a hug. I don't hug him back, but it feels nice to be held. I close my eyes and breathe in the scent of his spring-fresh laundry detergent, slightly covered by some sort of manly cologne.

"I'm sorry," I say. "I think maybe this wasn't such a good idea."

"You have nothing to apologize for," he says. "Want to go back to the car?"

That's exactly what I want to do.

I nod my head. He squeezes me tightly before letting go, then we walk side-by-side back up the trail over to the parking lot.

A police cruiser is pulled up to the curb when the lot comes into view. Leaning against it, his arms crossed and a smirk on his face, is Detective Craig Fritz.

"Hey, Lyla," Fritz says, looking menacing.

My stomach lurches.

"Do you know this guy?" Wrigley asks. He looks immediately repulsed by him.

"Wh-what are you doing here?" I ask the detective. I hate how small my voice sounds. How weak and afraid I seem. I hate that Detective Fritz can sense it, too. He eats it up.

"Do you wanna tell me what *you're* doing here?" he asks.

"I'm just hanging out with my friend," I try, avoiding his gaze.

"Is that a crime?" Wrigley asks.

Fritz ignores him and only addresses me. "You know, it's funny. You might not have realized this, but it's more common than you think."

I stand there and say nothing.

So he continues. "Culprits always seem to return to the scene of the crime."

CHAPTER 48

LYLA

When I wake up the next morning, I quickly realize that I haven't woken up at all and that I'm actually in some sort of dream.

I have to be.

Because I'm not in my bed. I am laying in a pile of fallen leaves, damp from the moisture in the air.

I slowly sit up and look around. I don't recognize this place.

I pinch myself on the forearm. It hurts. And the fact that it hurts, along with the cold chill running down my spine, makes me more alert. I'm not dreaming after all. I'm really here in the middle of the woods with no recollection of how this happened.

I scramble on my butt to quickly get to my feet. My breathing is shallow as I spin about myself, trying to get my bearings. Am I still in the Boldosa Redwoods? Where is Wrigley? Where did he disappear to? What happened with Craig?

I tug at my hair, feeling confused and frightened.

But then, as wakefulness spreads through my body, I begin remembering little things.

I came back from the Boldosa Redwoods yesterday with Wrigley. I had been silent during the car ride for a long portion of it because I was so uncomfortable and freaked out about how Freaky Fritz followed us all the way up to the lake. Wrigley played more of his amazing music and tried cracking jokes and being goofy to cheer me up. It had slightly worked.

So if he had dropped me off at home, how did I end up here?

I trudge through the woods, feeling like I have déjà vu. This reminds me of when I was in the Boldosa Redwoods before. During the upperclassman trip when I had buried Trinity's photo album in the woods so that it could feel like she went on the trip with us.

Wait a second.

I turn about myself, slower this time. These woods look familiar. I've been in them tons of times.

With Trinity.

I turn and start walking in the other direction. I see the tree that we joked around about, saying it looked like an old hag. We also said the bushes around the old hag looked like her millions of cats.

I keep walking.

Soon I recognize the fallen log that Trinity and I had sat on tons of times, talking, gossiping about boys we liked, and giggling with each other.

It hurts my heart to see it, but it also fills me with relief. At least I know where I'm going. I am in the woods behind Trinity Cruz's house.

I begin running slightly. The morning air is chilly and I'm wearing an oversize T-shirt and leggings with no shoes. My feet get pricked every few feet by some sharp twig or rock, but I ignore it.

When I get through the clearing, I am standing behind Trinity's house. I put my hands on my knees to collect myself for a moment because being back here is never a place I thought I'd find myself again. I check the bottom of my foot and pull out a thorn that had gotten lodged in it. I wince as blood bubbles out of the cut and then drips onto an orange leaf on the ground.

I hear the sound of something sliding open. I look up to Trinity's back porch. Her parents, Marty and Hilda Cruz, are emerging with coffee mugs in their hands out onto the back patio. They look the same, but in a way, they also look like they've aged ten years. Marty is incredibly tall and towers over nearly everyone whenever he goes places in public. He always dresses in crisp polos, and he always wears a gold chain around his neck with a cross. Hilda is tall and beautiful, just like Trinity. She looks like a retired model. Even standing there holding her mug of coffee wearing a fluffy robe and her hair a tangled mess, she looks like she could show new runway models a thing or two.

I feel like I'm going to vomit.

I know they've spotted me, but instead of trying to explain myself to them, I take off at a run again.

"Lyla?" I hear Mr. Cruz say.

"Lyla, wait!" Mrs. Cruz calls after me.

But I don't wait. I can't talk to them. Ever since the funeral, I told myself there was no way I would be able to look them in the eyes again. Yet, I just had.

My chest hurts more than my feet. The world around me is starting to go cloudy, and I feel like the breath is being sucked out of me. But still, I run. I feel like I'm dying. But from what I remember learning back when I went to a therapist after Trinity's death, I'm just having another panic attack.

Mom and Dad are right. I do need to go to therapy again.

CHAPTER 49

MADDY

"Another glass of wine?"

Steven and I look up at our waiter. We're inside an Italian bistro having dinner by candlelight at a cute two-person table with a white tablecloth draped over it.

"What do you think, Maddy?" Steven asks me.

I would love another one. I've been having an incredibly rough time lately, and I'm also still feeling nervous about being on a first date with someone as attractive and charming as Steven Hall. Another glass would put me more at ease, but I don't want him to think I'm some sort of lush.

"Oh, I shouldn't," I say instead.

Steven stares me down for a moment. Then he looks at the waiter again. "We will both have one more, thank you."

The waiter begins pouring us more of the delectable Chianti we've been sipping on.

My stomach erupts in butterflies.

How is it that he knows exactly what I'm thinking?

The waiter leaves, and Steven and I stab at our meals with our forks some more. He got the Cordon Bleu. I got spinach and mushroom ravioli. His looked super delicious when it arrived at the table, and I don't know if he saw me eyeing it or what, but he cut a piece of it off and plopped it on my plate, not even asking first if I wanted to try it. I'm pretty sure he is some sort of wizard. Some sort of superhero with the ability to read minds. I wonder if he can tell how amazing of a time I am having with him right now.

"And so, your son, Warner," Steven starts. "I hope you don't mind, but I asked Wrigley a little bit about him."

I raise an eyebrow, intrigued. "Oh really? And what did your son say about him?"

"Well, he said everybody loves him. That he's probably one of the most popular guys in the senior class. That he's nice to everybody, but that he's been acting different lately. Sucking on the football field—his words, not mine. And apparently, he got into a fight with his best friend? I really hope you already knew that and that I'm not throwing your son under the bus right now, though."

My heart constricts painfully in my chest. I stare down at my mushroom ravioli, no longer wanting to take another bite. "No, I heard about that," I say. "He is... going through some stuff lately. I haven't been much help. He doesn't like to talk to me. He's in his 'I hate my mom' stage or something. He's my everything, so it sucks, but I don't really know if there's anything I can do about it."

"Wrigley and I haven't always had the best relationship," Steven tells me. "It's hard for him to not have another parental figure around since I have to work out of town so much. He's a good kid, and he means well, but sometimes I feel like he's a little bit lost and I just don't know how to help him without putting my work aside. But the only reason I'm doing all of this work is so that he can live a comfortable life."

I'm not in any position to give Steven parenting advice. I wish I had money like he seems to have. And Warner has missed out on having a father his entire life. "I'm sure you're trying your best," I say. "Just like I'm trying my best." After all, I love my son. I would do anything for him. And I mean it when I say anything.

"Yeah, you're right."

I give him a little bit of a smile. "So you asked about Warner to your son. Does that mean he knows that you're going on a date with me tonight?"

He grins back at me, looking caught red-handed. "I couldn't help myself. I just wanna know everything about you, Madeline Carpenter."

I should be flattered by the compliment, but instead, I feel funny inside. I don't want him to know everything about me.

"Did I say the wrong thing?" he asks, noticing my expression. "I didn't mean to come on too strong."

I quickly shake my head and smile. "No, you didn't say the wrong thing at all," I try. "I'm just not used to dating such a good guy."

"No?"

"Unfortunately, not. Not for lack of trying, though."

He sips his wine, so I do, too.

"So, Warner's father..."

I nearly cough and choke on my beverage. I knew this question was coming. I just wasn't expecting it right this second.

Please don't judge me for this.

"He's... not in the picture," I say to him. I hope he doesn't ask me to elaborate.

"Fair enough. Another one of those not-good guys, then."

"Exactly."

I grin from ear to ear at him. He gets me in a way that nobody ever has before. And he doesn't seem to be concerned about why Warner's father isn't in the picture. He isn't trying to pry too much. He has a great sense of boundaries and really seems like he understands women. Or at least, me.

The rest of the date goes just as incredibly as the beginning of it. When we finish dinner, we decide to take a slight stroll outside through the downtown portion of Toxey. It's slightly windy tonight and I am in a cocktail dress with no sleeves, so when Steven notices that I'm cold, he is quick to take off his sports coat and drape it over my shoulders. I blush like a little girl with a crush, and I'm never the type of girl that blushes. I always demand to be treated right. But with Steven, I don't even have to try.

He walks me to my car parked on the side of the road outside the restaurant after we do our loop, talking about everything and anything. I opted to meet him here at the restaurant, even though he offered to pick me up from my house. I'm just not ready for him to see how poor I am yet.

"I'm really glad you could make it out tonight," Steven says to me outside my Hyundai. I'm so glad I got it washed yesterday.

"I'm really glad you're finally in town and were able to ask me out," I find myself saying. I don't know why I'm being so honest and straightforward with him. I don't usually let guys know right away how interested I am in them. I usually prefer to have some sort of mystery about me. Play hard to get. But I can't even control myself around Steven.

He chuckles. "For another chance to get to do this again, I'm going to try and be around more often."

"I'll hold you to that."

Standing in front of the driver's side door, I unlock my vehicle with my car keys. Steven steps forward, leaning closer to me. I stand there and wait, my heart skipping a beat as he reaches his arm out. Instead of it falling on my waist or trying to cop a feel, he is holding onto my car's door handle to open it for me. And while he's leaned in to reach for it, he gives me an effortlessly soft kiss on my cheek, lingering his face there for a little while afterward before stepping away with the door open.

No diving in for the kiss? No asking, "Your place or mine?" Is Steven really this much of a gentleman?

"I'll call you," he says to me.

"Oh—okay," I say with jagged breathing. Having him this near to me is making me turn to mush.

Nearly stumbling on my heels, I turn and get into my car. He flashes me his Greek god smile, shoots me a wink, and closes my door for me.

I am on some other planet, over the moon with happiness and giddiness about how wonderful my night had been as I drive home. But the more and more I think about it, the more that smile begins to fade from my face. The more the excited feeling inside me turns into dread.

Steven is wonderful. But that's the thing. He's too wonderful. And I've never had much luck with men. If I let myself get swept away by Steven, and if I fall for all of his charm and romantic acts, then I am setting myself up just to get hurt again. There's no way things with Steven can be going this well. He's too good to be true.

He's only going to hurt me again, just like all the other ones have. Why should I think this time with Steven should be anything different?

I am sick of getting hurt.

I go home, knock on Warner's bedroom door to let him know that I've returned, then I start getting ready for bed, feeling completely miserable. After my hair is brushed, my teeth are brushed, and my skincare routine has been completed, I fall into bed in my silk pajama set and check my phone.

Steven has texted me already. I should find that clingy and too eager, but I don't. I get the butterflies straight away by just seeing his name on the screen.

Steven: I had a great time with you tonight. And I'm not just saying that. It was so great that I couldn't even wait until tomorrow or whatever day I'm supposed to follow up according to the dating rules to tell you so. I really like you, Maddy.

And I really like him, too. But I don't want to like him.

So I don't reply.

CHAPTER 50

AUDREY

It's a rare occasion for me to be home alone at 8:30 on a Sunday night. Mom and Dad went on a date—which is surprising to me because they've been fighting so much lately—and Aunt Nora took Joey and Lyla to go see that new blockbuster film everybody's talking about. I already saw it with my friends a couple of days ago, so I opted to stay home. Besides, I figured Aunt Nora would probably prefer it that way anyway—she's not the biggest fan of me.

I hang out in my room, laying on my bed and holding my phone up in the air over my head as I reply to Ryan's texts. We've been talking back-and-forth all night, and I'm pretty sure this is the longest we've gone without not replying to each other. I am super excited to be talking to Ryan and that he's showing signs of interest in me. His texts have been somewhat flirty with the numerous compliments he's given me, but he hasn't asked me out on a date yet, so I'm waiting patiently for that to happen.

Somehow, I find myself on Instagram in between our text conversations, and I'm scrolling through Warner Carpenter's photo feed. He doesn't post on social media much. There are only a handful of photos, and I've seen them all plenty of times before. So why do I keep coming back to his page and creeping on him? Why do I smile big when I tap on the photo of him and his football buddies in one of their massive huddles, covered in sweat, shouting and smiling about their game win?

I go to zoom in on his face. He's smiling so happily in the photo that I want to get a closer look at it.

A heart appears under my thumb.

Oh crap.

I accidentally just liked the photo! And it's from weeks ago!

Internally, I panic. Should I unlike it, or do I just leave it? Do I want him to know that I've been creeping on his profile? If I unlike it, will he have seen that I liked it anyway, and will the fact that I unliked it just make me look more guilty?

"Kill me," I groan, dropping my phone onto my bed and covering my face with my hands. I decide to leave the heart.

The sound of something falling and shattering on the ground makes me bolt upright in my bed, my breath hitching.

What was that?

I sit there and wait for any more sounds, but all is quiet. Nervously, I get out of bed and walk out into the loft above the staircase. Peering down the steps, I see shards of ceramic glass splayed across the hardwood flooring by the front door. I tiptoe down the stairs. The vase sitting on the decorative hutch has been knocked off. I stand on the last step of the staircase, afraid to touch down on the ground in case I get a shard of it in my foot. A cool breeze brushes across the right side of my body, and I turn my head and see that the front door is wide open.

Terror ripples through me in an instant. Somebody is here.

"Mom?" I call out. Maybe she knocked it over and is somewhere in the kitchen finding the broom and dustpan to clean it up.

You know that's not what happened, Audrey. Come on.

By calling for Mom, I've just given away my location.

I turn to dash back up the stairs and hide in my bedroom. My phone is still up there on my bed. I'll call Mom and Dad to let them know what's happening and to see if maybe I should call the police.

A scream builds up in my throat when after I turn, I see a figure looming over me at the top of the staircase. They are dressed in all black. They have a plastic, shiny cartoon mask over their face. In their hands is a long, sharp butcher knife.

He's back.

I jump over the broken pieces of the vase, letting the scream out as loud as I can so that hopefully the neighbors or somebody will hear me and call for help or come to rescue me. I hear the sound of the person's loud boots thundering down the staircase after me as I run down the hallway past the office and into the kitchen. I hear more things breaking as the person clambers after me. They're knocking picture frames off the wall and more decorative vases off of the side tables my mom has artfully placed throughout the house.

"Leave me alone!" I shout, slinging one of the dining table chairs down on the ground to hopefully block his path and buy me some time. "Somebody help me!"

I make it back around the kitchen counter and towards the front door. I'm just about to make it over the threshold when suddenly, the masked intruder has a gloved hand on my wrist and is tugging me backward.

"Let go of me!" I screech, tugging away with all my might, but he's pulling me back, through the shards of glass. To avoid stepping on them, I fall on my butt, and the masked man nearly tumbles down with me, but he regains his composure and grabs onto my ankles instead and drags me further away from the front door.

"Please!" I shout.

Wordlessly, the man keeps dragging me backward. I pick up a shard of the ceramic vase as I slide through the pile of it, then I bring the sharp piece down on the man's gloved hand, but it doesn't pierce through.

"No!" I cry.

He lets go of one of my ankles to grab the knife that he has set on the floor. With my foot temporarily freed, I kick him in the face. He falls back, his hands flying over his mask to keep it on his face. I get to my feet and take off again, darting down the hallway toward my parents' bedroom.

I'm about to dive into the room and close and lock the door behind me, but then I realize that I'll be trapped in there with no escape. Nowhere else to hide if he's able to get into the room. I pivot on my heel at the last second, gripping the corner of the drywall, and see that the man is already back on his feet and stalking towards me with the knife again. In my haste to dash through the archway into the family room instead of down to my parents' bedroom, I twist my ankle and fall. The last thing I see is the man coming towards me before my head slams into the wood floor and everything goes black.

CHAPTER 51

Amelia

G entry and I did go to dinner, but it isn't a date. That's what we told the kids, however. In reality, we just need to have a lengthy, important conversation with each other that we don't want to chance the kids listening in on.

We drive in silence all the way back home afterward. When Gentry finally speaks, his voice seems extra loud because of how quiet in the car we've been for such a long period of time.

"Why is the front door open?" he asks.

I snap my head towards the front of the house as a Gentry nears the driveway to our garage.

"What?" I ask.

But then I see it. Our front door is wide open.

"Oh... maybe one of the kids—"

The rest of the sentence dies in my throat. Through the doorway, right inside the house, I see broken glass everywhere. I quickly grab Gentry's forearm.

"I think somebody broke in, Gentry!" I gasp, my heart quickly picking up speed.

Gentry pulls into the driveway, eyeing me with wide eyes. "Audrey!" he cries. Panicking, Gentry throws the car in park and we both jump out, running across the lawn over to the front door. I'm thinking the worst, even though I know I shouldn't. I'm supposed to stay calm in these situations. Everything is probably fine, right?

If everything was fine, Audrey would've called me.

We step over the glass in the foyer. I peer down the hall towards the kitchen and see picture frames knocked to the ground, shattered. Gentry dashes into the kitchen and I follow behind. I want to call out for Audrey, but I can't find any words in my throat.

"Audrey!" Gentry yells for me. Kitchen chairs are knocked over. There are no signs of Audrey, and she isn't replying to Gentry calling out to her.

I run into the living room; I don't see any signs of her in there, either. I turn back to go up the stairs as Gentry heads down the hallway towards our bedroom. I get one step up when Gentry's loud cry sends my heart nearly flying out of my butt.

"No!" he bellows. I step back down the stairs and run towards Gentry's voice. "Audrey!"

I turned the corner and see Gentry down on the ground, his back to me. In his arms, I can see long flowing blonde hair.

It's streaked with crimson red.

"Oh my God," I breathe.

"Come on, baby, wake up!" Gentry cries. I run to get to them, but it feels like the hallway has suddenly morphed into one of those never-ending fun houses. How could this have happened? Is Audrey dead?

For a moment, my mind is transported back to the night I drove past Lyla's car accident. The way I saw how it was completely crushed and destroyed, and that feeling that coursed through my veins as I wondered if there was any possible way she could've survived that.

This is a lot like that.

Finally, I reach Gentry and Audrey. Gentry is crying, his tears falling onto Audrey's cheeks. There's a small puddle of blood, but I ignore it as I sink down to my knees in front of them and stroke Audrey's face. She can't be dead.

"Call 911," Gentry demands.

I don't move right away. I can't stop looking at Audrey. I need to see a sign that she's still alive.

"Mia!" he snaps.

I pull away from her and fumble for my phone in my back pocket. As I call 911 and explain to the operator what has happened, I constantly look back at Audrey. I have already thought one of my children died before. I never thought I would have to feel this way again.

I can feel my body failing me. Giving up as I try to talk to the operator. I'm on the brink of fainting, but I have to keep it together. I have to know that Audrey's going to make it out of this alive.

CHAPTER 52

Audrey

When I wake up again after having a little nap, I'm alone in my hospital room with Lyla. She's sitting in a chair that she's pulled all the way up next to the bed, and I don't think I've ever seen her looking so pale. So unlike me.

"What time is it?" I ask, my voice groggy. "Why are you still here?"

Lyla's eyes snap to me, then they widen when she sees that I'm awake.

"Hey, how are you feeling?" she asks immediately, ignoring everything I've just asked her.

"I'm okay, Lyla," I say. "Really." It doesn't matter if I'm lying or not. It doesn't matter that my head is pounding and that the only reason my nap didn't last any longer is that I kept dreaming about the masked man. Lyla looks like she's on the verge of breaking, and I can't have that. I can't be the incident that sends her over the edge into a deep, dark depression that she can never crawl back out of. She's been through enough.

"I can't even believe you're alive," Lyla tells me, shaking her head repeatedly.

Me too.

"Of course I am," I say, even giving her a weak smile. But the truth is, I have no idea what happened to the masked man after I slipped on the tile wood floor and cracked my head open. When I came to again, I was in my dad's arms. He and Mom cried as they held me until the paramedics showed up and loaded me onto a stretcher. I went in and out of consciousness, but when I woke up a little while later, I had stitches on the back of my head. They had to shave the tiniest part of my hair in order to do it, but Mom told me she made sure they took as little off as possible so that it could still be hidden as long as I kept my hair down. I'm grateful for that.

Lyla leans forward and rests her chin on my hand, looking up at me with puppy dog eyes. "I should've stayed home. I should've been there."

"Don't do that, Ly," I scold. "Seriously. You can't blame yourself. You can't."

"Who was it?" she asks, knowing I don't know the answer.

I desperately wish I did.

The next morning, after I've gotten a little bit more sleep and woken up again, Lyla is still in the same chair, looking like she wants to fall asleep but isn't letting herself. Not only is she in the room, but Mom, Dad, Joey, and even Aunt Nora are here as well.

A nurse comes and checks on me, then Mom demands I get served something to eat and drink.

After I've nibbled on some oatmeal and a banana, Mom smiles at me as she begins asking questions. "Are you sure you're okay?" she starts.

I nod my aching head.

"Do you... do you have any idea who could've done this?"

Gentry and Joey are curled up together in a reclining chair in the corner, and Nora is standing by the window, biting on her thumbnail.

"I don't know," I say.

Mom looks as if she had been expecting that answer. "Well, the police have been to the house, and they're trying to find whoever did this, but I'm not sure how helpful they're going to be."

With someone like Craig Fritz working in the police department, I doubt they'll be helpful at all.

My family stays with me for another hour or so, all of them either trying to cheer me up, giving me pitiful smiles, or asking me if I need anything. Aunt Nora tries to tease me and tell me that I should've just seen the movie with them last night, but then Mom shoots her a look and she quickly apologizes for the stupid joke.

Eventually, Mom turns to Joey. "You need to get to school."

"I'll take him," Nora steps in.

"Are you sure?" Mom asks.

Joey slides out of the chair, not taking his eyes off of me. "I want to stay here with Audrey."

Mom brushes his hair back. "I know you do, sweetie, but Audrey's going to be okay. She'll be back home before school even gets out for the day."

Dad, still looking exhausted, nods his head at Aunt Nora. "Thank you," he says.

Joey walks to my bedside and looks at me nervously. "Am I allowed to hug you?"

I chuckle a little bit, even though it makes my head throb. "Of course. Get over here."

He smiles sheepishly and gives me a hug, then he and Aunt Nora leave.

"So..." I trail off as I look at my remaining family members. "Has anyone been in to visit me besides just you losers?"

"Uh... no," Mom says. "But I'm not sure that anyone knows what happened yet."

My heart falls slightly.

I don't know why some part of me had sort of been expecting it to be like in the movies or TV shows when a victim is brutally attacked and they are bombarded with their friends and crushes visiting and dropping off flowers, teddy bears, and get well soon cards. I don't have any gifts at all.

"I should probably go to school," Lyla says out of nowhere, slowly getting out of the chair. She looks dead on her feet.

I look at Mom, then back at her. "You don't have to go to school," I say. Thankfully, Mom and Dad nod their heads with me in agreement.

Lyla shrugs. "There's something I need to do there."

"But..." I trail off. Lyla gives my hand a squeeze, then she hugs Mom and Dad before she leaves the room.

Dad gets out of his chair and goes and stands next to Mom at the foot of my bed. "I think your mom and I should try to hunt someone down and see about getting you out of here, don't you think?"

I kind of wish I could just stay here in the hospital forever where it's safe and I'm being monitored at all times. But instead of telling them this, I nod my head. When they leave the room and I'm alone, I turn on the news. I get the feeling that in a small town like this, an event like last night won't go unnoticed. And sure enough, there on one of the new stations is my sad, broken-into house. The pretty anchorwoman is standing out on the sidewalk, giving out very little information about what happened to me last night because none of them have the details yet.

Has anyone at school even seen this? Is anyone even talking about it? I wish I could check my phone, but I don't have it. It's back at the house still.

The more I sit there in my bed with nothing else to do but watch the news, the quicker I realize that I don't like being alone here. And I can't believe I'm alone, too. Where are my friends? If I were in their shoes, I would've ditched school in a heartbeat to come and check on them.

My eyes begin welling up with tears because I feel slightly hurt, and because I haven't had time alone until now to think about everything that had happened to me last night.

Before I can let a sob escape me, a shadow appears in the doorway, and in walks Warner.

CHAPTER 53

WARNER

I only found out about what happened to Audrey when I got in my jeep to head to school. I was scrolling through all of my notifications on my phone before I put the car in drive, and a notification from the Toxey news app caught my eye. Then, instead of going to school, I went straight to the hospital, where the news article said Audrey was currently being treated for injuries.

She's alone when I get to her room.

"Hey, you," I say timidly as I linger in the doorway. She looks sad, but when she notices me, she perks up in her bed.

"Warner?" she asks. "What are you doing here?"

"I came as soon as I heard," I tell her. I hadn't even given it a second thought. It felt like the right thing to do. She had been attacked by somebody and it was probably the same person who was messing around with all of us. We have to be there for each other.

I step further into the room.

"Don't you have school?" she asks.

I shrug. "This is more important."

"I probably look like death."

I laugh. Of course, Audrey would be concerned about what she looks like right now. "Don't worry, you're still beautiful."

"Are you saying I do look like death, then?"

I open my mouth to reassure her that she doesn't, but then she cracks a smile. I take a seat in the chair pulled up to her bed. "Are you okay, though?" I ask. "For real?"

"I don't know. My head hurts—obviously. But as far as everything else... I think maybe I would feel a little bit better if I knew who had done this."

"Yeah, understandable. I wish we could figure it out." I can't help but feel like the time Audrey, Lyla, and I spent not talking to each other had somehow possibly caused this to happen. It was time wasted that we could've spent trying to figure out who was behind all of this and stopping them.

"It feels so unfair."

I nudge her hand gently with mine. "Hey, once you're better, you, Lyla, and I are going to put our heads together and get to the bottom of this. I promise. Whoever that psycho is, he's not going to hurt you again."

She gives me a kind smile, but I can tell she doesn't believe me.

A thought occurs to me.

"Hey. What was it you wanted to tell me that night? When you called and texted me and asked me to meet you?"

"Oh," Audrey replies. "That was the same night I was attacked by the masked man before. It was just to tell you about that."

She looks away from me, down at her hospital sock-covered feet. They're fuzzy and pink. When she looks at me, it's my turn to give her a smile. But this time, I'm the one who doesn't quite believe her.

When I get to school late, I take my time walking to my locker. I figure there's no hurry since I'm already missing most of my first-period class.

I put in the combo in my lock and open my locker door. The first thing I see is a white envelope. The front of it has the words, "*Don't open in front of prying eyes*" in blue pen ink and nothing else.

I look around me to see if maybe whoever slid it into my locker is still lingering around somewhere, watching me. I have a feeling that whatever is inside of this envelope, it's not going to be anything good. Another threat. More blackmail. Something from the person who's been messing with us. I could open it now, but I don't want to go the rest of my school day scared about the contents of it. So I wait.

CHAPTER 54

AMELIA

When Audrey promises me that she's going to be okay with just her dad in the hospital for a little while until she is finally ready to be discharged, I give her a tight squeeze and then make my way to a light fixture store for a client. I know that Gentry is going to stay with Audrey, but I still feel horrible about leaving her. I just didn't feel like being in the same room as him. I didn't want to deal with the awkward silence or chance another snippy conversation starting up.

As I drive in my Range Rover, a ringing sound plays through my car speaker and the screen on my dash notifies me that my mother is calling.

I press the button on my steering wheel to answer it through the Bluetooth system. "Hello?" I ask suspiciously. Susan Flynn does not call me often.

"Is Audrey alright?"

Of course, she would want to call to check in on her granddaughter. I let out a slow breath. "She's fine, Mom."

"I can't believe that happened to her. Poor thing," she says. I can practically see her sitting at her kitchen table, her forehead creased with worry as she stares at a baby photo of Audrey.

"She's a tough girl," I say. "She'll get through it."

"I don't doubt that. I am also calling for another reason."

"Yes?" I ask. My heart skips a beat.

"I just heard that Nora's been staying at your house."

"I wasn't trying to keep it a secret or anything..." I trail off.

"Sure you weren't."

"What's the problem, exactly?"

"I just—do you think it's wise to let her be there?"

"Wise?" I ask. "What are you talking about?"

"Well, has she been... I mean—how has it been? How is she doing?"

"She's been spending time with the girls and Joey, so that's nice. Other than that, she honestly keeps to herself." I think about telling Mom how Nora has overstayed her welcome, but for some reason, I get the feeling she will lecture me if I do, so I say the opposite. "It hasn't been a big deal at all to let her stay."

"Hmm."

"What?"

"Nothing. I'm glad Audrey is okay. Get your security system updated ASAP, and give everyone a kiss for me."

When we end the phone call, I sit in my car in the parking lot of the lighting store, my hand still gripping the steering wheel. I have no idea why Mom called me about Nora, and why she acted so strange. Does Mom know something I don't? Has Nora been talking to her? And if so, what is it that my sister has been telling her?

CHAPTER 55

AUDREY

I don't pay attention to anything the nurses give me or say to me. I never understand all of that medical mumbo-jumbo. All I know is that once I am administered something, I get sleepy and take another nap.

I wake with a start after having another nightmare of the masked man chasing me through my house. My eyes dart quickly to the reclining chair, expecting to see my dad sitting in it.

Someone is definitely sitting in it.

But it's no longer my dad.

Detective Craig Fritz is there in uniform, his ankle crossed over his thigh and his elbow resting on the armrest.

"You're awake," he comments.

It feels like the room has turned into an icy tundra. I shiver as I stare at him.

"That's good," he continues. "I've been meaning to ask you a couple of questions about what happened."

"Where's my dad?" I ask, looking over at the door. Maybe if a nurse walks by, I can summon her in here and she will make Fritz leave me alone.

"I won't be long, Audrey. It's just a couple of questions. After all, we want to find out who did this to you."

What if you are the one doing it to me?

I swallow and stare at him, trying to determine if he looks to be about the right size of the man who had chased me through my house last night. When he's sitting down like this, I can't tell.

I still feel groggy from the medicine. On the back of my head, my wound is throbbing slightly.

"Before I begin," Craig says, leaning forward in his chair. "I was wondering if you could tell me where exactly Lyla went that night that she snuck out of your tent during the upperclassman trip."

"I don't know," I snap. Then I realize my mistake. "I mean—she didn't leave the tent."

Craig gets to his feet, grinning at me. He points his pen in my direction before biting the cap off of it was his mouth and jotting down something on his small notepad.

"She didn't leave the tent," I say again. But the damage has already been done.

"It's funny," he tells me. "I have suddenly completely forgotten what it was I wanted to ask you about last night. It's probably for the best, though. You do need your rest and all of that."

He leaves, and I sit there, stunned. Guilt creeps in and I feel my face heat up. What have I just done?

I look around for the nurse button on my bed so that I can ask someone where my dad went. I see that my phone is sitting on the tray attached to the bed. Somebody must have gone home and gotten it for me.

I practically lunge for it, desperate to text Lyla and Warner to let them know what just happened. But then I check my notifications. Warmth fills me when I see that I have a ton of them. Text messages, Instagram messages, and Snapchats from people. So many of my peers were checking in on me and asking if I'm okay. Sophia texted me to let me know that she and the girls tried to visit but that my parents weren't allowing visitors. I'm irritated that my parents didn't bother to tell me this, but at least now I know why nobody has visited. Except for when Warner snuck in earlier.

Ryan's text to me—after I never replied to him last night, and he found out the reason why—is especially nice.

Ryan: *I heard what happened. I am so sorry, Audrey. I came to the hospital as soon as I could, but I got stopped by your parents. They told me they don't want any visitors because they don't know who attacked you and they don't want to take any chances. I'm just really glad that you're OK. Let me know when you get out of the hospital and if you get your parents' approval, since they've met me now, so I can bring you all your favorite things to cheer you up.*

CHAPTER 56

WARNER

I am holding the envelope in my hand when I walk inside my house after school. I am just about to open it when I realize that Mom is home. Not wanting her to pry, I toss it on the counter casually and pretend like I haven't noticed her as I get a drink and a snack out of the kitchen.

"How was school?" Mom asks, getting off of the couch and walking towards the kitchen over to me.

"Audrey Bailey was attacked by somebody in her home last night, did you know that?" I ask, just so I can gauge her reaction.

She stops walking for a second. "I—I didn't know that," she says in a slow voice. "Is she okay?"

"She's going to be fine. It's scary, though. They don't have any idea who did it."

"That's... that's horrible," she says. "I hope they can catch him."

"You don't actually feel bad, do you?"

"What are you talking about?"

"You don't even like the Bailey twins. The whole Bailey family."

"I—just because I don't care for them doesn't mean I don't feel bad that something tragic happened to Audrey. Do you seriously think I'm that heartless, Warner?"

I shrug and say nothing.

"Do you think maybe it was a friend of Sydney's?" she asks.

"Excuse me?"

"The person that attacked Audrey. Maybe something happened between Sydney and Audrey that night during the trip, and maybe a friend of Sydney's was trying to retaliate, or something."

I shake my head and step away from the counter, ready to head to my room so I don't have to keep having this conversation.

But then she asks me something that makes me pause.

"Are you seeing Audrey?"

"What?"

"Maybe Sydney was seeing someone, too. Maybe they were thinking that you did something to Sydney—for whatever reason—so they were trying to get back at you by attacking her. Is that possible?"

The granola bar I've just taken a huge bite out of feels dry in my mouth. I don't want to swallow it but I can't spit it out, either.

I can't believe her right now.

I force the bite down my throat as my blood boils. "Are you insane?" I snap. "How many times do we have to have this fight, Mom?"

"I know that you're keeping something from me, Warner, and we're going to keep having us fight until you tell me the truth!"

I round the corner of the kitchen and get in her face. Suddenly, I'm screaming. "I DIDN'T DO ANYTHING TO HER!"

Mom flinches and steps away from me involuntarily. I can tell that I've scared her. But right now, I'm too angry to care. I throw the rest of the granola bar on the ground and walk back out of the house.

CHAPTER 57

MADDY

With shaking hands, I walk over to the counter and pick up the envelope Warner had placed down.

Don't open in front of prying eyes.

The envelope is still sealed. Warner hasn't read it yet.

Now, on top of being scared about the way Warner had just yelled at me, I'm also terrified about what the contents inside of this mysterious envelope might be. I know I shouldn't read it. I know it's a huge invasion of privacy. But my worries get the best of me, and I find myself tearing it open. I pull out a lined piece of paper inside it and read the letter:

Warner,

You deserve to know the truth. It might be really hard for you to hear, and you might be really confused and angry at first. You might not even believe me. But I promise you that I'm telling the truth.

Your mother has kept your father's identity a secret from you her entire life. She's told you she has no idea who he is, but that's not the case. She's always known. Your father is Dean Reeves. There's no reason for me to know this, but I couldn't keep the secret to myself any longer.

Sincerely,

A concerned friend

If I hadn't distracted Warner, gotten him angry enough to storm out of the house like that, he would've opened this. He would've opened it and found out about the one thing I never want him to find out. My worst fears would have come true.

I burst into tears and set the note on the counter. It's just not fair. I know it's wrong of me to make Audrey keep this huge secret to herself, but she has no right telling Warner the truth. She has no idea why I made the choice that I did and what I went through when I was only a little bit older than she. Dean doesn't deserve to be a part of Warner's life. Getting to be his teacher and coach is already more than I can stand. He has no right showing up now after so many years of abandonment.

I love Warner and I only want to protect him. If Dean didn't want him all those years ago, then I highly doubt he's going to want to stay involved in Warner's life for the rest of his existence. All I want is the best for my son.

Audrey has broken our deal. And I told her if she did, she would pay.

I know that Amelia and I just recently started being friends again. I know I shouldn't do anything to jeopardize that because I've missed having her in my life and I've missed having a best friend to talk to.

But Audrey has to pay.

CHAPTER 58

AMELIA

Because of last night, I am more anxious than ever to figure out who Sydney Hutton was and why she came to Toxey in the first place.

It's well past any normal person's bedtime, but I'm in Gentry's home office, sitting at his computer, trying to look up more information. I managed to somehow come across pictures of Sydney from the upperclassmen camping trip. I read news articles about how she had been staying with a foster family. How the foster family was devastated to learn about what happened to her, but they hadn't had her very long before that fateful night occurred. It seems like before that, Sydney Hutton just ceases to exist.

Outside the door to the home office, I hear our front door open and close. Suspicious, my stomach dropping, I jump up from the desk. What if that masked person Audrey told me about is back for more? Back to finish what he started? I don't know if that man had the intention to kill Audrey or not, but I didn't want to take the chance of finding out.

I grab a baseball bat from behind the office door before I leave the room, and I hold it steady as I creep down the hallway, checking my whereabouts. When I reach the foyer, I don't see any signs of a disturbance. I creep up the staircase and go immediately to Audrey's room. The door is cracked open, and when I peek my head in, I see that she is sound asleep. Relief fills me, but I still feel nervous. I check Joey's room next at the end of the hall. He, too, is asleep. I go to Lyla's room. The door is closed. I'm extra careful to be quiet when I open it. But inside, Lyla's bed is empty.

Confused, I go out front to check if she's out there. I walk out to the sidewalk in my slippers and peer down both ends of the street. I spot Lyla in one of her all-black outfits as she crosses underneath a streetlight. She's walking casually with her head down, and she's alone.

Where is she going?

I go to call out to her, but then my yell dies in my throat. My thoughts are still lingering on Sydney Hutton. What if where Lyla is going has something to do with what happened to her that night?

Against my better judgment and all my beliefs as a parent, I decide to follow her.

After about twenty minutes of sneakily trailing behind my daughter and getting my white slippers dirty to the point where I'm going to have to toss them after this, I watch Lyla arrive at the cemetery. She easily slips in through the bars of the closed gate. I wait until she's a safe enough distance away, then I do the same. Thankfully, I slip through the bars almost as easily.

Why would Lyla be coming to the cemetery in the dead of night? Is she meeting somebody?

Oh God, what if Lyla has gotten into drugs and this is where she meets her dealer?

I jump behind a tree when Lyla looks over her shoulder. I wait a few seconds, then I carefully peek around and watch as she stops at a headstone. She stares at it for a long while, then she sinks to her knees, and a loud wailing sob pierces the silent night air.

The sound of it nearly breaks my heart into a million pieces. A lump forms in my throat instantly.

How long has my daughter been coming here and doing this? I thought she was getting over what happened to Trinity. I thought she was moving on. I didn't have any idea she still had this much sadness inside of her about the loss of her friend.

I decide that I don't care if she hates me forever. I emerge from behind the tree and run over to her. I sink down in the grass beside her. She jumps at first, but when she sees that it's me, instead of saying anything, she continues to sob. I wrap my arms around her, feeling almost sad that she's letting me hold her instead of pushing me away. She continues to sob while I squeeze her close to me and kiss her hair. I can't offer any comforting words because the lump in my throat is so large that if I speak, sobs will start escaping me, too.

"I thought Audrey was dead," Lyla says between her gasps for air. "I was so scared, Mom. I was so, so scared."

At this, the dam inside me bursts open, and I start to cry with her.

CHAPTER 59

AUDREY

It's not until late at night when I finally get discharged from the hospital. Then, Dad drives me home, asking me repeatedly if everything's okay and if I'm sure I'm feeling all right enough to leave the hospital. What he doesn't know is that physically, I am okay. I'm just being deathly quiet because of my incident with Detective Craig Fritz and the fact that I accidentally let slip to him that Lyla had left her tent during the upperclassman trip. I'm trying not to beat myself up too much about it because I know Craig purposely waited for an opportunity like one where I was coming off of a heavy amount of medication before he tried to question me about it.

When we get home, I'm greeted by my entire family, all of them giving me big hugs like I've been gone for months. Everything has been picked up that was damaged when the intruder had come after me yesterday. Even the broken picture frames are somewhere out of sight. My guess is that Mom doesn't want me to see anything that would trigger the fresh memory of the horrible thing that happened here. Too bad it's all I can think about.

Well, nearly all I can think about.

When Lyla hugs me tightly, I almost want to push her away. I almost want to tell her I don't deserve her love. I want to tell her that I'm stupid and I messed up, but it's not exactly something I can say to her right in front of everybody.

As the night goes on, I get sick of everyone's attention and go to bed early.

The next day at school, I still can't find it in myself to tell Lyla what happened. I know I need to do it soon, before Craig Fritz gets to her first. I just need a little bit more time.

Everyone is incredibly sweet all morning long. My friends give me a group hug that lasts forever next to Sophia's locker. Several people ask me for details about what happened, but I tell all of them that I don't want to talk about it. That I'm not ready. Still, it does feel nice to have it out in the open. Before, I felt like I needed to keep the masked man and what he did to me a secret.

Sophia has been so nice to me all day, so when we separate briefly in the cafeteria so that I can go sit at the table with Danielle and Olive while she gets in line for our food, and then she storms over to the table after, the angry look in her eyes is unsettling and alarming to me.

"Are you kidding me?" she asks, flinging her tray down on the table with such force that a few pieces of lettuce from her salad fly out of it.

"What's going on?" I ask quickly. At first, I think she's mad at something that happened to her and not at me.

"You've been hanging out with Bryson?"

I look over my shoulder to make sure she's not talking to somebody behind me—because that's definitely not true. I have never hung out with Bryson before in my life.

"Wait, what?" I ask.

"Don't play dumb!" she screeches. Heads are beginning to turn to look at us. "I have messages on my phone about it, Audrey!"

I slowly get to my feet, feeling like I need to be at the same eye level as her for this conversation. I have to back her off of her ledge. "Sophia, I promise you—"

"Stop lying! That's all you ever do anymore! You and your sister are nothing but attention-starved wannabes! I can't believe you would do this to me, Audrey!"

"I didn't!" I plead, my voice rising in pitch.

She rolls her eyes and scoffs dramatically. "Please. Cut the innocent act. Do you know what I think? I think you deserve what happened to you yesterday. If it even really happened. For all we know, you probably staged the whole thing just to get more attention. We all know how sick you are of Lyla hogging it all."

I look across the cafeteria at my sister, who is sitting alone at a table by the window. Her eyebrows are furrowed as she watches the show.

"Sophia, come on," I try. It seems like everyone in the cafeteria has stopped to watch us now.

Before I can further explain myself to Sophia, she reaches over the table quickly. At first, I think she's about to hit me, but then she grabs the drink off her tray and throws the contents inside of it right at my chest.

The cafeteria collectively gasps. When I peer around at everyone, I can see a majority of them videotaping us on their phones.

Sophia storms away while Olive and Danielle remain seated at the table, looking like they have no idea what just happened.

But I know what happened.

The same person who hurt me that night is doing this to me now. I'm beginning to think I'm never going to escape him.

CHAPTER 60

Audrey

When I wake up from my nightmare-filled slumber the next morning, the first thing I do is check my phone. Maybe I will find that Sophia has texted me to tell me she was just kidding and that she knows I would never try to steal her crush from her.

I don't have a single message from her.

Instead, what I do have, are hateful messages from my fellow classmates who are on Sophia's side. And of course they took her side—Sophia is the queen of the school. Therefore, she is always right.

At least some people are being nice about it.

I also have messages from my classmates telling me that what Sophia did to me in the cafeteria was messed up. That they know I wouldn't do something so heartless and that Sophia was way out of line.

Taking a deep breath and willing myself not to cry, I go through everyone's stories on Snapchat. I have to witness about fifteen different videos of myself getting soda dumped on me from all different angles, but then I also see on someone's story, a clip of the news. An anchorwoman is standing outside my house again, and the stuff she's saying is almost too ridiculous to believe.

"Sources tell me that Audrey Bailey and her closest friend got into an argument at their school yesterday over Audrey Bailey allegedly hanging out with her best friend's boyfriend. Could it be that her attacker had been her best friend, wanting to get her revenge on Audrey for what she did to her? As you can see for yourself,"—the camera pans over to my car in the driveway— "her friend is clearly very upset about the situation."

My jaw drops open and I fly out of bed. I run out the front door barefoot and over to my car. Back in the house, I can hear my family calling after me.

The reporters are gone now. They have already gotten their story.

But my beautiful baby blue Mini Cooper has been messed with. In sloppy red paint all across the side of it, it reads, Boyfriend Stealer.

I burst into tears right there on the driveway. I can't believe Sophia would go to these lengths over some text message she got that's not even true. How much worse is this going to get before it gets better? How am I ever supposed to get her to believe me? All year long so far, I've been struggling to keep our friendship afloat enough as it is. Now, I have little faith that I'm even going to go to school today with any friends at all.

"Audrey!" Lyla's voice cries behind me as she runs over. I turn and she throws her arms around me, and I cry into her hoodie. "I didn't do anything!" I say in a muffled voice.

"I believe you. But Sophia is not the friend you thought she was if she isn't going to take your side on it."

Thankfully, Mom lets me take Lyla's White Toyota 4Runner instead of my poor, humiliating car. When I get to school, Lyla asks me if I want to hang out with her on the front steps instead of going into the building and seeing everybody. But I tell her that I will find her later, then I storm into the school. I'm not going inside to see Sophia, Danielle, or Olive.

I'm going to find Bryson Anthony.

I find him upstairs, hanging out in the hallway by the trophy case with some of his friends.

"Hey!" I shout to him when I get up the steps. His friends make low, "Oooh," noises when they see what's happening, and Bryson's face falls when he notices me. I march over to him.

"Hey, Audrey," he starts off uncomfortably.

"Don't hey me," I snap fiercely. I'm not even shaking as much as I thought I would be. Apparently, I'm getting pretty good at this whole confrontation thing. Little meaningless fights like this seem like nothing compared to getting chased through my house by a man with a knife.

"Why haven't you told Sophia the truth?" I demand to know.

"Can you chill out?" he tries.

I step closer to him. "We've never hung out before, Bryson! But since Sophia doesn't believe me, she's ruining my life!"

"Audrey, just calm down, okay?"

I want to hit him. The only reason I don't is that I can't afford to be suspended right now. Instead, I stand there fuming, waiting for his explanation.

"Look," he begins, looking over his shoulder and his friends as if they're going to somehow give him back up. "I've already tried to talk to Sophia. I promise. She won't listen to me. I honestly didn't even know that she had a crush on me until yesterday."

"Well... get her to listen," I say, my tone losing its muster. "I-I can't talk to her. She doesn't want to see me."

"Uh..." Bryson trails off, his eyes looking at something down the hall. My stomach knotting, I follow his gaze. At the other side of the landing, down the hall, Sophia is standing amongst the throng of students making their way to their first-period classes, watching us with a heated expression.

"She probably isn't gonna want to see you even more now," Bryson tells me. Then he shakes his head and he and his buddies walk in the other direction.

I try to give Sophia a look that explains that I was just trying to clear up the misunderstanding.

She remains standing there like she wishes she could slit my throat. Like she wishes she could summon the masked man to come back and finish what he started.

***

When school gets out, I tell Lyla I can give her a ride home today. I know Coach Green is going to make me run so many laps for skipping practice yet again, but I don't even want to think about the kind of torturous thing Sophia has planned to humiliate me during practice today. I'd rather get in trouble with Coach Green. I'd rather have to run fifty laps every day for the rest of my life than face Sophia.

Sophia's specialty is tearing people down and being mean. Usually, she just does it for fun. When she's fueled by anger, it's downright terrifying to be on the receiving end of it.

Lyla and I pull into the driveway outside our house, driving past my vandalized car again.

"Wait a second," Lyla says, opening her car door before I even put the vehicle in park.

"Lyla!" I whine. I slam on the brakes and she hops out and runs over to my Mini Cooper. I groan and, even though it's only halfway pulled into the garage, I get out and see what she's doing.

She's holding a folded piece of paper in her hand.

"What is that?" I ask. Had that been there this morning?

Lyla unfolds it and reads, then she looks back up at me. "Audrey, I don't think Sophia did this to your car."

"What are you talking about? Of course she did." I step over and read the note she's holding in her hand.

It had to be done.

Lyla is right—Sophia wouldn't have left a note like this.

"The person that's been messing with us did this?" I ask in astonishment.

"Who the heck is this person?" Lyla wonders, her eyebrows clashing together, storm clouds brewing in her eyes. "It seems kind of strange that they would go from trying to stab you with a butcher knife one moment to vandalizing your car like some petty teenager the next."

I crinkle the note in my hand. "I don't know, Ly," I say, my tone resigned. "But I'm really sick of it."

"Me too."

I'd been too lenient before. I hadn't been working hard enough.

Now, I'm determined more than ever to figure out who's doing this to us. I need to put a stop to it. I need to go back to snooping around places I shouldn't and looking for information.

When Lyla retreats into her bedroom and nobody seems to be around, I creep down the hallway, a flashback of when I fell in front of the masked man appearing briefly in front of my eyes as I step over the spot where Mom and Dad had discovered me unconscious. Then I go inside my parents' room, check that I haven't been seen, and slowly close the door behind me.

CHAPTER 61

MADDY

I feel a little uneasy when I get home from work that evening. I pull into my driveway and hop out of my Hyundai, and I see that Warner's jeep is already here. At least he is home, where he's safe.

I walk down the driveway to my mailbox on the street. The sun has just finished setting, and the sky outside is still a gray-blue. It's twilight.

I look to my right and see a car's headlights shining on me as it drives slowly up the street toward me. I try to ignore it and open the mailbox to pull out various coupons, past-due bills, and junk mail telling me I pre-qualify for this or that. Then I close the mailbox and start heading back up the driveway, but my stomach sinks when I notice the car slowing to a stop outside my house.

Is this why I was feeling uneasy? Was somebody following me home the whole time I was driving, and my subconscious knew it?

Carefully, I stop walking and turn back around to face them.

A beautiful new silver Mercedes G-Wagon is parked outside of my house. The person rolling down the window is smiling brightly at me.

It's Steven Hall.

I put a hand on my heart.

"Steven!" I cry out. "I thought you were here to kidnap me or something!"

My heart is pounding, but I don't feel much relief about him being here right now. I hadn't wanted him to see where I live yet. My house is probably small and pathetic compared to where he lives.

"I know this isn't the most ideal way to go about this," Steven says to me. I step closer to the car. Despite everything, I can't help but smile slightly. He does look incredibly handsome in his white button-down with the sleeves rolled up.

"What are you doing here?" I ask.

"I can't stop thinking about you, Maddy." He looks unapologetic about it. "And you aren't returning my texts or calls. I just wanna know why."

I chew on my bottom lip, trying to pick my words carefully. "Steven, you're amazing," I start. He immediately rolls his eyes. I laugh. "No, it's true!"

"Then what's going on with you, huh?" he asks. "Because I had an amazing time with you on that date. I don't know what I did to mess it up, but I am here to grovel and hope that you'll give me another chance."

"Wait... how did you even figure out where I live?"

"Well, it's kind of not hard to know when we live in such a small town."

"Right..."

He sticks his arm out the window, his hand held out to me.

I look over my shoulder to see if Warner is peeking out at us through the blinds. He doesn't seem to be, so I turn back to Steven and take it.

"Please give me another chance?" he asks.

"You did nothing wrong," I admit. "I've just been dealing with some personal stuff. Dating gets harder when you get older."

"I couldn't agree more. That's why when you find someone that you know you have a connection with, you have to work extra hard to see it through."

Those dang butterflies are back, swarming around wildly in my stomach. He's so right. I need to stop worrying about him turning out to be like every other guy who has hurt me before. I feel something for this man, and I need to see where it takes me. Even if that means getting let down by him. There's always a chance that's going to happen. But there's also always a chance that it won't.

"You know what? I couldn't agree more," I decide. He grins from ear to ear, making me melt.

I give his hand a gentle squeeze, then I lean in and kiss him on the cheek, just as he had done to me after our first date.

"You won't regret this," he tells me. "I'll call you?"

"I'll be waiting," I reply.

He gives me a wink. When he drives away, I stand there with my arms crossed, holding my mail and watching him go. I don't look back down at the mail pile until he's out of sight completely.

I start walking up towards the front porch, sorting through the stack. My hands pause when I get to a bright red envelope. It's completely unmarked, not even a stamp on it. Does that mean someone hand-delivered it?

Curiosity gets the better of me, and I open the envelope right there outside the house.

What's inside of it confuses me. Then it makes my blood run cold. It makes the color drain from my face. It makes my stomach feel like it's going to fall out of my butt.

Inside the envelope is a picture of Dean. I can tell that the photo was taken when he was in college because Dean is wearing a college T-shirt. He's with Amelia Bailey. They're on a beach somewhere, and they're kissing.

CHAPTER 62

AMELIA

My phone will not stop vibrating. Not only is Craig Fritz texting me repeatedly, but he is also calling me nonstop. I keep declining him, but he keeps calling right back immediately. I'm too afraid to block the calls because I'm not sure what he will do if it gets to that point.

"What's going on?" Gentry asks me as we sit at the dining table together. It's just the two of us, our kids busy doing homework and who knows what upstairs. It's one of those "fend for yourself" nights.

"What do you mean?" I ask shortly. Then I decline another call from Craig. He sends a text immediately.

Craig: *You can't avoid me forever, Amelia. We need to talk.*

"Who is blowing up your phone right now, Mia?" Gentry asks.

I glare at him. "Who are you texting?" I ask him in return.

He's holding his phone, and his fingers pause over the keyboard of it as he realizes I've caught him.

"I'm going into the office," he says shortly, getting to his feet and storming off.

Craig calls me again. There's no way for me to get this to stop. Not unless I do what he says.

I look around me to make sure nobody's near, then I finally answer him.

"What do you want from me?" I hiss in a whisper voice.

"There she is!" Craig says happily. "Mia, let's talk."

"I'm not going to talk to you over the phone like this."

"In-person then? Even better."

We pick a place to meet and I hang up on him abruptly. Without letting anybody know that I'm leaving, I sneak out of the house. I drive to the edge of the woods a little outside of our neighborhood. There's a parking lot where everybody goes, leaves their cars to go on one of the many hiking trails, and that's where I've told him to meet me.

Once I arrive, I have to wait a little bit for him to get there via his car. He pulls up in the old brown jalopy, and I'm amazed he still has the same car he had in high school. The fact that he isn't in a police car makes me wonder if he is even handling the Sydney Hutton case legally.

Most likely not.

Craig gets out of the car. He looks unshaven and unkempt. Tired and maybe even a little bit not sober.

"Let's get this over with, then," I say immediately. When he approaches me, I take a step back. I want a good amount of distance between us. It seems like we're the only two in the entire world out here right now.

"Mia, Mia, Mia," he starts, his voice slurring a little bit.

"Why am I here, Craig?" I demand. I cross my arms and stare at him firmly, but I feel my body begin to tremble.

"I know you already know the answer to that question," he tells me.

"I actually don't, though."

He shakes his head. "This isn't about Sydney Hutton."

Of course it's not. It's about my past. The one I've spent years with Maddy trying to keep hidden.

But I feign ignorance. "What are you talking about?"

"What happened to Carson Price, Mia?"

My stomach rolls. The world around me sways slightly, and I wonder if I'm going to be sick right here in the parking lot.

"He disappeared, didn't he?" I ask.

"I don't know, did he?" Craig deadpans. He takes a step toward me.

I take a step back.

"Mia!" he snaps suddenly, his voice getting much louder. "You need to tell me what you know! Did you kill him?"

It's the first time I've ever outright been asked that question. By anyone. Ever.

I'm slapped with the reality of the situation, and suddenly, I can feel my eyes filling with tears.

"Ex-excuse me?" I ask, stuttering.

"You heard me!" he shouts. "I asked you if you killed him! Well, Mia? Did you? Did Maddy? I'm sick of playing these games! It's been too long! I know you two did something!" Still, he's stepping toward me. I take four large steps back this time. My heel trips over a pebble and my ankle twists, but I ignore the pain. In fact, I don't even feel it.

"Craig, listen to me," I try, hating how weak my voice sounds. "You don't understand. You don't even know what's going on. There's so much that you don't know."

"Oh, I understand," Craig says. "But I also know a lot more than you probably think. So start talking, or I swear, Amelia Flynn-Bailey, you are going to regret meeting me this evening."

At least he's right about one thing.

I already do regret doing this.

CHAPTER 63

WARNER

I'm in the middle of reading an email from Mr. Reeves through the school's portal about some tips for my college applications when I get a text message from Audrey. I pick up my phone and see a pin on a map. She has sent me her location.

I text back.

Me: *What's going on?*

I try to get back to concentrating on my college applications until she replies, but I can't focus on them anymore. Why would Audrey just send me her location out of the blue? Has something happened? Is she in trouble?

Audrey: *I need you to meet me. Lyla too. There's something I need to tell you guys.*

That can't be good.

I exit the email and slap my laptop shut, then I shove my feet in my Vans before running out of my bedroom. I pass by Mom in the hallway, who freezes, her hands holding a frozen TV dinner and a glass of wine.

"Where are you going?" she asks.

"Gotta run!" is all I offer.

"Warner!" she calls after me. But I ignore her and grab my keys off the hook and run out the door.

As I'm driving along, I see Lyla riding her bike. I honk my horn and pull up alongside her. She looks wide-eyed and terrified at first, but when she realizes it's my jeep, she relaxes. I pull over so she can put her bike in the back and get a ride.

"I thought you were here to kill me," she breathes uneasily as she gets in.

"Sorry, I didn't even think about that," I say.

"It's okay."

"Do you know what this is about?" I ask as I keep driving. Audrey's pin location is just up ahead a little bit further. I can tell it's in the woods, so I'm going to have to park on the street, and Lyla and I are going to have to walk a little bit.

"No idea," she admits. "I didn't even know she left the house."

"Huh."

I park and we get out and walk through the woods together. "You don't think something happened to her, do you?" I ask.

"What do you mean?" she replies.

I'm picturing a dead Audrey in the woods, and I'm picturing that the killer stole her phone and sent us her location so that we are the ones to find her body, but I figure I shouldn't and tell Lyla this. I don't want to freak her out. So I take a deep breath to call myself. "Nothing. It's probably nothing."

We step through the woods, standing very close together. I move apart some branches for her so that she doesn't get things snagged in her hair. She gives me appreciative glances as I help her climb over logs, too. I can't tell if it's just the moonlight out or if she's looking more pale than usual.

"Hello?" a voice calls in the distance, making Lyla and I freeze at first. But then I realize it's Audrey's voice.

"Audrey!" Lyla calls, picking up the pace. I rush after her, then I nearly slam into her back when she comes to a sudden stop. I peer over her shoulder and see Audrey in front of us, looking scared and shaking.

Now that's a person who is ghostly pale.

"Audrey?" I ask, coming around Lyla to step closer to her. "Are you okay?"

"I—I didn't know where to meet you guys so that no one would overhear me," she starts.

"Ree, what's going on?" Lyla asks. "You're scaring me."

Audrey swallows audibly and shakes her head.

"Whatever it is, we're here for you," I say truthfully. But being out in the middle of the woods like this late at night and seeing her looking so afraid—it has sent chills down my spine. I know whatever she's about to tell me isn't going to be good.

"Audrey?" Lyla tries again. Audrey is taking forever to form the words.

Finally, she meets our eyes and opens her mouth to reply.

"I don't really know how else to say this, so I'm just going to say it, I guess. I think... I think our moms killed Carson Price."

CHAPTER 64

AMELIA

With Craig's sudden interest in what happened to Carson Price, Nora suddenly showing up at my house out of nowhere and making herself at home, and my mom's strange warning on the phone call with me not long ago about Nora, I feel that it's all starting to add up. Craig thinks I killed Carson Price. Nora must have questions about it, too. That's why she came back. It has to be.

I am shaking and sobbing when I get home. I have to sit inside my Range Rover for a good fifteen minutes to calm myself so that I don't seem so weak and pathetic when I go inside to talk to my sister. I check my reflection in the rearview mirror, sit up straighter and keep my head high, then I take a deep, shaky breath and get out of the car.

Luckily for me, Nora is heating up some leftovers in the microwave when I walk in through the mudroom.

"Nora," I say in a dark voice.

She looks me up and down in suspicion. "Where have you been?" she asks.

"Outside," I demand, ignoring her question and motioning with my head to the back door.

"But I was just about to —"

"Now."

She holds her hands up in surrender as the microwave beeps. She doesn't bother to get the leftovers out of it. Instead, she turns and walks out to the back patio, and I follow her.

"What are you doing here?" I ask, crossing my arms and putting my weight on one foot as we stand towards the edge of the pool.

"Are you seriously asking me this again?"

"Why did you come back?" I persist. "Why now? Why are you suddenly so interested in your nieces and nephew when you never were before?"

Nora crosses her arms, too. "You know what, sister? I have a question for you."

My stomach sinks. Is it going to be the same question Craig had for me about Carson Price?

She continues. "Why didn't you ever visit me?"

In a way, this question hits me even harder.

"Nora..." I trail off, unsure of the best way to respond.

"Why?"

I hadn't expected her to turn this around like this.

"Because!" I stammer. "I... I didn't understand what was going on. What was happening to you."

"I had nobody there, Mia. No one."

Nora is referring to the time she spent in the mental institution. Back in high school after Carson Price went missing, Nora sort of... fell mentally ill. When Mom and Dad didn't know what else to do, they decided to send her to an institution. She kept saying Carson Price was dead. She kept acting out. She wouldn't eat. She hardly slept. The fact that the police never found a body made everything more confusing. I think my parents were just afraid.

I was afraid. It's part of the reason I didn't visit.

"I'm sorry, Nora," I try. I do regret not going to see her. I just couldn't bring myself to do it. It was too hard. Too scary. Terrifying.

"You know, I wish that was good enough," she tells me.

"Nora, you weren't completely alone. I know Mom and Dad came to see you. Dean said he tried to write you a letter and that you never wrote him back."

This makes her laugh. Actually, laugh. The kind where she throws her head back and her entire body shakes with it.

"What's so funny?" I demand.

She tilts her head and calms herself down. "You know what? Stay right here. I'm going to go get something."

She goes back inside the house. I stand there tapping my foot, keeping my arms crossed. Mainly because it's cold outside and less because I'm mad. I'm still terrified about this whole situation. I didn't think we would be talking about Nora's time in the mental institution tonight. I was trying to get answers about why she decided to show up at my house. I don't want to talk about this.

When she comes back, she's holding a folded piece of paper in her hand. She holds it out to me, but I hesitate to take it.

"Go on," she urges, nearly shoving it in my hand. "Read it."

Trying my best not to show how much my hands are shaking, I unfold a note. It's a letter.

From Dean.

He wrote it to her while she was staying in the institution all those years ago:

Nora

I'm so sorry this happened to you. I don't know where Carson is or what happened to him, but I really hope he is alive and out there somewhere. I know you truly believe you saw him dead, and maybe he is dead. But I think it would be better if he wasn't, don't you?

I hope you're doing okay in there. I hope that it at least beats being here at Blackfell. It's pretty sucky here right now.

I know we didn't really ever get a chance to talk again after the prom. I'm sure you probably already know this, but Maddy dumped me. And I liked her, so it sucked. I don't even really know why I'm telling you. There's actually an entirely different reason why I am writing this letter to you in the first place, Nora.

I'll always love you. Like a sister. Like a best friend. We grew up together, in diapers. You grew up as my best friend, and it's hard to see you as anything other than that.

But it's different with Amelia. I grew up with her always just sort of there... just out of my reach. Not really ever my friend. She was sort of like an older sibling that came from a divorced parent, who I only saw every once in a while. But then at some point, I don't know what changed, but I have to be completely honest with you. I fell for her.

I'm so sorry if this causes you any pain. The last thing I want to do is hurt you. But I don't want to keep hiding it from you. And I don't want to lie. I've loved her for years. I've always loved her. And I probably always will.

I can understand if you hate me and never want to speak to me again. But I really do hope you write me back. If you do, I will schedule a time to come and visit. If not, I'll get the message.

You will, forever and always, still be my best friend.
Dean

I can only think of one sentence in my head when I finish reading. It replays over and over as I stand there staring at the letter Dean wrote to my sister.
Oh. My. God.

CHAPTER 65

LYLA

I'm still in the woods with Audrey and Warner. Audrey has just told us that she thinks our mother and Warner's mother killed Carson Price.

"Audrey, why would you say that?" I ask her, trying to remain calm.

"I heard Mom talking on the phone to somebody. She told them she would meet them somewhere private. I had a feeling it was Freaky Fritz. So... I followed her. I-I heard them talking in a parking lot nearby."

"Oh my God," I say.

"What did they talk about?" Warner asks. "Tell us everything."

"Fritz demanded to know what she did to Carson. He just kept asking her. He said he was sick of waiting around and playing games. He asked her if she killed him, and she told him there were things he didn't understand. Things he didn't know."

"Okay..." I say slowly. "That doesn't mean that they did anything... right?" I look at Warner to back me up. But it doesn't seem like he wants to. He seems like he very much believes that this could be true.

Could my mother really have killed someone?

Audrey shakes her head and looks down, her forehead creasing like she's about to cry. It appears as if it's torture for her to get the words out.

"And then, as I stayed there hidden, watching, Craig... grabbed Mom and started shaking her. Literally shaking her. She burst into tears and ran away from him."

I put a hand on my heart. The mental image of it even makes me want to start crying. "What is his problem?" I ask, instantly getting mad. "Should we do something?"

"Absolutely not," Audrey says. "This is serious stuff, Ly. Mom could be in trouble. So could Madeline." Then suddenly, she starts to cry.

Warner is quick to step forward and wrap his arms around her tightly. She sobs into his chest as I stand there, feeling dumbfounded. I can't believe this is happening.

"We'll figure this out," Warner says in a reassuring voice.

Audrey sniffs and steps away from him. Her face is puffy and her eyes are bloodshot. She looks exactly how I do when I cry.

"I just don't see how," she says. "It's not like we have the police to help us. They are... they're practically the bad guys."

"Well, hey—your mom didn't outright admit that she killed Carson, right? That my mom killed him?" Warner asks.

"Yeah?"

"Then there's still a chance that maybe she didn't. We have to go with the whole 'guilty until proven innocent' thing, right?"

She sniffs in response. Then Warner looks at me. "Don't you think?"

"Um... yeah," I mutter.

Audrey still looks so broken that Warner gives her another hug. I guess maybe I look a little more put together than her or something. She accepts the hug gratefully.

"You guys have a tough mom," he says afterward. "Everything's gonna be okay. It was good of you to fill us in though, Ree."

He calls her Ree now?

"He's right," I say to Audrey. She gives me a weak smile.

"I should go," Warner says. "You guys need a ride back?"

"No," we say together.

He nods his head and gives me a hug goodbye. "I'll leave your bike out for you," he says into my hair before he pulls away. Then he rubs Audrey's shoulder briefly and disappears down the woodsy trail.

I turn to Audrey. "Are you going to be okay?" I check.

"I don't know. I think so. You should've seen it, Lyla. It was awful."

"Have me come with you next time," I demand. I don't like the thought of her being out there all alone around Craig Fritz. Or around my potential murderer of a mother.

She nods her head.

I don't know if it's jealousy or what, but a question forms and then comes out of my mouth before I can even process it in my head.

"Do you... have feelings for Warner?" I randomly ask my sister.

She gives me a stunned expression. Like my question had come completely out of the blue, but I have my reasons for asking. They had just seemed so... cuddly moments ago.

"Warner?" she asks, sounding like I've asked her if she likes someone from that group of guys that spends their lunches playing Dungeons & Dragons in the cafeteria. "Definitely not."

I nod my head. "Sorry, that was a dumb question."

"Um, yeah," she agrees. Of course she wouldn't like Warner. She's obsessed with that senior, Ryan Copeland. And why would she like a guy who had rumors going around about him having a crush on me over her?

I'm probably just losing it.

She links her arm through mine. "Let's just get out of this creepy place."

CHAPTER 66

AUDREY

After all the horrible stuff that's been happening lately, the last thing I want is for Lyla to bike home by herself.

"Please, just let me give you a ride?" I try. My damaged Mini Cooper won't fit her bike, but we can come back in the morning to come to get it—when it's daylight outside and there are people around going on their morning walks and jogs.

"Um... no thanks," Lyla says. "I want to bike home."

"Lyla..."

"I'll be okay, I promise," she tells me. Then she gives me a long hug. I can't imagine what it would be like to be an only child and have to go through this alone. There are some moments like these when I am especially grateful to have her.

We get to the road, and she picks up her bike where Warner carefully left it up on its kickstand. I unlock my Mini Cooper and she waits for me to get safely inside of it before she starts biking away. I start the car, lock all the doors around me, but I don't leave immediately. I'm still having a hard time processing everything that's happened.

I pull out my phone and check social media again. I've been doing it more lately than I used to. It's as if it's my coping mechanism. Watching people's Snapchat and Instagram stories, living their normal lives, is making me feel distracted from how crazy mine has turned this year.

But when I open up Sophia's story, it feels as if my heart has shattered. The tears instantly start flooding out of me again.

It's a Snapchat story of her hanging out with Ryan Copeland.

In her bedroom.

They're giggling and using stupid filters to make each other look like vampires and bunny rabbits.

I know that it's directed at me. I know she wants the whole school to see that she has stolen the guy I like just because she thinks I stole hers.

CHAPTER 67

MADDY

When Mia calls me, I am still a shaking, angry mess over the image I've just found of her and Dean together. Seeing red, I answer the call.

"Yes?"

"Maddy?" Mia asks, her voice shaky. It sounds as if she's crying. I had been about ready to confront her, but hearing the tone of her voice stops me.

Don't do it, Maddy, I tell myself. You don't know the full story.

"What's wrong?" I ask her instead through clenched teeth.

"It's Craig," she says. "He just made me meet him and... oh my God, it was horrible, Mads. He... he accused me of murdering Carson."

"What?!"

"Yeah. And then when I got home, I had a horrible confrontation with Nora and she left. I asked her why she came to visit me in the first place, and she wouldn't give me a straight answer."

I know I should be feeling sorry for her, but I'm having a hard time doing it right now. I can't stop looking at the photo of her and Dean together. Since Dean is in a college T-shirt, then this has to be in Amelia's sophomore year, since she is older than him. As far as I thought I knew, she and Gentry were together then. Does Gentry even know about their little fling?

"Mia, just try and calm down," I say.

"I know, I know," she says, taking a deep breath. "I just wanted to call you to let you know that C-Craig might try to come over and do the same thing to you. Or he might tell you that he knows Warner did something to Sydney. He'll say anything to try and get something he can use as a confession out of you, I just know it. You have to be careful."

I run a hand through my hair. "Thanks for the heads up," I say curtly. "I gotta go."

"Okay," she says pathetically, sniffing. I don't want to comfort her, but I feel like I have to.

"It will be okay."

"Thank you."

We hang up and I get up out of my bed. When I leave my bedroom, at this point, I am officially desperate. I'm not the kind of mother that invades her child's privacy. Or at least, I didn't use to be. But if Craig is on his way over here and he tries to say something about Carson's or Sydney's death, I have to be prepared.

I enter Warner's bedroom.

His laptop is sitting on his bed. If there's anything that will tell me the truth about what happened between him and Sydney, it will be on there.

Looking over my shoulder and making sure I don't hear the sound of Warner returning through the front door, I go to his bed and open his laptop. Thankfully, it's not password protected.

The screen wakes up, and I press the start key, ready to go through his files, but then I pause when I see what's already been pulled up on his web browser.

He has multiple college applications pulled up.

I click through the tabs and see that each school he's applying to is somewhere in Florida.

It shocks me to my very core. Warner has always told me he will stay here for college. I told him I needed him. I begged him not to leave me. He said he wouldn't.

But he has been lying to me.

Out of everything I could've found on his laptop, this is what breaks me. This is what makes me fall to my knees as I burst into body-racking sobs. The most important person in my life is planning on leaving me. Planning on moving all the way across the country. And I feel like I have nobody to blame but myself. I am an overbearing, immature, irresponsible mother, and Warner can't wait to get as far away from me as possible.

Somehow, I end up in my bed again. I don't even remember getting there. All I know is that I keep crying and crying, and then eventually, at some point, darkness swallows me.

CHAPTER 68

WARNER

I drive home in a hurry. I've decided I'm just going to do it. I'm going to go home, barge into Mom's room, and demand to know why Craig Fritz would think she and Amelia Bailey killed Carson Price. I'm going to demand to know the truth. I think I've gotten good enough over the years to be able to tell when Mom is lying to me, and I'm not going to stand for it any longer. Tonight is the night I will finally learn the truth. If Mom did kill Carson Price, then maybe it's somehow related to why we've all been getting tormented. Maybe the person torturing us is the one who wants the answer so badly—Craig.

I pull into the driveway, put my car in park, and hop out, nearly tripping when my knee gets stuck under my steering wheel and flying out headfirst. Thankfully, I land on my feet.

I take the first step towards the front porch to go confront Mom. But then something happens out of nowhere.

Mom's car beside me bursts into flames. It emits a boom so loud that, confused; I think an atomic bomb has been dropped. Suddenly, I'm flying through the air. I hit the ground hard and everything goes black.

CHAPTER 69

MADDY

A loud, booming noise jolts me awake from my sleep. I sit up in bed with a start, adrenaline instantly pulsing through me even though I don't know what's happened. But then, through my bedroom window, I see a strange orange glow outside. I leap out of bed and dash down the hallway and out the front door.

The first thing I notice is my car in flames, the front of my house damaged from it. I cry out in fear, but then I realize that this isn't even the worst of it.

Out in the middle of the street, Warner is laying there, not moving.

"Warner!" I scream, running over to him. Still, he doesn't stir. I drop to my knees and hover my hands over him, not even sure which parts of him are unharmed. He's not moving. He doesn't even appear to be breathing. His body is bent at an awkward angle and he's bleeding in several places.

"Warner, wake up!" I plead. I cup his bleeding face in my hands, but he doesn't stir. "SOMEBODY HELP ME!" I scream at the top of my lungs. I keep my gaze fixed on my son. "Warner, please, baby, wake up!"

I don't understand what's happened.

Who in the world could have done this to my son?

CHAPTER 70

LYLA

I want to ride my bike home because I haven't quite been able to gauge how Warner has been handling the news about his biological father, and I want to sneakily try and check on him.

Warner hasn't mentioned anything to me about finding out that Dean Reeves is his father—I had been the one who wrote him the letter and stuck it in his locker. I did it to protect my sister. After she was attacked by the man in the mask, I wanted to ensure that it didn't happen again. If Warner found out about his father at school while Audrey was in the hospital, then it cleared her name from the list of people who could have told him.

The time I round the corner on my bike onto Warner's street is the same time I see the fiery burst of flames from Maddy Carpenter's car. Then I see Warner go flying. I start peddling faster, my heart pounding in my chest. It was the tormentor. He was back.

I slam on my bike brakes, nearly flying over the handrails of them, when I see Maddy running outside to Warner's aid.

"SOMEBODY HELP ME!" she screams.

I pull my phone out and dial 911 as nearby, I spot Jackson rushing out his front door. Warner isn't moving as I give the details to the operator. If I had only gotten here moments earlier...

No.

It's too horrible to think about. Warner can't be dead. He just can't be.

LYLA

Even though it's the middle of the night, it seems as if all of Blackfell High is in the waiting room at the hospital wanting to see Warner. I got here first, and I told Audrey what happened, but other than that, I don't know how the word got out. One by one and in chunks, students started arriving, looking horror-struck by what had happened to Warner.

Danielle, Olive, and Sophia approach me in the waiting area while I'm sitting there with my knees tucked up under my chin as I stare at nothing. Apparently, they can't tell that I don't want to talk to anybody. I just want to hear the news that Warner is going to be okay.

"Hey, Ly," Sophia says in a sweet voice. When I look at them all, I'm slightly confused. Why do they all look like they're in full hair and makeup for the occasion? Weren't they asleep before they heard the news? Or at least in their pajamas in bed? Mostly everybody else here looks a mess in their sweats and makeupless faces. All of the guys seem to have a serious case of bedhead.

"Hey," I say weakly.

"This is all so... crazy," Sophia says. Next to her, Danielle and Olive nod their heads.

"It is," I say numbly.

"Have you heard anything about Warner? Is he going to be okay?" Sophia asks.

"Where is Audrey?" Danielle chimes in.

"In the bathroom," I reply. She lasted all but five minutes before she ran away with tears streaming down her cheeks.

"Are you doing okay?" Sophia continues to ask. "People are saying you're the one who called 911. Is it true?"

I can't take any more of it—all of their niceness is fake. Even their niceness during the sleepover after Wrigley's party had been fake.

All they want is to gossip. To be informed and know things before anybody else.

"You know what, Sophia?" I ask, getting to my feet and getting in her personal space. She looks alarmed, as do the other girls. "Can't you just back off?"

Heads turn to look at us.

I don't care.

"You don't actually care about what happened to Warner!" I continue. "You don't care what happens to anyone except for yourself. Audrey is supposed to be your best friend, and yet you're choosing to believe a lie about her hanging out with your stupid crush over her when she told you she never talked to him! And to hang out with Ryan just to get back at her... What is wrong with you?"

"Lyla, come on," Danielle says, trying to come to Sophia's aid. I whip my head to her next.

"Don't even start with me!" I hiss. "How could you and Olive side with Sophia about this? You know Audrey would never try to steal a guy from her. You're just too cowardly to stand up for her because you are worried about what Sophia will do to you if you do. It's pathetic!"

A hand grabs my arm and pulls me away from them.

"Let me go!" I yell, ready to throw a punch at Sophia. But then I look up and notice that it's my dad pulling me away.

"What are you doing here?" I demand.

"I came as soon as I heard what happened," he replies, continuing to pull me away from the waiting room and into a secluded hallway out of earshot of everyone.

"This isn't the place, Lyla," he tells me.

"I know, but... I just couldn't take it anymore."

"Look, why don't you just come home and get some rest?" he asks. "You're supposed to be grounded, anyway."

"Please don't make me," I say, instantly getting tears in my eyes. I don't want to leave Warner. I don't want to miss the news when he gets out of surgery. "I need to know that he's going to be okay," I say. "Please."

Dad reaches out and wipes a tear from my cheek. "I'm sure he's going to be okay, honey."

I throw my arms around him and hug him. If only Warner had a dad in his life to care about him as much as mine cares about me. A hug from a dad is one of the best things you can get.

He rubs my back and puts his chin on top of my head. "I suppose there are a lot of other kids here. You and Audrey can stay. I know he's your friend and that you both care about him."

He's so much more understanding than Mom.

I hug him tighter.

After Dad leaves, Audrey comes out of the bathroom to tell me she's going home. She still looks deeply upset.

Then a couple more hours later, I'm informed Warner is awake. He's still in the ICU, and he's still weak, but he's awake.

CHAPTER 72

WARNER

I am in and out of consciousness all night long, but the first time my eyes are open where I am actually aware of what's happening around me, the only person in the room with me is Lyla Bailey.

She's sitting in a chair pulled up close to the bed, and when she sees my eyes open, she leans forward eagerly, a smile on her face.

"You are one popular dude," is the first thing she says to me.

I chuckle weakly. "What?"

"The whole school has been in and out of here all night long. You've got a lot of people that care about you."

I'm flattered that a lot of people are here to visit me, but I am mainly glad to see that the only person I wanted to be here is right in front of me.

"Oh," I say, my eyes fluttering closed and opening back up again. I don't want to fall back asleep with Lyla here. I need to soak up this alone time while I can.

"Warner, I... I saw the explosion happen." She hiccups, then suddenly, she's crying. She reaches forward and takes my left hand, the one not in a brace. "It was so scary. I thought you were dead."

I try to give her hand a reassuring squeeze, but I am still so weak. *I can't believe she's holding my hand.*

"I wouldn't do that to you," I try to joke.

She laughs pathetically. "I have to be honest with you, Warner."

I wait, my heart starting to beat faster. I don't feel any pain in my body, and I have a feeling it's because she's here distracting me from it all.

She sighs. "I know this is probably messed up of me to say, but I don't care. I literally thought you were dead. And it put a couple of things in perspective. I... I wish you had been the one to send that text to Jackson." She scoffs and shakes her head. "Stupid, right?"

Is this real life? Or did the doctors give me one heck of a drug?

"No," I tell her. "Definitely not stupid."

She sniffs. "I—I remember you visiting me in the hospital after my accident," she says. "I know I've never told you that. I just felt like I shouldn't because you hadn't come to visit me with Jackson. It was just you. All the time. I had a feeling you wouldn't want him finding out. But... it meant the world to me, Warner." She wipes her eyes on the back of her free hand, refusing to let go of the one that's holding mine.

This is everything I've ever wanted her to tell me. For someone who was just in a horrible accident and had been clinging onto life for a moment there, I am one happy dude.

CHAPTER 73

AUDREY

I leave the hospital because I can't take the dirty looks everybody is giving me about the whole Sophia thing. Nobody has any idea what really happened between us, and yet everyone seems to have decided to side with the queen of the school over me.

But I want to see Warner, still. So, as soon as I get the text from Lyla telling me that he's awake and accepting visitors, I shower and get ready for the hospital. When I get there, there aren't as many people now because everyone has finally started to go back home to get ready for the school day. But I would have come back anyway, even if everyone was still here. It wouldn't let them all stop me from seeing Warner.

I walk down the hall towards his room, hating the reminder of how I had been a patient in this place not very long ago. And I have no doubt in my mind that the tormentor had done this to the both of us—the same person who chased me around in my house is the same person who caused Warner to have his accident.

When I reach room 207, the door is open. I pause, seeing that he already has a visitor with him—one that looks just like me.

Lyla is sitting in a chair moved all the way up to Warner's bed. The two of them are giggling, smiling, and making lovey eyes at each other.

I don't believe what I'm seeing. I had told Lyla I didn't have a crush on Warner, but maybe I would've said otherwise if I had realized she had a crush on him. I didn't think she would go for Warner. She had told me before that she doesn't like him like that. Warner is Jackson's best friend. Isn't that a little... wrong?

I do have a crush on Warner. But based on the way he's looking at my sister, I have the feeling I've missed my chance.

Instead of making my presence known, I turn around and leave the hospital.

CHAPTER 74

LYLA

I get to school late. I had stayed in Warner's room talking with him much longer than I thought I would. But the moment I get to Chemistry in second hour, everyone is staring at me. I give my late pass to Mrs. Winston cautiously, interrupting her lecture.

Then, to my horror, somebody yells out, "Yo, that's the chick that killed Trinity!"

"She didn't kill her," Danielle says. She looks right at me, a hatred in her eyes that I've never seen before. Danielle has always been the sweet one out of the three of them. I know she's probably mad at me for yelling at her in the hospital earlier, but can you really blame me? I always stick up for my sister. I get the feeling that this new look she has for me has nothing to do with that, though. "But she is the reason that she's dead."

The class bursts into chatter all at once. They're talking about how it's all my fault that Trinity is dead. That I had been texting while driving. That I had been texting Wrigley Hall while driving. That he's the reason I got into the accident that killed her.

"That's enough everyone!" Mrs. Winston says.

But the chatter doesn't die down.

"So then, did you kill Sydney, too?" somebody calls to me. I can't even tell who it is. The voices seem to be getting louder and louder, swirling around inside of my head, almost as if they're trapped in there and can't get out.

I feel the blood drain from my face. I don't know how this could've happened. How did they all find out? I haven't told a soul.

No one except for my therapist. And Sydney.

CHAPTER 75

MADDY

I've been back-and-forth from the hospital all day, getting stuff for Warner and running errands for him. I know that Lyla Bailey has been in here visiting him in between the times I've been gone because I spotted her leaving this morning when I was getting out of my car. Still, Warner is frail right now, so I don't say anything to him about it when I visit him.

When I bump into Jackson, however, I pull him aside, asking if he can talk.

"Of course I can, Mrs. Carpenter," he says to me.

"Miss," I remind him. Jackson has been one of Warner's best friends for how long now? He should know that I am single.

"Right, sorry," he tells me. Still, I appreciate that he's calling me by my last name in a professional manner instead of just Maddy, like a lot of Warner's other friends like to do.

"Have you gotten to talk to Warner much?" I ask him.

"On and off," Jackson says. "He's asleep all the time when I go in there. But I don't wanna go to school today. My parents said it's fine if I don't. I just wanna make sure he continuously has company. I can't expect you to stay with him all day long. I know you have stuff to do and I'm more than happy to help."

I've always liked Jackson. He's always been such a sweet kid.

"I really appreciate that, Jackson," I say, giving him a smile. He grins back. "So you guys have made up, right?"

"Yeah. For the most part," Jackson says. "I know he and Lyla don't have a thing."

"They don't?" I ask. It's news to me. The way Lyla acted when she was in the hospital waiting room with me late last night told me otherwise.

"That's what he told me..." Jackson trails off.

I nod my head slowly. What other information can I get out of Jackson? Maybe something... Sydney related?

"I have something else I've been meaning to ask you," I decide to say.

He waits for me to ask.

I clear my throat. "Jackson, this whole Sydney Hutton thing... What exactly do you know about it?"

Jackson looks down the hallway to his left and then to his right. When he looks at me again, he seems like he wants me to listen closely. I lean in a little bit.

"To be honest, Miss Carpenter, I think I know something about the Sydney thing that no one else does."

"Jackson," I say very sternly, my heart skipping a beat. "Warner could be in some real trouble about the Sydney thing. I need you to tell me everything you know."

He nods, seeming like he completely understands me. I am eternally grateful for it.

"Great. Well, the thing is... I'm not exactly sure what went down that night, to be honest. But he did tell me something that makes me feel a little concerned."

"What is it?" I demand.

"He told me that he wished Sydney was dead."

"What?" I ask, my mouth going dry.

He nods. "I don't know, Miss Carpenter. I don't really see Warner as the type of guy to do something to her. But I just can't help getting the feeling that maybe—I really hope you don't hate me for saying this—but maybe he did."

CHAPTER 76

AMELIA

I meet Maddy at the hospital. I brought her a real lunch from a popular drive-through salad place, along with some caffeine for the long night I'm sure she had to endure.

We sit at one of the tables in the hospital's cafeteria, and I reach across it and squeeze her hand. She smiles appreciatively and starts unboxing her salad.

"I'm so sorry about all of this, Maddy," I tell her. I do truly feel awful. Not long ago, my daughter was in the hospital for a very similar situation. It makes me wonder what's going on around this town. Who is doing this? Are the incidents related?

"Thanks," she says quietly.

"Do you know who did it?" I ask.

She shakes her head. She's not in the most talkative mood, not that I can't understand why.

I feel uncertain and uncomfortable in places like hospitals. Institutions. It constantly reminds me of terrible, terrible things. It reminds me of my sister, and how she ended up going into a place similar to this. A place sterile and heavily monitored.

Maddy is having trouble opening the packet of nonfat Greek Caesar dressing, so I take it from her and rip it open with my long acrylic fingernails.

"Thanks," she mumbles again, pouring it over her kale and spinach mixture.

"He's going to be okay, Maddy," I try, wanting to be reassuring.

"You know, maybe we should talk about something else," Maddy suggests.

"No problem," I say.

"Has it been weird with Nora gone?" she asks.

I'm pleased she's brought this up because I want to talk about it.

"A little bit," I admit. "I had started to forget what it was like to not have her around. Even though she mainly kept herself and stayed up in her room. The whole situation was just so weird."

"I wonder what suddenly made her change her mind and want to be a part of your kids' lives," she says.

I shrug. Then, after a few moments of silence, I bring up the question I've been wanting to ask.

"Did you ever stay in touch with Nora?" I ask. "You know, over the years?"

Maddy finally looks away from her salad and meets my eyes. She seems almost startled slightly. Taken aback. "I haven't talked to Nora Flynn in years," she tells me. "Not since the Carson thing."

"Right. I figured."

But the thing is, I know she's lying to me. Even though we became friends again, she's still lying to me about things. And I'm still lying to her about things. In a way, it feels exactly like everything is back to normal. Even when we were friends in high school, we kept things from each other.

The night that Nora and I got into an argument and she left my house, she told me the truth about her and Maddy. It was after I read the letter that Dean had written her.

"You know who the only person that visited me besides Mom and Dad was?" she had asked.

"No," I admitted, too afraid to look her in the eye because I was ashamed of what I had done. How I hadn't been there for her. She would never understand. It would just be too hard.

"Madeline Carpenter," she informed me. "She's the only one."

"What?" I muttered.

"Yeah. Turns out, she was more of a sister than you ever were."

"I..." I trailed off, not even knowing what to say.

"Surprised to hear it?" Nora spat. "Well, you better believe it, sis. Maddy and I have stayed friends throughout everything. Always."

CHAPTER 77

LYLA

After school, Mom and Dad want to talk to me in the office inside our house. They never bring me in there, so immediately, I'm concerned.

I follow them inside, and then dad waits so that he can shut the door and lock it behind me.

"What's going on?" I ask. I feel completely and totally drained from the day I've had. I didn't sleep at all last night because of Warner's incident. Then I had to go to school and deal with everybody blaming me for Trinity's death. Now this?

Honestly, while I'm thinking about it—I've hardly slept since Audrey's accident. I can't sleep. It's nearly impossible. I'm scared all of the time. A man with a knife chased my sister around our own home. They could be anywhere at any time, ready to strike again. Ready to take my sister's life. Ready to take Warner's life. I don't want that happening.

I regret going to the therapist at all. Sydney is dead, so I don't think she's the one that would let my secret slip to the world. Somehow it came out because of the therapist. It had to have. I don't know how else it would be possible. How else could that secret have gotten out? It makes no sense. I should've never gone.

"We've heard some concerning things from Principal Mathers," Dad starts off the conversation. Mom sits in the chair behind the desk and Dad leans against the front of it. I am sitting in one of the club chairs facing them. My hands are grasping the armrests firmly, elevated because of how high the armrests are.

I bite my bottom lip and look away from them. I should've known this would be about Trinity. I should've known it would get back to them in an instant. "Okay," I say.

"Lyla, honey," Mom says. "We need you to tell us the truth about it."

"I'm sure you've already heard from everybody else," I say, defeated. It's out. I don't know what's going to happen to me now. I don't know what that means. I can't even think about how Trinity's parents are reacting right now. Surely somebody's already told them. I deserve to be in jail. Prison. Maybe that's where I'm about to go. Maybe the police are already waiting outside to handcuff me.

"We heard rumors that you were texting and driving," Mom says carefully.

I nod at her. What else can I do? Try to lie now?

"Oh," Mom says as Dad sighs heavily.

"I'm sorry," I manage to get out. The lump in my throat is huge, but I don't want to cry anymore. I'm so sick of crying.

"Lyla," Dad says, speaking in a firm tone and looking me directly in the eye. It's so intense that I can't help but look back at him. "You seem... tired. You have been acting... unwell, lately. Not following the rules. Snapping at us. Falling behind in school. You have lost interest in the things that you used to enjoy doing. You've cut your hair."

"Okay..." I trail off, uncertain of where they're going with this.

Dad and Mom look at each other. I don't like the expression that they're sharing.

Mom licks her lips before she speaks. "I think it might be a good idea if we send you somewhere to help you recover from all of this. It was my impression—and your father's—that you were doing better about the whole Trinity thing. But maybe with Sydney's death, it brought back all kinds of thoughts and feelings, and maybe you aren't doing so well after all."

I want to say, No duh, I'm not doing well. I want to say, How can it not be any more obvious to you people? I want to say that if they paid me one ounce of attention, they would have seen it in an instant.

"I can't believe you didn't even tell us that you were still going to visit Trinity's grave," Dad says. I give Mom an agitated expression. I know I didn't outright ask her not to tell Dad about what she had seen when she followed me to the cemetery that night, but I figured I could trust that she wouldn't say anything about it to him.

How stupid I had been.

"So you... want to send me away?" I squeak out. Don't cry, Lyla. Don't cry. "Like... like to some sort of mental institution?"

"A wellness spa," Dad corrects. But it's the same thing. I just know it is.

I can't stop the tears this time.

This is really happening. My parents really want to send me away.

CHAPTER 78

WARNER

There's nothing I can do about it when Detective Craig Fritz comes into my room in the hospital. Of course the police would have questions to ask me about the mysterious explosion that happened outside of my house. If only it had been any other officer besides him. If only there was a way I could request someone else. Or request to have him removed from my presence.

Instead, all I can do is lay there in my bed and let Fritz speak.

He doesn't look good. His facial hair is overgrown, even though I'm pretty sure that's against the rules as a police officer. I think I heard somewhere that the only facial hair they're allowed to have is a mustache. Yet, it seems as if Craig Fritz now has a full-grown beard.

His eyes are sunken in with dark circles under them. It doesn't even seem like he bothered to look in a mirror to fix his hair before leaving his house today.

"What are you doing here?" I say in a flat voice, hoping I make it plain on my face how much dislike I have for him.

He makes himself comfortable in a chair at the foot of my bed. He leans back in it and puts his hands behind his head. On his lap is a manila folder.

"How are you doing, kiddo?" he asks in a mocking tone.

"Tell me what you want, or get out of here," I snap.

He chuckles. "If you really want to get right to it, then." He takes a deep breath before continuing. "I have been in and out of the hospital since your accident. I've had to wait until the doctor said you're well enough to be questioned. But while I was waiting, I noticed something. I noticed your football coach and former English teacher, Dean Reeves, coming in and paying you a visit. None of your other teachers paid you a visit. I just thought it was slightly strange. So I went back to the precinct and I did some... digging."

"What are you talking about?" I demand. He's making absolutely no sense. Of course Coach would come to visit me. I'm one of his favorite students. And over the couple of years I've known him, he's been almost like a father or uncle to me.

Craig holds up the folder. He looks sinister. *Giddy*, even. It both confuses me and makes me feel incredibly uncomfortable. "You're gonna wanna take a look at what's inside of here."

"I thought you came here to ask me questions about the incident," I say. I don't want to look inside his stupid folder. I don't even want to know what it is he thinks he can try to show me. I just want him out of here.

"Oh, I already know what went down with that," he says. "In fact, I'm almost no longer even interested in that. Because this information here is so much juicier."

I say nothing and glare at him. But fine. He has made me curious.

Curious, and afraid.

He tosses the folder on my lap. "This is all the information I've gathered so far. I gotta warn you; it's quite shocking stuff, Warner Carpenter. I think it shows pretty concrete proof."

"Proof about what?" I ask. I want to look, and I don't want to look. He's got to be bluffing, right? He can't have anything on me that will shock me as much as he claims it will, right?

"You're gonna have to open it and find out," Craig says. Then he gets to his feet. "I would love to see the look on your face when you read it, but it's probably better that I give you some privacy."

He leaves the room, and I sit there staring at the envelope, not touching it. If it's from Fritz, it's probably a bunch of garbage. A bunch of made-up lies.

But still, the longer I stare at it, the more curiosity seeps into my brain and wills my fingers to move of their own accord. The next thing I know, I find myself opening the stupid folder.

It takes me a second to comb over everything inside of it. All it makes me feel is confusion. There are birth records. There are pictures of Maddy and for some reason, of Coach Reeves, too. Pictures of them together as kids. High schoolers. There are also other documents that I can't quite make sense of. Still, I continue flipping and re-flipping through it all. Then I see the yellow sticky note at the back. It's written in Detective Fritz's messy handwriting:

Reeves is the father?

I drop the folder and its contents into my lap. That is when it all clicks into place. Everything inside of this manila folder shows the evidence that Dean Reeves is my biological father.

CHAPTER 79

Amelia

When Dean asks me to meet up with him again after work that Friday, I don't even hesitate before I say yes. We've met up a couple of times since that day inside his classroom. I haven't told anyone about it, and it's not as if it's in a romantic way or anything, but as it turns out, we both have been trying to figure out what happened to Sydney. What actually happened. I had been emailing Dean repeatedly about my efforts, expressing my concern over the Craig and the Sydney thing and how they might be related to each other. Dean had been expressing his concern over how it might be affecting Warner's well-being. Then the next thing I knew, we were telling each other we would give each other any information we discover about Sydney. And when Dean says he needs to meet with me today, it sounds urgent.

He has me get in his car with him in the school parking lot. I pull up next to it, park my Range Rover, and let myself in his passenger seat. His car is one of the only ones left in the teacher's parking lot, so I'm not worried about anyone spotting us.

Dean looks a little tired today. He is rubbing his eyes as I open the car door and get in, and when he pulls his hands away, he almost looks startled to see me, as if he hadn't been the one who messaged me to tell me to meet him here. But then he smiles kindly.

"Hey," he tells me. "How is Audrey doing?"

"She's been going to your class, right?" I ask, getting concerned instantly. Is that what this is about? Not the Sydney thing?

"Oh, of course. I just meant about the hospital incident," he clarifies.

"She is... I don't know," I say, not even ready to talk about that right now. I'm sick of finding my daughters in situations where I think there might be dead. My heart can't take much more of it. "Why did you want to meet?"

"Hey, are you okay?" He asks it in such a soft tone. Dean looks so genuine and full of concern that a lump forms in my throat. But I don't want to cry in front of him. I can't right now. I have to be okay. I have to be strong. I always am.

So I just nod my head and look away from him.

He clears his throat and continues. "Well, I have something that has to do with Sydney. Or at least I think it does," he says, changing the subject.

"What is that supposed to mean?" I ask. How could he think it does and not know for sure?

He reaches across me, and at first, I'm confused as to why he's in my personal space, but then his hand goes to the glove compartment box and opens it. He pulls out a flipped-over piece of paper and holds it up for the both of us to read the other side together.

"I found this," he tells me.

It's a missing person flyer. The girl on it looks just like Sydney Hutton. However, that is not the name on this flyer. The name on this flyer is Megan Young.

"What is this?" I whisper.

"I think I figured out why it's so impossible to find information on Sydney Hutton."

I look closer at the paper and notice the date. It's from years ago. And in the photo, Sydney has dark brown hair and looks much younger. More like somebody who is the appropriate age to be in high school. I always wondered why she looked so much older than the other kids every time I saw her before.

"Oh my God," I say, realizing what has happened.

Sydney Hutton never existed.

CHAPTER 80

LYLA

Last night with Mom and Dad in our home office, there had been a lot of crying. Not just from me, either. I made both of my parents cry because of how worried they are about me. They told me they just wanted me to get better, but I told them that sending me away wasn't going to make that happen. In fact, I threw such a fit that they tabled the discussion and said we would continue it later. I haven't had heard anything about it since. And I hope they just drop it and never bring it up again.

I leave for school this morning earlier than Audrey so that she can't offer me a ride. Instead of going to school, I ride my bike to the hospital. I spend the entire day hanging out with Warner. Yes, Madeline Carpenter catches me inside his room multiple times, but to my surprise, not once does she tell me that I have to leave and stop bugging her son. Warner and I decide to take it as a sign of her possibly coming around to the idea of the two of us being friends.

But he's been weird all day. Moody and quiet. And he keeps staring off into the distance, in his own little world. I keep asking him what's wrong, but he won't tell me anything. I wonder if it has to do with the fact that he knows Dean Reeves is his father.

Eventually, Warner makes me leave. Only because when he says I look like I'm going to fall into a coma right there in the chair by his bed, I admit to him that I haven't slept much lately.

The whole bike ride back home, I wonder why he didn't want to say anything to me about his father. A handful of times, I even contemplated coming clean and telling him I had been the one that wrote the note. But then I didn't want to take the chance that he would be furious at me for not telling him as soon as I found out. And I didn't want him to be mad at Audrey, either.

I am so glad to have Warner's friendship back, and I had meant it when I told him that I wish he had sent that text to Jackson about having feelings for me. I have feelings for Warner. I think I have for a while. It's making me feel incredibly confused, because I know I also have a crush on Wrigley. But I feel a little bit hurt by Wrigley, too, because not once has he reached out to me since he found out that texting him back is the reason why Trinity ended up dead. The fact that he hasn't said anything hurts. A lot more than I thought it would.

When I get home from the hospital, I go to get off my bike, but I'm so tired that I don't move my leg over all the way and I tumble down, the bike falling on top of me. Hearing the ruckus, Joey rushes into the garage through the mudroom door.

"Lyla!" he cries out, sounding worried. He helps me to my feet, and I give him a tired smile and ruffle his hair.

"I'm fine," I say. "Just tired."

"Have you seen Aunt Nora?" he asks.

I pause, turn, and look at the street through the open garage. No sign of Aunt Nora's car.

"You know what? No, I haven't," I realize.

"I snuck into her bedroom when I got home from school today. All of her stuff is gone. She didn't even say goodbye."

"Aunt Nora is gone?"

"I'm pretty sure."

Why wouldn't she say goodbye? Why wouldn't Mom and Dad say anything to let us know? Something isn't adding up.

"I'm...I'm sure she'll be back. Maybe there was an emergency she had to deal with. Maybe you could give her a call?"

"I don't even know her number," Joey says.

"I'm sure Mom will give it to you," I say, my eyes half open as I limp back into the house with Joey. My leg is throbbing, and I know I've scraped my elbow from the fall.

"It's just weird."

I can't even focus right now—I am borderline delirious from the lack of sleep. Still, if I close my eyes all the way, I picture the most horrible, gruesome things you can imagine. Usually, it involves Audrey or Warner being dead. In a brutal way.

I trudge up the stairs, my feet feeling like lead, and then I go into the bathroom. Audrey's in the shower, the floral curtain closed tightly, so I know she won't mind me barging in. We do this to each other all the time.

"Lyla?" Audrey asks.

"Just getting something," I tell her. I open the medicine cabinet and take out my PTSD medication. I don't normally like to take it, but I'm hoping it will help me sleep and not see such horrible images when I do. I take a pill out, close the lid, and put the bottle back in the cabinet. Before I'm about to walk back out the door, I see Audrey's phone light up with a text.

"Where were you today?" Audrey asks from the shower.

"The hospital with Warner," I admit. I don't feel like trying to keep anything from her. I'm too exhausted.

"You ditched school to visit him in the hospital?" she asks. "Do Mom and Dad know?"

"Who cares?" I pick up her phone. Why does she have a text from an unknown number?

My face is identical to hers, so the facial recognition on the phone mistakes me for her and unlocks itself.

I read the message.

Unknown: *If you really want answers to what happened to Sydney Hutton the night she died, then you'll want to meet me.*

Underneath the text is an address. I stare at it, confused. Is this the person that's been messing with us? The man who chased Audrey around the house and nearly killed her?

"You need to be careful, Ly." Audrey is lecturing me inside the shower. "Mom and Dad are starting to really freak."

Without much of another thought, I delete the text message.

I have to protect my sister. I cannot take the chance that Audrey will go anywhere near this person. Ever.

CHAPTER 81

AMELIA

Dean gets out of his car and walks me back over across the parking lot to mine.

"Thanks again for meeting me," he tells me.

"Of course," I say immediately.

"I'm gonna keep digging in on this, and I'll send you an email as soon as I find out anything else."

Before I can stop myself, I reach out and touch his forearm. "Call me," I suggest instead. "I'll answer."

He stares down at my hand on him and raises an eyebrow. "Are you... sure?"

I know he's referring to Gentry. He doesn't want to be disrespectful or cause any problems between us. Little does he know, Gentry and I are already full of problems.

"Um, yes," I say, pulling my hand away and tucking some hair behind my ear.

"Mia..." Dean says. I can't stand that I love the way he says my name. I can't help but take a couple of steps toward him. We're right outside my car door, his hand is on the handle of it. He stands frozen, still as a statue, as I move closer.

"Dean," I say. "It's been really nice hanging out with you again."

"It... has?"

Why does he seem confused? "Well, yeah..."

He steps away from me. I feel the stinging heat of rejection nearly slapping me in the face.

"What are you doing, Mia?" he asks, suddenly sounding upset.

I tilt my head. "I—what do you—?"

"I'm serious!" he interrupts.

"Dean, what's wrong?" I ask, feeling incredibly confused.

He runs a hand through his hair, messing it up but still looking beautiful.

"You know what?" he asks. "This was a bad idea. We shouldn't have met up."

"What are you talking about?" I ask, feeling hurt even more by him. What did I do? How have I somehow said the wrong thing?

"Because... Dang it, Mia!" he snaps, suddenly yelling now. "You're flirting with me and you very well know it! And you know how I feel about you!"

"Dean!" I gasp out. I knew how he used to feel about me. I learned about when he kissed me for the first time. When we had a short fling my sophomore year of college. Then when I read the letter he wrote to Nora—that was the one that really taught me the truth.

But even then, that letter was from years ago. I had no idea that he still felt the same way now.

"No, Mia, I'm serious," he tells me. "I don't know what I was thinking. I hate myself for not being able to stay away from you. Maybe we should just stop talking to each other." His chest is rising and falling rapidly, and his jaw is clenched tightly as he looks out in the distance. I'm waiting for him to tell me he doesn't actually want that.

For a moment, I consider telling him the truth. The truth about Gentry and me. It's seconds away from falling out of my mouth. It would help him understand. It would help him see why I am acting this way.

But at the last second, I decide it's too risky.

I know he's lashing out because I've hurt him. But it's not fair of him to hurt me, too. Quickly, my defense mechanism kicks into action.

"Fine," I say, crossing my arms. "You're right. This was stupid."

He doesn't answer.

I shake my head, feeling defeated. Then I get in my car and leave.

CHAPTER 82

AUDREY

I approach Joey with a twenty-dollar bill in my hand. "How would you like to make some quick cash?" I ask him, wiggling my eyebrows. It's late, and Mom has been in Dad's home office for quite some time, working away diligently on her laptop. Dad had an emergency work trip to go on, so he left earlier today.

"For twenty bucks?" Joey asks. Then he rips the money out of my hand. "I'm all yours."

I chuckle. "Good. I need you to distract Mom and get her away from her laptop. Don't ask me any questions about it. Just do it."

"On it."

Joey runs up the stairs to his bedroom. Moments later, while I'm sitting in the living room drumming my fingers on the armrest of the sectional, I hear Joey. "Mom!"

"Joey?!" Mom's voice calls from the office. Then I see her running down the hall, a frantic look on her face as she sharply turns the corner to dash up the staircase toward Joey's voice.

Perfect.

I go through the archway in the living room into the hall leading to the office. I try to avoid going into these areas at all costs because of the horrible thing that happened to me when the masked man was here, but this has to be done. I need to know what Mom is working so diligently on her laptop on.

I enter the office and get on the computer. I shake the mouse, snapping the screen awake. She thinks we don't know what her password is—that if she told us one time, we would forget it and never use it again. But she had used Lyla's and my birthday, so it's kind of hard not to forget it.

I enter the password, and the screen unlocks. I think it's strange that she even took the time to lock it before going to check on Joey in the first place. What was so important that she needed to keep it hidden?

When I see the reasoning, my jaw drops open. I had expected to see something about the Carson Price situation. To see that she had been typing up her confession letter, or that she was emailing Maddy about everything that had happened all those years ago. It's nothing like that at all.

My mother has been making an online dating profile.

CHAPTER 83

AMELIA

Since it's Saturday and Gentry and Nora are gone, and I've been feeling like a horrible mother lately, I decide to get up early to not only finish up some chores around the house, but to also make my children breakfast this morning. I want the four of us to sit down as a family. I want to start getting back on track with my relationship with them. Things have not been easy lately, and I know part of it is my fault. I need to do better.

I'm making everybody ham and cheese omelets, homemade hashbrowns, and whole-wheat toast with olive oil spread.

When it's ready, I go over to the stairs.

"Kids!" I call up the stairwell. "Wake up! Breakfast is ready!"

I stand at the bottom of the steps, waiting for a moment. When I don't hear anyone stirring, I frown. "Kids!" I try again. "Come on! Up and at 'em!"

When I still hear nothing, I make my way up the stairs. I suppose it is the weekend, and it's only seven o'clock. But Joey needs to get up anyway because he has a soccer game later.

I open Audrey's door first. "Sweetie, wake up, I made breakfast!" I say, trying to use an extra cheery, chipper voice. Whatever problems I have going on in my personal life, it's none of their business, and it's nothing for them to need to worry about. I can't let them see that I'm struggling.

"What?" she says in a groggy voice, sitting up, her hair in every which direction. I smile fondly at her.

"Breakfast. Ham and cheese omelets. Come and get it."

"Oh, okay," she says, still half asleep. I make my way across the hall and go to Lyla's room next. I knock and open the door.

"Lyla, breakfast," I say in the same sweet, timid voice. I know she's especially mad at me for sending her back to therapy and suggesting that she should go to a wellness spa.

"Lyla?"

I step into the room and take a look around. Lyla isn't here.

That's strange.

I leave the bedroom and go to the hall bathroom that she and Audrey share. The door is open and nobody's inside it.

"Lyla?" I call around myself. Where could she have gone?

I go back into Audrey's room instead of going to wake up Joey.

"Have you seen your sister?" I ask. Audrey is slowly getting herself out of bed. At the mention of me being unable to find Lyla, she seems a little bit more awake.

"She's not in her room?" she asks, still sounding groggy.

"No..." I trail off. Then I go down the hall to Joey's room. I swing the door open without even knocking.

"Joey, have you seen your sister?" I ask, even though it's apparent that he hasn't because he's still dead asleep. "Joey!"

He snaps his eyes open and sits up. "What's going on?" he asks.

"We can't find your sister," I say. "Oh, and I made breakfast."

I leave the bedroom and enter Lyla's room again. Maybe I had been seeing things, and she actually is asleep in her bed.

But no. Her bed is still made.

I get a sinking feeling inside my stomach as I race down the stairs. I grab my cell phone off of the kitchen counter and check for any missed calls or texts from her. Nothing. I give her phone a call. She doesn't answer.

"Lyla!" I yell louder this time. Then I open the back door and walk around the yard, seeing if maybe she made it out here somehow. I'm scared to even check the pool in case maybe she fell in and something horrible happened to her. Thankfully, the pool is empty, minus the vacuum cleaner slowly moving about.

"Lyla!" I call, in case she is somewhere beyond the back fence, wandering around. She hasn't been the best at following rules lately. I know I probably shouldn't be freaking out. She might've even gone to her friend's house for a sleepover and didn't tell me. She might've gone to the cemetery to visit Trinity's grave and then fell asleep out there.

But even as I try to think such thoughts as those, I don't feel any better.

I check out the front yard next, and still, I don't see her anywhere. I call her phone four more times. I have Audrey try to call her phone, too. Joey, even. Then I call Gentry, even though I desperately don't want to. He tells me he hasn't heard from her, and that he'll try giving her a call, too.

He calls me back twenty minutes later and says he hasn't heard a word.

The fully cooked breakfast I had made on the kitchen counter sits there untouched and cold. My kids are still searching about the house, calling for Lyla. They're going in and out of the garage and the front and back door.

"Where could she be?" Audrey asks, her face full of concern when she passes by me in the kitchen as I try to call Lyla's phone for the millionth time. It rings, so I know it's still on—she's just not answering.

"Mom, what if something bad happened to her?" Joey asks. He walks over to me and I throw my arms around him and hug him tightly. Upon seeing us, Audrey comes over and hugs us as well. I stand there embracing my children, tears threatening to spill over the waterline of my eyes. I don't want Joey to know it, but I am thinking the exact same thing as him.

CHAPTER 84

MADDY

When Amelia calls me a couple of hours after I've woken up, she's frantic again like she had been during our last phone call.

"Mia, what?" I say, feeling confused. "I can't understand anything you're saying. Calm down."

"Lyla!" she screeches. "I can't find her anywhere! Please tell me you've heard something! Please tell me she's been at the hospital with Warner or something?!"

I have never heard her this freaked out before. I have never heard her talk in such a shrill voice. I have never heard her sound so panicked. I totally get that whole "mother's instinct" thing—so if Mia thinks something horrible has happened to her daughter, I get the feeling she might be right about it.

I spend the next twenty minutes trying to calm her down. I tell her I can be over at her house as soon as I can, but she tells me it's not a good idea because her other kids are home. I want to say screw it about that whole "pretend friends" situation because who cares if we're friends or not when a matter like this is occurring? But still, I respect her wishes and tell her to just call me if she needs anything.

I feel sick to my stomach when I drive to the hospital. I'm hoping that I'll see that Lyla has just spent the night inside Warner's room so that I can call Amelia back and tell her that everything is fine.

I'm disappointed when I go into room 207 and see Warner staring at his phone, the room empty except for him.

"Good morning," I say in an uneasy voice. He's been very short with me every time I've visited him since the explosion. Heck, he's been short with me for months now. But still, something feels different about it now. I can't tell what it is.

"Have you seen Lyla?" he asks right away. No, Hello to you, too. No, Good morning, back. I know that he's expecting to see

Lyla. She's been visiting nonstop ever since Warner first arrived at the hospital. He was expecting her to have been here when he woke up.

As much as I don't like it, I know Warner has feelings for Lyla. It's going to make it hard to break the news to him about this. But still, I have to do it. I don't want to lie to him anymore. Especially not about this. If I don't tell him, somebody else is going to.

I sit down in the chair next to his bed. "Honey," I start.

He squints at me. "What? Have you seen her or not?"

"I'm trying to tell you something," I say, my voice getting a little irritated. I take a deep breath to calm myself down.

Not now, Maddy.

"Warner, it has come to my attention that Lyla has gone missing. As of last night."

He mouths the word missing, staring at me with a dead expression in his eyes.

"Warner?" I ask.

Still, he stays silent, staring me directly in the eyes.

I take his hand and squeeze it, but that's when he rips it away from me.

"You know what, Mom?" he snaps. "Go away!"

I jump back slightly in my chair. "Warner?"

"I mean it!" he shouts. "Get out of here!"

"What's going on?" I ask, my heart pounding.

"Just leave me alone! Go away!"

I practically fly to my feet, not able to get out of the hospital room fast enough as he keeps yelling at me.

I walk down the hallway, gripping the wall as I go in fear that I'm going to fall. Then I collapse onto the nearest bench and begin sobbing. I have no idea what just happened.

But as I keep crying, everything just feels worse and worse. I've spent my entire life running away from my past, and it seems like it keeps catching up with me, no matter what I do.

I don't know why I ever thought I could get away with what happened all those years ago.

CHAPTER 85

WARNER

I don't know how, but I just know that all of this is tied to what my mom and Amelia Bailey did to Carson Price all those years ago. It has to be. It's all Mom's fault. All my mom has ever done her entire life is lie to me.

Like how she lied to me about who my father is.

Dean Reeves.

Now that I think about it, I'm pretty sure every adult I've ever known in my entire life has lied to me.

It all makes sense now why Coach had been so kind to me over the years. Why I felt closer to him than his other students had. It's not some teacher's pet sort of situation. It's because he knows he's my freaking father! And he never bothered to tell me! Nobody did!

I hate that I'm stuck in this stupid hospital bed. I hate that all I have is my phone to rely on to get information about Lyla's sudden disappearance. I hate that all I can do is just lay here all day long, checking my phone repeatedly, texting my peers and listening to the news for updates.

What could've happened to her? Who could've taken her? Where could she have gone?

I can't stop picturing Lake Oshwana. I can't stop picturing how just like they had pulled Sydney Hutton's body out of the water, what if they pull Lyla Bailey's body out of the water, too? What if Carson Price's body is also in there?

What if someone has done something horrible to Lyla?

I'm too sick to my stomach to eat anything all day long, and it concerns the nurses and makes them want to keep me at the hospital even longer. I try to explain to them the reason why I don't have an appetite, but they don't seem to listen to me.

By the time the night falls, I'm so upset that I can't even focus on anything. I can't just sit here and deal with this. I can't sit here while

Lyla is out there somewhere, potentially waiting to be rescued by someone. I have to find her. I have to at least try.

I wait until the nurses do their next round of checkups on me. Then, as soon as they're out of sight, I rip all the cords off of me, and gritting my teeth, I rip the needle out of my skin, too. It bleeds, but I ignore it as I fling myself out of bed. I grab my shoes off of the counter on top of my bag of clothing items that were destroyed in the explosion, so I don't even bother to grab those. Not even putting my shoes on—I'll wait until I'm out of here—I run for it.

I have to get to Lyla.

CHAPTER 86

Audrey

Since a masked man broke into our house recently and chased me around until I fell and became unconscious, everyone seems to take Lyla's disappearance pretty seriously from the get-go. Dad even races back home from his trip. The neighbors come over to console us. The news vans show up pretty early on, and then by the time the sun starts setting, it seems like all of Toxey is standing outside of our house, waiting to hear the newest update on my twin's disappearance.

I've been crying on and off all day long. I've been trying to keep it together for my mom's sake, and for Joey's sake. They're both a mess. Joey hasn't stopped crying at all, and Mom has been frantically running around the place, talking in a voice I've never heard her talking in. She doesn't even shower or get changed. She doesn't ever let anyone see her the way she has let pretty much the entire town of Toxey see her today—in her pajamas with her hair pulled back in a messy ponytail, not a lick of makeup on her face.

I send my sister another text.

Me: *Lyla, please. I don't know where you are, what you're doing, or what's happened, but if you have ANY way at all of letting me know you're safe, please do it. I'm so worried about you. I feel like our twin telepathy isn't working like it's supposed to.*

Writing the text out makes me begin to tear up again, so I go to the bathroom and splash water on my face. Then I grab a towel to clean up the mess I've made around the rim of the sink, and I wipe down the mirror. I pat my face dry on the towel and take a deep, soothing breath, breathing in the scent of the dryer sheets we use through my nose.

It's going to be okay; I tell myself.

But I know I'm full of it.

When I go downstairs, I peek through the window in the front room—even though I'm not supposed to be in here—and see how many people are gathered outside. News vans, police officers, reporters, investigators, and our neighbors. Mom and Dad are about to release a statement to the press. It makes me realize just how serious this whole disappearance thing is.

I'm told I shouldn't step outside because it might make some people confused if they don't realize that I am a twin of Lyla's. They don't want anyone getting us switched around and thinking that Lyla's been safe this whole time and that this has all been just a huge act. So I'm sneaky as I look out the window at everyone. Mom and Dad are standing on the front porch, a bunch of microphones stands in front of them from different new stations. Many people are taking pictures and videos of them, and flashes of light keep going off in their faces.

Behind the crowd, on the street, I see somebody in an old, faded gray Mustang. In the driver's seat, a familiar arm is dangling out the window as they watch the scene before them.

"Jackson?" I say to myself, catching the face of the person in the vehicle.

When I go to look more closely at him, the car drives away. I slide down the couch I am peeking out the window on.

How strange had that been? I think to myself. It looked a lot like Jackson had been sitting in his car, staring at the scene unfolding in front of our house, like he didn't want anyone to know he was there.

But that wouldn't make any sense. Jackson doesn't have a car.

I lean forward again as far as I can until my face is pressed up against the window, to try to catch a glimpse of the faded Mustang again. I don't see anything.

It makes me wonder if I even saw Jackson at all.

CHAPTER 87

WARNER

Not knowing where else to go, I decide I will go to my thinking spot, the abandoned train station. I'm just going to sit down on a bench and try to figure out what I should do first. How I should go about finding Lyla and finding out what happened to her. Every time I've tried to call and text her, she hasn't answered. Besides, I feel that concentrating on this will distract me from the huge bomb Craig Fritz dropped on my life about who my father is. And I don't even want to waste time thinking about that when the girl I am kind of crazy about has disappeared.

Dean Reeves isn't even worth it.

I put my shoes on when I'm safely out the hospital doors and around the corner, hidden behind a dumpster. Then I take off at a run, even though I'm feeling incredibly dizzy and weak. My body is drenched in sweat within seconds of running, and I know I should probably still be in the hospital, but I can't care about that right now. Not when Lyla could be in trouble.

I can't lose her. Not when I've come this close to potentially having something more than just a friendship with her.

When I get to the abandoned train station, I sit down on the bench and try to call Lyla again. Stones gather in my stomach when, instead of her line ringing like it usually does, it goes straight to voicemail.

Either her phone has died, or somebody has turned it off.

"Crap," I mumble, sending her another text. It shows up as green instead of blue in our text messaging thread—another sign that her phone is not in service at the moment. "No!" I cry out. As my voice echoes away, I hear something else. A rustling noise. The sound of whispers. I look over my shoulder. In the distance, out in the overgrown parking lot where I usually park my jeep, I see a figure. It's just their shadowy outline, at first.

I duck down behind the bench so that I'm not spotted by whoever it is. Then I'm more careful when I look back at them again, trying to spy and see who they're talking to.

After a few moments, I make out Detective Craig Fritz. I can't see who he's talking to because he is standing in front of them, talking animatedly in a voice too quiet for me to hear. But my stomach drops as I contemplate who it might be. My thoughts take me to Coach. Mr. Reeves. My father. Whatever he's called.

What if Fritz and Mr. Reeves are working together, for some reason? Detective Fritz is already one creepy, weird dude. And if my biological father has potentially been holding in this secret about me being his son all this time, then what other secrets is he harboring along with it?

Eventually, Fritz moves out of the way slightly, and I figure out who the second person is. If it wasn't for the brown hair, I would've thought maybe it was Lyla.

But it's not. It's Nora Flynn.

"What on earth...?" I trail off, shocked to see them together. I can't hear what it is they're saying to each other, but I see it very clearly from the light of the moonlight when Craig reaches out and takes Nora's hand. I can also see clearly that Nora looks stressed out about something. Whatever that something is, Craig looks as if he's comforting her. As if he's being a surprisingly decent human being towards her.

Craig seems like he hates every single person in Toxey. So why is it that he seems to hate every single person in Toxey except for Nora?

What the heck is going on around here?

CHAPTER 88

LYLA

Seventeen Hours Earlier

I slip out of bed silently and walk over to my closet. I open it up, making sure it doesn't make any creaking noises. Then I walk straight to the back of it, not bothering to turn on the light in case anyone notices.

I open up one of my storage boxes, and then I pull out the long blonde wig inside of it. When I leave the closet, I glance at the clock on my nightstand. It's two in the morning—I'm right on schedule.

I stand in front of my mirror, put the wig over my head, and make sure it's perfectly placed, securing it with bobby pins. I can't take any chances of getting found out.

I am determined to make things right. I'm determined to clean up this mess and make it all go away. I want things to go back to how they used to be. Maybe not all the way back to how they used to be, but I at least want to get rid of this mess involving the man that's been tormenting us.

The thing is, I don't want Audrey to do what that text had told her to. I can't let anything happen to her. I can't take another accident. I'm already scared enough as it is. And I'm going to keep being scared until something is done about it.

So, before I deleted that text message the anonymous person sent to her, I memorized the address on it. I wrote it down as soon as I got back to my bedroom.

I don't want Audrey going to that address, but it's not going to stop me from doing it.

Dressed up as my sister, I take a deep breath, then I sneak out of the house to go meet up with the mystery person.

Hopefully, I'll finally get some answers.

CHAPTER 89

MADDY

April 25th, 1998

"It's your little sister. Nora!" My classmate, Mindy, screams at Mia and me. Mia and I have just finished getting in a fight right in the middle of the prom dance floor, and everybody is staring at us. I want nothing to do with Mia anymore. I'm so sick of being her friend. So sick of having to play by her rules and do everything she says. She is a complete stick in the mud, and I have had enough of it.

"What about her?" Mia asks Mindy, wiping tears from her eyes and looking around at everyone who is staring at us instead of dancing with each other.

I look around, too. Nora is nowhere to be seen, and neither is Carson Price.

"She's in the bathroom, sobbing!" Mindy continues. "I can't get her to come out of the stall."

I try to make eye contact with Mia, but she won't look at me. Instead, she races after Mindy, who is leading her to the bathrooms outside the gym, in the hallway. I run after them because I care about what has happened to Nora, too.

As soon as we enter the bathroom, I recognize Nora's loud, wailing sobs.

"Nora!" Mia calls out, running over to the stall she's locked herself in.

"M-Mia?" Nora asks between her sobs.

"Nora, let me in," Amelia says.

The stall door unlocks, and Nora lets it fall open. When I peek inside, I see blood everywhere. It's all over the floor and the toilet seat, and it's all over Nora.

"Oh my gosh, Nora!" I gasp, slapping a hand over my mouth at the sight of it. It had not at all been what I was expecting.

Nora is on a ball on the floor in front of the toilet.

Mia squats down and hugs her sister, grabbing a bunch of toilet paper from the roll to hand it to her as Nora leans into her, continuing to cry.

"Nora, what happened?" Mia asks. Then she helps her sister by dabbing at her nose with the toilet paper.

"I think it's broken!" Nora sobs. When Mia touches the paper to her nose again, she winces. "Ow! It hurts, Mia! It hurts!"

"I'm sorry!" Mia says in a shrill voice. I don't know what to do. I can hardly move. "Who did this to you? Tell me right now!"

"It—it was," she gasps out, hiccupping so hard that she can barely speak. "It was C-Carson!"

I feel like a complete jerk. All along, Amelia had been trying to warn me that Carson was bad news. I told her she was judgmental. I told her that if Nora was happy, then she should be happy for her sister. I thought Amelia was being judgy because Carson was the new kid who didn't dress as cool as everybody else. Carson seemed like a loner and didn't like to smile much—and Amelia had always been more of the judgmental type.

But I should've listened to her all along.

"Where is he?" Mia asks. Nora throws her arms around her sister and continues to cry. She's getting blood all over Mia, but she doesn't seem to mind.

"You were right, Mia, you were right!" she says. "I'm so sorry!"

"You don't have to apologize, Nora!" Mia says to her. "It's okay! Shh, it's going to be okay!"

"It was him the whole time. It's always been him," Nora continues. I could kill him.

"Nor, where did he go?" I demand. It comes out gravelly and weak, but that's not how I feel.

"I don't know! I'm too afraid to go back out there. Please help me." Nora is hyperventilating as she squeezes her sister tighter.

"H-how did this happen?" I ask. Then I turned to the other girls in the bathroom. "Can you guys get lost?!" I shout at them. They scurry away, but now they're only lingering by the door instead of right behind us because they want to stay and watch the drama.

"He wanted me to spend the night with him!" Nora says. "I-I told him I didn't want to! That I w-wasn't ready!" Nora chokes out. "So he—he punched me!"

"I'm so sorry, Nor," Mia whispers in her ear, still hugging her.

"Mia," I say. "Her nose is bleeding a lot. We need to get her out of here."

Mia stands up and pulls Nora up with her, so I step forward and help.

"Hold this to her nose," Mia snaps at me, handing me the wad of toilet paper. "And be careful!"

I do as instructed, while Mia puts Nora's arm around her shoulders and carefully starts walking with her out of the bathroom.

"Can't you guys mind your own business?" she snaps at the brats who are still watching us. They giggle and turn away.

When we get out in the hallway, Dean Reeves, Parker Fritz, and Craig Fritz are all waiting for us out in the hall.

"What happened?" Dean demands instantly, looking horrified as he races to my side to help me with Nora's bleeding nose.

"I took pictures," Nora manages to say. "I have record of every time he's ever put his hands on me."

Every time? How long has he been doing this? I can't stand it.

I watch as Amelia points a shaky hand right at Craig. "I told you so, Craig!" she snaps at him. "I told you he needed to stay away from my sister!"

"Nora," Craig breathes. Then he looks at Mia. "Mia, I—"

But I'm mad at him, too. "Save it!" I snap, seeing a crowd starting to gather around us. "Don't say another word. Just go. And keep your friend away from us!"

But Craig looks hesitant to leave.

"Now!" Dean shouts at him.

At this, Craig finally leaves.

His brother, Parker, looks appalled as he stands next to us. "I can't believe it," he says. "I can't believe my brother was friends with that guy! How did he not know this was happening?!"

"He defended him, even!" Mia roared.

"We're going to get you cleaned up, okay, Nor?" Dean says. I watch as he stares at her more like a caring brother would.

"Carson can't get away with this," I say. I am making eye contact with Amelia for the first time since our fight. I know we're not seeing eye to eye about things right now, and I know I have a huge dislike for her, but I also know we can both put everything aside for this. It's the one thing we seem to have in common.

Nora.

For some reason, I'm able to tell exactly what Mia is thinking. And I know she can tell exactly what I'm thinking, too.

Dean, Nora, Amelia, and I walk into the parking lot together.

"Are you sure you got her?" Amelia asks Dean, who has his arm around Nora and is still supporting her bleeding nose.

"Yeah. I'll take her back to my place so that way your mom and dad aren't asking any questions."

"Thanks."

The two get into Dean's car, Nora muttering about how sorry she is and how stupid she feels. Then when Dean drives away, Amelia's left hand swats my shoulder. I whirl to her, annoyed. But she's pointing at something out in the distance.

"Look!" she hisses.

I follow her finger and see a familiar car with a stripe driving out of the school parking lot, going in a different direction than Dean and Nora.

Carson.

"Let's go," I say quickly. We run over to my jeep and get in. Then I follow Carson Price, wherever it is he's going.

I had no idea Carson was planning to drive all the way out to the Boldosa Redwoods.

"Is he ever going to stop?" Amelia asks, sitting in the passenger seat.

"I don't know," I say. What if he's running away? What if he's planning on fleeing the country and going to Mexico, and we're stuck following him this whole way? At what point am I supposed to stop and turn back around and give up? I don't want to give up. I want Carson Price to pay.

Finally, he exits the highway, and then I find myself traveling through the quiet, dark woods behind him.

"Where the heck is he going?" Amelia whispers even though we don't have to be quiet inside my car.

"No idea," I say. We stay back as far as possible so that he doesn't suspect us following him. Then when he turns right into a gravel drive, I hang back, parking on the side of the road. I think he's just turned into someone's lake house.

"Is this where he wanted her to go with him?" Mia asks.

"Probably," I say. We wait a little bit before getting out of the car. Then we follow the long gravel driveway until the trees clear and we can see the lake house. It's a large A-frame cabin with a massive front porch that wraps around to the back. I catch a glimpse of Carson entering through the front door and closing it behind him.

"He went inside," I say.

"Well, let's go then," she says.

"Do we have any idea exactly what it is we're going to do when we find him?"

I had known without even having to talk to Amelia that this is what her plan was. To confront him. To threaten him about something terrible happening to him if he ever laid his hands on Nora Flynn again.

"Yeah," she says. "We're gonna make sure he never touches her again."

She creeps forward to the porch steps. I follow behind her, but then my eyes catch on a shovel that's laying on the ground in the dirt by the steps. So I pick it up. Mia looks over her shoulder, sees me holding it, and nods approvingly.

Not that I need your permission, I think to myself.

We're quiet when we open the door. We sneak inside the house, not seeing any sign of Carson at first.

The A-frame cabin is magnificent inside—expertly decorated with oriental rugs, a beautiful stone fireplace, and animal heads mounted on the walls, their antler sticking out far.

"Where is he?" I mouth to Amelia. She looks around, uncertain. We both look up when we hear the ceiling creak above us.

He's gone upstairs.

As we sneak towards the staircase, I look out the window and notice the massive pool outback. Just beyond it is the lake. I can barely make out the body of water through the cluster of trees in between it and the pool.

We tiptoe up the staircase. Amelia still doesn't have a weapon to use, but I hold onto my shovel tightly.

When we get to the landing, we still don't see Carson anywhere. Then Amelia nudges just me. The back door to the balcony is wide open. He must've gone out there.

Swallowing and feeling slightly afraid, I move first. Amelia has suddenly turned to stone behind me. It's as if the closer we get to Carson Price, the more she realizes what we're doing.

I creep through the open doorway. When my foot steps onto the balcony, it creaks under my bodyweight, and Carson whirls around, startled.

"What are you guys doing here?" he asks, a cigarette in his hand.

"We know what you did, Carson," I say immediately. I look over my shoulder, surprised that Amelia is hanging back further than I thought she would be.

Coward.

Carson's eyes go to the shovel in my hand. "I don't know what you're talking about," he says. "Did you seriously follow me all the way out here?"

"We know what you did to my sister," Amelia says behind me.

"Wait, what did she tell you?" he asks, his eyebrows lowering over his eyes. His blonde hair is unkempt and overgrown, and his knuckles are bloody like they always are. Carson is notorious for getting into fights. And punching his girlfriends, apparently.

"Who do you think you are?" I ask him, stepping closer to him again, holding the shovel up. "What makes you think you can lay your hands on a woman?"

"Especially that woman being my innocent little sister!" Amelia adds.

He huffs out a sarcastic laugh. Then he takes a puff from his cigarette. I'm annoyed that he isn't more threatened by the fact that I'm holding a shovel I could whack him across the head with.

"You wanna know something?" Carson asks. He flicks his cigarette to the ground and squashes it with his thick black boot. "Nora Flynn is crazy."

I'm about to talk back, but a wild, animalistic scream sounds behind me. Before I know it, Amelia is ripping the shovel out of my hand. She runs toward Carson with it, and I watch in shock as she whacks him across the side of the face with the back of the metal scoop. He flies into the wooden railing of the balcony, and the whole thing gives out with ease, as if a simple flick of the finger would've been enough to do the job. Then suddenly, Carson is falling.

"Mia!" I shout as Carson goes over the edge. She gasps and drops the shovel. Then she slaps a hand over her mouth. I hear a splash down below, but neither of us moves for what feels like a long, long time.

Then carefully, I step towards the edge of the balcony where the railing gave out.

Carson is face down in the pool. There's a massive cloud of blood around him in the water, lit up by the pool lights.

Carson isn't moving.

"Oh my God, what did you do?" I screech, then I take Amelia's hand and pull her away from the balcony. The whole thing is creaking like it's going to collapse at any moment. It's easy to tell that the weather has rotted the wood away, or that it was poorly constructed in the first place.

I pulled Mia back inside the house. She looks paler than I have ever seen her.

"I-I didn't mean for that to happen!" she cries out.

I believe her. I believe she meant to just hit him across the face and break his jaw or whatever. But I say nothing as I race down the stairs. I run out the back door and go over to the pool. Still, Carson isn't moving.

"Help me get him out!" I demand. She nods her head and comes over to help. We reach in the water and grab his ankles and start pulling. When we have him out, we roll him over on his back. His cheek is cut open, but that's not the main source of all the blood. It seems as if he's hit his head on the edge of the pool when he fell. There's a gash on the back of his skull, and blood is pouring out of it.

"Maddy," Amelia whispers.

I shake Carson to try to get him to wake up.

This can't be happening.

Amelia shakes my shoulder. Then she slowly gets her feet. "Maddy!" she shouts at me.

Finally, I let go of Carson.

He's dead.

Amelia and I killed Carson Price.
TO BE CONTINUED IN THE NEXT BOOK, "TRAPPED BY A LIE"

"Up Next"

I hope you enjoyed "Sealed With A Lie". If you've read these first two books in the series, you now pretty much have the rhythm down. Each book gets more exciting as you go along, and there's a cliffhanger at the end. I promise it just keeps getting better. But you don't have to take my word for it. Just read the reviews for Book #3 below.

Oh yes! About the next book!

"Trapped By A Lie" is ready for you right now. Here's a taste of what's to come next...

Audrey Bailey's twin sister is missing. The dead body of the last missing girl was discovered last week.

Audrey is riddled with guilt since Lyla was masquerading as her when she was taken. It looks like the stalker who has been attacking the Bailey and Carpenter families has raised the stakes.

A twisted web of threats, accusations, and lies is spreading like wildfire from the Bailey and Carpenter families and enveloping the entire community. Audrey and her friend Warner, along with their parents, risk their lives, their jobs, and their sanity to find her.

The most likely culprit is someone who was presumed dead twenty years ago. The only people the police are investigating are the Baileys and Carpenters themselves.

Will Lyla be found, or will the tormentor succeed in destroying these families and their town?

"Trapped By A Lie" is the third thrilling novel in the 5-book *"Moms Who Lie"* domestic psychological thriller series by Brett Monk and McKenna Langford.

If you like **twisty psychological thrillers** with **relatable teen and adult characters** and a **drop-the-mic cliffhanger** at the end of each book, then you'll love *the "Moms Who Lie"* series!

———

Here's what the reviewers are saying about "Trapped By A Lie"...

"Trapped By A Lie by Brett Monk and McKenna Langford is nearly 400 pages of thrills, fear, and questions, and when I got to the end I desperately wanted more! I can't recommend this series enough. If you love psychological thrillers, then you'll love this book. If you don't like psychological thrillers, then you'll still love this book! Buy it, read it, and then join the large list of antsy readers not-so-patiently waiting for the last two books in the series! And as a personal note to the authors, can you please hurry with the other two books? No, seriously, CAN you?"
- **The International Review of Books**

"Brett Monk and McKenna Langford once again deliver a fast-paced mystery in *Trapped By A Lie*, the third book in their *Moms Who Lie* series, which gets better with each installment. By now we know the players, or at least we think we do, as the investigation of a teenager's disappearance in the seemingly idyllic town of Toxey reveals more about the town and its denizens, coloring in elements from previous installments. The authors are experts at letting the mystery unfold piece by piece until reaching a satisfying conclusion, which hooks readers in for another installment. The book's many short chapters flit between the main characters, without skimping on detail, bringing a breathless sense of action that never lets up from the very start."
- **Self-Publishing Review**

"Trapped by a Lie is the third book in the Moms Who Lie series. Each book in the series is more suspenseful than its predecessor. The town is still in shock after the disappearance and subsequent death of Sydney Hutton, a high school student. Now another student, Lyla, is missing. Who is terrorizing this once peaceful and safe town? This book is excellent. It is well written and thought provoking. The events that occur can realistically happen anywhere. No matter how much parents try to protect their children or how careful they themselves are, there is no guarantee that nothing bad will happen. I experienced a wide range of emotions while reading this book. At times, happiness at others fear and sadness. The character development in this book is perfect. I highly recommend this book. It is a must read."
-Elizabeth M., Amazon Reader

Afterword

We hope you thoroughly enjoyed *"Sealed With A Lie"* and that you'll join us for the rest of the books in the series.

Also, If you want to learn what happened back when Maddy and Mia were in high school, the night Carson disappeared, you can download the free bonus novella, *"The Lying Begins"* at the link below.

https://www.brettmonk.com

When you join the community, you will not only get free books and other content by me and some of my friends, but you will get the inside scoop on discounted products and upcoming releases. Plus, I share some personal thoughts and "behind the scenes" photos and notes about my life, media adventures, and favorite grilling recipes. :-)

Community members also get to vote in polls and make suggestions for upcoming books and projects. You might even want to consider being a "beta reader" or an "advance review reader", both of whom get to read the books before they're available to the public!

Best Regards and Happy Reading!
Brett & McKenna

About the Authors

Brett Monk

Brett Monk is an author, movie director, and voiceover artist.

He holds degrees in Communications and Psychology and spent over 30 years writing and directing films for businesses and government agencies in the Washington, DC area before turning his focus to creating books and audiobooks.

He also directed and co-wrote two feature-length murder mystery movies which are in worldwide distribution.

Originally from the Shenandoah Valley area, he now lives in Northern Virginia with his family and a rambunctious Bernedoodle named Merlin.

McKenna Langford

McKenna lives in Arizona with her husband and two goofy Boxador brothers.

Before she dove into the world of ghostwriting and co-writing, she got her bachelor's degree in interior design and published her first five novels. She worked in a boutique interior design firm in the valley for two years, moved to Seattle with her husband to explore for another two years, then moved back to Arizona and made writing her full-time career in 2021.